DATE DUE

INDIGO AUTUMN

ETHYLIND GRIFFIETH

S0-EAY-436

TXu1-866-457
ISBN: 149045733X
ISBN-13: 9781490457338

This is a work of fiction. All characters and events in
the novel are fictitious.

DEDICATION

For all those of the light who have the courage to come to planet Earth and do the dirty work.

ACKNOWLEDGMENTS

The author wishes to thank David for his patience in formatting my one last edit—how many was that now, David?

Prologue I

The Previous August

Ledger Griffieth was on his way to Geneva, Switzerland. He had tried to sleep on the night flight but his mind kept returning to his elderly uncle who had summoned him to his bedside.

The phone call from the hospice where Uncle Rutger was being cared for had prompted the flight to London and on to Geneva. Ledger had not realized the seriousness of the old gentleman's state of health until the phone call. Uncle Rutger had been an outdoor winter sports enthusiast all his life—robust and hardy of constitution—never any negative health issues until now. It seemed after a very long life fate was dealing with him.

The staunch elderly gentleman had been as his father before him, a partner in the same long established law firm handling the legalities of some of Europe's most prominent families.

Ledger had spent many winter holidays skiing the Alps with his parents, Uncle Rutger and a solitary friend of Rutger's known only as Zorloff. Ledger had never known Zorloff's last name. The man quietly kept to himself—even on the slopes he always skied alone or behind their group. He contributed little in conversation but regardless, always seemed to enjoy being a part of their gatherings.

The phone call had conveyed an impelling last request of Ledger relayed by Rutger's caretaker, one of great consequence that could only be carried out face to face. Ledger wondered what that could possibly mean and why him—why not another of Rutger's closer relatives? He felt himself to have always been a conservative person of no great mystery except for his work in Astrobiology which at times called for discretion since some of his work was done for the government. What could his uncle want with him now in these last moments of his life? True, they had always had a comfortable affection and enjoyed the family skiing trips, later, the après conversations of life and all its attendant curiosities. He hoped he could be a comfort to Rutger now. Finally Ledger slept, awakening as the plane landed in Geneva.

He arrived at the hospice late in the evening after all was done, meeting with Rutger's personal caretaker right away. He was told not to stay long as the old gentleman was very weak. He quietly peered around the doorway of Rutger's room seeing what had once been a vigourous man now seemingly asleep. Intravenous lines ran from his long frame to bags of fluid. At first he thought Rutger was not conscious but as he stepped over to the bedside intense blue eyes flew open. The man's hand flew out to grasp Ledger's.

"Ledger, I was so afraid you wouldn't make it in time—I didn't expect I was so near."

"Uncle Rutger, always I have enjoyed your company—what can I do for you—are you being kept comfortable?"

"Yes, yes, there is so little time and there is a great responsibility I must transfer to you if you are willing, it is time for it to be carried out—it is of monumental importance as you will see."

Ledger didn't know what to say.

The elderly man continued. "Look in the nightstand drawer—a black leather notebook lies there-in. Rip the lining loose and feel for a small key—it is one that fits an old form of file cabinet in the storeroom where my firm's earliest original documents are stored."

The young man did this baffled at the meaning of his uncle's words. He fished the key from inside the lining exposing it to the ailing man.

"Very well." Rutger seemed relieved. "Now, to carry out what you must do, first you shall know what history is behind your errand."

"I am only the second keeper of the secret—my father before me was the first. Before his death he recounted to me an encounter he had in 1937 Broyles, France between himself and a couple he believed were time-travelers from the future."

Ledger was astounded at what such words could mean.

Rutger continued. "They proclaimed themselves to be archaeologists from America on holiday in France. My father stayed in that region of France for a week as he had business there. Several nights they had dinner together, the three enjoying the speculative aspects of their conversations, some of which he refused to convey to me. In the end, they entrusted to him an experiment, one he was to tuck away and at the right point in time make arrangements for it to be dispersed to the right party in the manner described by them. It is now time for the disbursement of the document to be carried out—what will come of it, I can't imagine. I hope you will take on this last request of mine."

Ledger nodded his acquiescence.

Rutger continued. "It must be sent by Fed-Ex overnight—the address is on the outer container, and, as I discovered only ten years ago—also inside. Because of the age of the outer container it no longer held its confidentiality and revealed the letter inside. I couldn't resist. The message inside is cryptic and would add to its suspicion knowing its background. I have enclosed a letter explaining the firm's position—that is all that is necessary." Rutgers breathing seemed labored as he continued, seemingly short of breath with the effort. "I'm entrusting you to now take care of this for me before I leave this existence. I have alerted our offices you are to recover a document of import for me, so you will have easy access to the antiquated file cabinet." Rutger appeared even more fatigued. "Ledger, I would have passed this responsibility to my dear friend Zorloff, as we, over the years have had many understandings of life but the sudden onset of my frailty prevented my discovering his whereabouts." Rutger drifted off momentarily and then roused startled that he had. "You must advise him that what we discussed has been carried out by yourself Ledger—this is important." Rutger's strength seemed to be failing him ever faster and with what little remained in his long frame grabbed Ledger's hand pulling the young man close to his face as his voice weakened further. "There are certain *protocols* for contacting Zorloff." The old gentleman's voice was now barely a whisper as he related to Ledger what steps would be necessary to locate Zorloff. With those last words the old man seemed to drift off to sleep once more.

Ledger squeezed his old friend's hand and quietly left the room. Such a request he had never in his wildest imaginings considered. Uncle Rutger was not the sort to be delusional not even at the end of life. But being of concern for his uncle's last wishes Ledger would do what was asked of him as a courtesy. He too would find Zorloff following Rutger's instructions considering the mysterious nature of events.

After a nights much needed sleep Ledger arrived early at the law firm's offices and was shown the packed storeroom where past decades of documents were available. It didn't take long to locate the particular file cabinet he had been directed to look for. Rutger had suggested Ledger bring along with him a small can of lubricant as the lock was old and might be difficult to open. He need not have for the little key responded with an immediate click revealing exactly what it had held in secret all those years.

Ledger brought the package back to his hotel room to examine it before sending it on to its final destination. He photographed the yellowed document and its container. And—he was reluctantly in agreement with his uncle that this smacked of time travel, there was no other logical explanation. How could someone in 1937 know of the Fed-Ex of the future? This had to be some sort of communication from the past to this Peter Steffington in the states.

As a scientist, Ledger had always suspected mathematically speaking, that somewhere there would be evidence of time travel. What could this mean? How had his uncle's curiosity held him at bay all these years? Yes, this was something he would carry out for Rutger and those archaeologists, but it was something he intended to do a little investigating of on his own. He cut off a snippet of the letter. He would have it's age analyzed, but then he thought, it would be better if he did this himself so as to keep this document and his effort of it's disbursement out of the curiosity of others. He went to the nearest Fed-Ex location in the city and sent the documents overnight as uncle Rutger had requested.

Later that day in the darkness of the early evening Ledger received word that his uncle had passed away. He extended his stay only long enough for Rutger's funeral. The following day he took an early morning flight back to Boston to begin his search for Zorloff, knowing this was of great importance, particularly for the time frame that the package was designated for. He considered just what he had been a party to—only a shadow of concern crossed his mind as he felt nothing ominous was involved in what he had done. He slept soundly on the flight home to prepare for what he knew he must do to find Zorloff with this urgent message.

Prologue II

End of Summer 1920

On the French side of the English Channel a dark, clandestine figure worked frenetically from the topmost floor of an old mill long abandoned by its miller-owner. Dr. Zachery Frank had found it necessary to use the forces of nature to engage his first attempt with the science he had long sought and serendipitously come across in an old journal found by workmen renovating a Chateau in the French countryside. A behemoth of a late-day thunderstorm was almost upon this locale, slightly elevated from the coast—so perfect for what Dr. Frank set about—to successfully complete, his first attempt at time travel!

A small private boat chugged its way through the increasingly rough water of the English Channel to beat the raging fury of the monstrous storm about to engulf it. Storms this power-ful were seldom seen here. Electrical in nature, heavy air and thick, dark slow-roiling clouds indicated a fearsome promise of destruction to come to any foolish enough to be in its path. The lateness of the day made the atmosphere as dark as midnight. Wind began its powerful surge just as massive amounts of rain hit the water second only to the demonic bombardment of the unnatural lightening turning the storms darkness into blinding flashes that obliterated reality.

The captain of the small boat would ordinarily not have left shore with such a storm approaching but his greed at the pros-pect of profit from a last minute request offering double the fee had over-ridden his caution of the impending tragedy nature promised to the reckless. Now he regretted his decision but it was too late to turn back.

The three young passengers strapped to an attached bench outside the wheel-house window of the rising and plunging boat had missed the earlier ferry and would have missed their train to London and then on Northward to boarding school in Scotland if their escort Mr. Bordelaine had not quickly found them alter-nate transportation across the Channel. The gentleman accom-panying the three young passengers (two adolescent boys and an only slightly younger, quiet oriental girl with blue eyes) was eager to be done with his part of the responsibility of delivering the three to their destination. He wanted to be finished with this errand and on his own way. As a last resort he solicited this willing captain and his boat. The extra fee solved his problem. He watched the little boat leave in the increasingly choppy waters. Not one to be haunted by guilt he turned and hurried away to catch his train.

The vessel bravely ploughed on through the treacherous waters barely able to keep afloat. The twin boys, frightened themselves, tried to comfort the young girl while their captain worked at keeping them all afloat and alive. The storm would not have an ending soon. It seemed to rage and hover over this particular spot on the planet, unable to use its self up.

Back inland Dr. Frank stood before the glassless window frame of the deserted mill gauging the exact moment he dare join nature to his adaptation of the instruction in the journal— to be the master of time! He had at long last been able to interpret the journal and prepared what he realized was an archaic arrangement of equipment needed for this first go. His great deficit had been his lack of a fully functioning power source for this initial working model—so as a last resort he had turned to nature itself.

In the distance he watched the small boat struggle its way through the storm. The very air was electrified in a strange sort of way—even so this was the storm he had needed—longed for. Dr. Frank had all in place and waited until the pinnacle moment he felt the storm would release its greatest energy.

He had long been obsessed with the esoteric sciences of the ancients, alchemy and all such ventures promised those inventive enough, the disclosure of their obscure secrets. This impeccably dressed man with slicked-back dark hair wore a black-rimmed monocle and exhibited an inscrutable air of sophistication and arrogance. He personified one who elevated themselves to a place far above the rest of humanity, a species who had no valued relevancy to himself.

He strode to an apparatus in the middle of the rotting wooden floor where he cranked up through the partially missing roof a thick, needle-like projection intended to pull down the power of the lightening itself.

Back at the window he zeroed in on the small boat. He cared not whether it made it to shore or sank, for at this moment in time and happenstance it would serve his purposes.

He pulled on thick black rubber gloves and a long protective coat of the same substance. He exchanged the monocle for protective goggles then grasped a long metal cylinder he had prepared swinging it toward the window and the channel in the direction of the boat.

He was ready—the hellish bolt struck the projectile above— hit so hard the old mill reverberated with the inflow as *it* became the power-surge Dr. Frank had awaited. The boat of fear-filled passengers was in his sights as he threw the conversion switch at his side.

Glued to the scene in the distance, Dr. Frank was awestruck when at the same moment his beam directed at the boat was intersected above the vessel by a lightening bolt as powerful as the energy beam he had attempted to control.

Such a conjoining of energy momentarily turned all existence blue-white rending time meaningless. For a mere instant in time he perceived the very fabric of reality twist and yaw out of stability. Then a massive swirling portal of blinding white light opened up in front of the helpless craft pulling it into the swirling vortex of energy. It disappeared into the portal. Abruptly, the passageway into another realm blinked out as if it had never existed.

The boat and its passengers were gone—gone! But where?

This was Dr. Frank's first attempt to control this science and it had gone terribly wrong. This was not what he had expected to result from his endeavours. He would have to rethink all he had assumed he understood—start over somewhere else—no more electrical storms! His beginning plans had been too grandiose and impatient. He must not be so eager—more methodical and calculating.

The boat and its occupants were of no consequence to him—only a convenience for his use at the time. He left the mill giving instructions to the driver waiting below to have everything packed up and moved to a new location on the morrow. There was much he had to do.

Chapter One

The Present

Autumn lingered unexpectedly soft and warm for a part of the coast so far north, gentle days, yet chilly nights. By sunset the trees on the ridge along the road to Smugglers Cove would be silhouetted by an indigo sky filling with stars. Very soon the full Harvest Moon would add its brightness to the seaside community of New England's coastal dwellers.

But for now, golden grasses of wild grains gently swayed and bent their seed heads beside the black topped county road as two young women bicycled their way east to Smugglers Cove and then north up the Old Coast Road to the home of their father's long time friend, Serpentine Pendergast.

The two had arrived the previous evening on a transatlantic flight from London where both lived very different but successful lives. They had simultaneously decided a hiatus was needed to restore their creative energy, not a long one, just a week or so away.

Smugglers Cove, a quaint and as yet undiscovered little New England coastal town had been recommended by their father, Marc Patrone, as a retreat he occasionally snuck away to himself—a perfect place of anonymity for those seeking it. Their father was to join them in three days to spend time together; something the three looked forward to and had always made a great importance in their lives no matter how busy they were.

The two bicyclists, Ombline Patrone and her twin sister Georgianna, were as unalike as midnight and noon. Ombline, fair as the morning light, enigmatic lavender-blue eyes and hair the colour of moonlight, the rare beauty of a Nordic ice-queen was in startling contrast to the blue-black raven-haired Georgianna, her topaz cat-like eyes a draw to all she came in contact with. As different in appearance and personality as they were, they had had a connectedness from birth few sisters enjoy in life.

Bicycling in the autumn's early afternoon sunshine was a treat that had not been experienced by the two for quite some time—both needing to be away from the bustle of a cosmopolitan existence—a simple joy of nature reclaimed.

So far, they had encountered no traffic on the narrow meandering road through an autumn meadow of foliage—copses of trees readying for their eventual slumber; but for now, one last hurrah for what summer had been up to in its prime, a bounty of nature—seed pods, grasses and inedible fruits of the sort only wildlife would find tantalizing, a place of unique beauty, all in harmonic balance. Both bicyclists felt that rooted magical renewal only nature at its best can bestow.

Upon arrival the evening before, they had settled in as guests of Serpentines in an unfinished Victorian mansion being restored out and away from town. Their hostess had purchased the previously crumbling monstrosity comprised of local stone work for a restoration project as a diversion for her restless nature. She had not yet decided whether to sell it when completed or run it as a resort of sorts. The stone and millwork had been restored to the original design. The shutters framing the windows were sealed with a grey stain as the rest of the building's woodwork in keeping with the effect the harsh North Atlantic's coastal storms would eventually have on such a material as wood.

The suites were complete as was most of the interior but with the punch list yet to do. Georgianna and Ombline had delighted in the elegant décor combining an upgraded modern version of a sort of Victorianna with a few larger pieces of what they were sure were locally purchased antiques so as not to be suffocating with an over-powering Victorian theme. Every amenity of comfort had been accounted for, none overlooked because of the out of the way location.

They had arrived at sunset just as Serpentine's landscaper, Esmeralda Marrs, and her crew were leaving for the day. Serpentine had put a rush on to finish before the first snow to complete all the fall plantings and final landscaping touches. It was her goal to at least for now, have a grand opening before Thanksgiving and the holidays to come since cross-country skiing had become popular in the backcountry of the area west of Smugglers Cove.

Esmeralda had exited husband number four several years ago, and, to change her life to a new direction, been mentored by one of Boston's major landscaping firms. Discovering the undiscovered Smugglers Cove she had found *home* and had become one of the most successful entrepreneurs in the state.

Esmeralda had introduced herself before leaving for the day and offered what assistance she could if any problem arose, leaving her business card with the two young women.

After Esmeralda left, Ombline called Serpentine to apprise her of their arrival, that both were exhausted and required only hot showers and to bed. Serpentine invited them to lunch at her estate the next day and informed them that there were bicycles and safety helmets for their use if they so chose in Grey Hall's (a name Serpentine had decided upon for the old Victorian mansion) multiuse garages.

So, instead of taking their rental car to the estate for lunch they had decided a bicycle trip on such a beautiful autumn day was preferable. Two and a half miles to town, left on Main Street, then north, which became the Old Coast Road that ran parallel to the rocky cliffs along the Atlantic. Three miles north of town they were to turn west into Pendergast estates set well back from the Old Coast Road on a hillock of land—a promontory with a view of the ocean out beyond the cliffs.

Serpentine had related that the area was rife with old stories of marauders of both land and sea. One could view the waves crashing onto the mighty rocks below the cliffs on the eastern side of the road. Smugglers and pirates of long ago needed a lookout at the top of the cliffs to spot their passing prey in the dark blue waters out to sea. It was a place where the imagination could easily get away from one on storm-whipped nights.

There had been brochures laid out on the reception desk at Grey Hall describing the area's notorious past. Georgianna, always a romantic, pointed out that there might have been secret caves below the cliffs where boats could have been kept hidden for boarding the ships the smugglers looted, then, back up the cliffs and on to town with their rich booty, or, maybe store it in the caves. The locale certainly seemed to have had a rich history outside of the law.

"Oh-h-h-fun—pirates!—And a yo-ho-ho me Matey!" A gleeful Georgianna had exclaimed, thumbing through printed material from the reception desk upon their arrival the previous evening. "Look at this Ombline, maybe Grey Hall was originally a smuggler's hideout, or a transfer spot for stolen loot." She waved the brochure in Ombline's direction.

"I don't think so Georgianna, it's not old enough to have existed when Pirates controlled things hereabouts." Her sister quickly glanced through it and placed the brochure back on the desk.

Ombline picked up her bags and headed up the long staircase. Georgianna had followed. They both needed rest. They intended to relax and restore while at Grey Hall, then explore the quiet quaint town of Smugglers Cove and its coastal area, but they would enjoy what modern civilization had to offer weary travelers first.

Morning had found them both famished. The kitchen had not yet been stocked, only English muffins and cream cheese in the fridge. These had been opened and probably left there by workmen. At least there was strong coffee to brew in the Butler's pantry. Freshly invigourated, off they went pulling out two bicycles from the garages in back of Grey Hall.

Georgianna, in her dusty plum and light grey plaid jacket, jeans and short black boots looked more cosmopolitan than Ombline in her natural coloured fisherman's sweater, jeans and sneakers; but that was Georgianna's nature—fashionista whatever the occasion. It would be past lunch time when they arrived at the Pendergast estate—a late lunch.

Their route east to town was an easy ride—no extreme hills—rolling countryside to their left, to their right, a rambling ridge that paralleled the road. Groves of trees in autumn hues grew up the ridge's sides and along the top, their colours splashed everywhere.

Ombline remarked, peering up along the ridge line. "This could be a bit spooky out here at night, kind of perfect for All Hallows Eve, if for some reason one were out here in the dark just before sundown, gnarly-looking old trees up there—great for scary silhouettes that would appear to reach for you with their spindly hands." She exaggerated a shivering and laughed, looking askance at Georgianna who had always been easily caught up in some tall tale of Ombline's devising.

"Well, sister dear, I don't intend on being out here at night so my thoughts will not even go there—only the most pristine of experiences do I allow to loiter up here (Georgianna tapped her head) *while* I'm here—I don't even intend to have a flat tire on this bike, nothing but pure serenity!" She knew what Ombline was doing—all their lives from childhood on, Ombline had loved to rope her in with the creative embellishment of even the most mundane of *whatever* her mind chanced upon.

"Georgianna! Don't curse us with what you will and what you won't—you'll just bring *it*—whatever *it* is on us." Ombline laughed.

Her sister joined in her laughter. "Bring *what* on us? Don't be superstitious—what could possibly happen in such a peaceful place as this—I'm already so relaxed I might just fall off this bike!" Georgianna turned and stuck out her tongue at Ombline illustrating her complete confidence in her statement, just daring fate to take a whack at them on such a beautiful day in such a beautiful place. There had not been even a single piece of traffic on the road. It seemed they had it to themselves.

They peddled on in silence enjoying the beauty of the autumn day as the sun warmed the air. The further they rode, the higher the ridge along the road rose until at its highest point a blue-tiled roof could be seen on its summit. The building was sizable and seemed to occupy the highest point of the ridge. It was, like many of the local structures they had seen driving through town the night before, constructed of stone. Possibly a quarry nearby had made this a cost-effective and easily accessible building material.

From their vantage point they could see the unusual steep pitch of the three divisions of roof—the main body of the building and two smaller wings partially hidden by trees. Each section of roof had substantial lightening rods extending well above tree height.

"Isn't that odd?" Georgianna said turning to look at her sister pedaling beside her. "A blue roof, something you don't see everyday, and lightning rods, so lofty as to reach the sky—just waiting for a monster of an electrical storm to suck down its energy—or something; could that be the sort of arrangement needed for ham radios do you think?"

"That, I would not know." Ombline said as they peddled on down the road closer to the blue-roofed curiosity above the road. They could see that a drive snaked its way down the hillside through trees and thick underbrush to a gated entrance, not a sizable gate but a simple swing-out iron-barred one negating entry. A no trespassing sign was attached to the top.

Suddenly, a sizzling electric blue flash linked the three lightning rods up on the building's roof creating one formidable horizontal blue bar of energy turning from blue to deep purple and back to blue again, then it was gone, as if it had never existed—so unusually bright for the light of day.

They brought their bikes to a halt mesmerized by the unexpected electrification of the lightening rods, if that was what it had been.

Without turning away from what they had just witnessed, Ombline asked, not expecting an answer. "What *was* that? Such an intense jolt of energy!"

"It must have been some sort of freakish atmospheric lightening, or, they have a serious electrical problem." Georgianna said. "But then, I understand lightening can strike from as much as a mile away from its source even when there are no clouds around—not unheard of." She turned to Ombline scanning the sky. "There *are* no clouds—maybe some mad scientist lives and works up there."

"Or, maybe it's none of our business." Ombline finished for her.

"That, would be my guess." Georgianna agreed as they resumed the ride to town, all the while wondering what they had seen up on the ridge top, certainly a curiosity—such eye-catching and seemingly omnipotent powerful horizontal blues. The route through Smugglers Cove attested to the tucked away sea coast town's reputation of being a hidden jewel on the New England coast; quaint antique shops seemed to be the primary business of it's citizens—that, and restaurants, each proclaiming their own seafood specialty, most surely a fresh day's catch considering the fishing boats in Smugglers Cove's small harbour. The sun glinted off the water as it lapped against both fishing boats and those of a recreational nature as well, tied to old fashioned wooden docks. They took a quick bicycling tour around the little harbour and then continued the trip on up the coast road. The town they would explore later.

Chapter Two

There were no gates guarding the Pendergast estate—just a black top lane bordered by clipped hedges leading to an imposing (once again) stone residence affirming it's claim to the land it resided on; a decorative waist high stone wall encompassed the immediate grounds of the structure, more definitive than protective. Untouched forest provided a picturesque backdrop from the grounds as if nature was allowed a sanctuary from mankind. Rolling hills of forest merged with a distant blue haze of mountains far to the west.

The grand old trees on the grounds were occupied by a flock of cawing ravens only concerned with some food source they had noticed in the foliage left on the trees. Squirrels squawked their agitation at the black bandits, anxious they would be robbed of their winter's stash of food stuffs by the sudden invasion of the interlopers from the skies.

Georgianna and Ombline had worked up an appetite by the time they arrived. The ride north out of Smugglers Cove had been more arduous than to town—more uphill as the coast road wound it's way northward along the Atlantic. Spray from waves crashing on the rocks below had added an extra saltiness to the air. They parked their bikes to the side of the drive and rang the bell. A dark-haired Butler answered the door then escorted Georgianna and Ombline down the entrance hall of dark generational antiques against the backdrop of yellow-washed walls to the rear of the building's ballroom-sized solarium. There was no indication of such a vaulted glass repository of nature from the road or up the drive.

They entered the lofty glass enclosed dome expecting to see their hostess; a group of three turned in their direction, the taller of the women turned to them smiling and excused herself from the others to join her lunch guests introducing herself as Serpentine Pendergast.

"I'm so glad you could make it. Your father described each of you perfectly. You of course, are Ombline, and you, are surely Georgianna," she smiled, acknowledging each. Serpentine seemed truly delighted they had arrived. The older woman had a very likable kind of aggressive quality about her Georgianna thought later. Serpentine would have impressed anyone. She was sure her father's friend had once been one of the world's great beauties-even so now. She had an adventurous quality, sort of an Indiana Jones—maybe leather breeches, boots and even double revolvers had possibly not been at some time unknown to her; she exuded a daring fearlessness. Georgianna wondered if Serpentine's lineage was that of the smugglers—if so, they must have been dashing and very disarming swashbucklers themselves considering the woman's magnetic persona. She wondered how her father had avoided Serpentine's charms considering his six defunct marriages, but then maybe he hadn't since only now his daughters had been introduced to her after so many years of their friendship—a secret love in his life all along? *What was their history?*

Serpentine dressed simply—if elegantly, in a beige sweater and slacks, brown knee-high boots into which the legs of her slacks were tucked giving her an even more adventurous edginess. Thin by nature her still brunette hair and flashing dark eyes evinced a person who took life by the horns and enjoyed the tussle—even so—her warmth and kindness were obvious by several cats and five happy multi-breed dogs (surely shelter mutts) lounging in the solarium, now in a loving home. Three came with tails wagging when the girls had entered the room. Both bent to pet and return such open affection being great lovers of animals themselves.

Lunch had been an unexpected delight, nothing stuffy or formal. Serpentine's cook had prepared a veggie pizza, one of the best Ombline said she had ever had.

"Delia was trained in the culinary arts in California," Serpentine explained. "We greatly enjoy her fresh take on cuisine. I'll have her prepare a few of her freezeable specialties and send them over so all you have to do is heat them. While you're away from Grey Hall for the day the kitchen and pantry are being stocked so you needn't be concerned about dinner."

A pleasant two hours were spent with Serpentine who offered them a ride back with the bikes loaded in the SUV, but they declined saying how much they had enjoyed the ride and looked forward to biking back realizing it would be almost sunset by the time they arrived at Grey Hall. Still, it would be a fun adventure in the fresh autumn air.

Earlier, upon arrival, they had only been in the solarium long enough to be met by Serpentine and her dogs, but both were taken with the space in the process (they were told) of being decorated for the Harvest Moon Ball which Serpentine made a point of inviting them to, saying it was one of the town's most treasured yearly events. They were particularly taken with a centrally located piece of arresting statuary in the solarium over eight feet high and had not had the opportunity to inquire about it before they sat down to lunch. What was *its* tale—so very unusual?

During lunch Serpentine had momentarily excused herself to address the concerns of those involved in decorating the solarium for the ball. Ombline had remarked to Georgianna while digging into the pizza slice in her hand. "That statute in the solarium—it's remarkably similar in style to the twelve faerie statues on the Steffington estate—don't you think?" (The Steffington estate, located in north central Michigan, had been prominent in the twin's childhood. The faerie statues were the focal point of a garden maze the twins had played in as children with their cousin Chloe Steffington, the Steffington's grand-daughter, or as they thought of Chloe, as their sister in heart. In reality the three *were* cousins. Chloe's maternal grandmother, Lilly Patrone, had been the wife of their father's long ago miss-ing brother Alon, and, had maintained close ties through the years with Marc and the Steffingtons. Even now Chloe worked closely with her grandmother Lilly in the discovery aspect of Lilly's Art merchandising business in Michigan. The three little girls had always said they were triplets—not just twins plus one because they had so loved being together—so—they had pro-claimed themselves to be sisters—triplets)!

"This piece though, is much larger than the faerie statues, its wings are massive, very impressive and that one encompassing horn on top of the head spiraling it's way into such a spectacular headpiece—fantastic!"

"Do you think it could be by the same artist—that they are somehow related?" Georgianna asked.

"Possibly. It's certainly executed to convey the physical prowess of the male body," Ombline said, "a dominant nature spirit—beautiful of form—even frightening if you allow it to be."

Just as Georgianna intended to say more, Serpentine returned, she had obviously overheard the last of their discussion. "Yes, it is remarkable—a gift from an old friend many years ago. Are you enjoying your lunch?" With this she seemed to dismiss their inquisitiveness and changed the subject abruptly.

Later they thanked Serpentine for a gracious afternoon and headed back to Smugglers Cove and on to Grey Hall. Shadows had begun to lengthen by the time they reached town, for the dark now came much earlier this time of year. The temperature had dropped considerably and encouraged a faster pace back to the warmth of Grey hall.

Chapter Three

The sun was lowering toward the west and would soon present the almost bare branched trees on the ridge as Ombline had predicted, like spooky silhouettes of black gnarled hands appearing to reach for anyone unwary and brave enough to be up there after sundown.

They peddled a little faster remembering many of New England's ghost stories. The temperature was dropping even more rapidly now and both were eager to settle in for the evening in front of a warm fire in the mansion's main gathering room.

Dried autumn leaves skittered across the road in front of them in the gathering dusk in cadence with a gentle wind meandering down the ridge. The dried leaves' curled edges sounded like scurrying small feet as they were blown across the pavement. Along the far distant mountains to the west a deep blue line of dark purple storm clouds brewed—suggestive of a rainstorm later in the night—but for now, dust and the dry calm of a chilly disquieting autumn evening reigned. They pedaled faster choosing not to glance up to the ridge of gnarled trees anymore as they sped down the road knowing it was better not to spook themselves up.

The closer they came to that part of their ride where the blue-tiled house dominated the ridge, they did slow, expecting just what neither voiced, but it drew them. And then, out of nowhere a black Bentley emerged unexpectedly behind the iron gates crossbars, hardly a sound to indicate its ghostlike sudden appearance. The no trespassing sign jiggled as the gate swung outward. The black luxury car sped out and the gate swung back with a heavy clang. They quickly pulled to the side of the road standing by their bikes as far back as they could get as the Bentley sped past them all too close, not seeming to take note of them in the darkening countryside. Leaves were whipped up in explosions of dried brown in the wake of the car's passing, littering the two with a tornado of the crisp refuse.

Barely discernible in the darkened window of the speeding vehicle sat a woman unconcerned with the pedestrians beside the road, her dark hair worn in the braided coronet style of a previous era complementing the dark austere designer suit she wore—cognizant only of the failed attempt of her mission.

Georgianna shook her fist and shouted at the receding tail lights as the car sped away from them back toward Smugglers Cove. "You want to take another whack at us? We're not road kill yet in case you weren't sure about it!" Infuriated, she looked to Ombline passing the back of her hand across her forehead indicating relief that they had not been side-swiped by the unconcerned chauffeur of the dark woman passenger.

Ombline pushed her bike back onto the road. "Come on Georgianna just in case they come back to take another go at us. What ever is going on up there, (she paused only long enough to glance up the once again barred drive to the darkened hill-top house) I don't think we want to be around out here in the dark."

They jumped back on the bikes and peddled even faster down the road as the sun finally sank behind the mountains to the west leaving them in darkness. They sped up Grey Hall's drive and around back to the garages.

Motion detector lights came on as soon as they pulled up to the building to put away the bikes, likewise, lights came on lighting up all the entry doors to Grey Hall, a welcoming comfort to anyone just arriving from an unsettling experience in the dark.

They entered by a side door, turned off the alarm and reset it after locking the door behind themselves, then, set about laying a fire in the fireplace just as the first rumblings of distant thunder could be heard.

Georgianna mocked in a ghostly voice. "Woo-woo-o-o-o, a stormy night in a haunted old smuggler's mansion—need me to sleep with you tonight Ombline?" She teased her sister as she handed her kindling to start the fire.

"I don't think so." Ombline laughed. "Only if I have to beat off some ardently romantic swashbuckler of a spirit, besides this isn't exactly your ordinary old, cob-webby haunted house—the best of everything—a ghost wouldn't feel at home in all this clean modern comfort. Let's eat! I'm starved with all this outdoor life."

Ombline found the pantry and freezer full as Serpertine had promised and popped a pizza in the oven while both showered, later sitting in front of the fireplace each with a glass of wine and half a pizza. The storm had rumbled its way to Grey Hall. Heavy rain drops beat on the windowpanes as the thunder rolled across the dark landscape; flashes of lightning illuminated the wind-whipped tree branches outside the windows making the comfort of the fireside even more delicious.

Ombline nibbled at a slice of pizza for the second time in one day. "If we're going on a pizza diet we're going to have to ride those bikes sun-up to sun-down or we are both going to be waddling home."

Georgianna gave a knowing nod. "Back on track tomorrow, let's bike back to town for lunch—hopefully, not to be run down by any mysterious chauffeured Bentley in the light of day."

"Agreed"

They sat in front of the firelight a while longer just listening to the rain on the window panes and metal roof. Eventually the relaxed calm of the day out-of-doors called them both to a night's rest with the rain still a-patter outside. Through the night the storm rolled across the countryside and eventually on out into the Atlantic leaving the earth cleansed for autumn's glory.

Chapter   Four

The storm of the night before being long gone had produced a beautiful sunny morning. A morning most anyone would be eager to find something to do involving the outdoors. Again, Georgianna and Ombline prepared for a bike trip, this time to lunch in town and then, where ever wanderlust directed them for the rest of the afternoon. Maybe farther up the coast, having been told the scenery became even more compelling as the road wound up the old Atlantic coast's original highway.

The ride to Smugglers Cove was pleasant and uneventful. Nothing out of the ordinary seemed to be associated with the blue-tile house on the ridge, deserted as it seemed to have been initially. No dark strangers in Bentleys attempting to run them down or sizzling blue lightening bolts to mar the day.

They racked their bikes out front of what Marc Patrone had recommended to his daughters as the best place to have lunch in town—Contraband—an establishment of fine cuisine with an unusually large and varied menu, evidently a gathering place for dinner as well with a considerable wine list for such a small town; it seemed to cater to all tastes.

"Seems larger inside than outside, as in *Dr. Who's TARDIS.*" Georgianna commented, being a fan of the long-running British science fiction program, as if this tongue-in-cheek comment could in fact be reality.

Ombline turned to look at her sister and just shook her head smiling. "You're so easy Georgianna!"

"What?"

"Nothing. Nothing anyone but me would understand—as you have been known to say more than a few times—lets eat!"

Contraband seemed filled to capacity for lunch. They ate at the bar knowing it would most likely be faster than being seated at a table.

They agreed on lunch when their bartender/waiter took their orders for salads with cheese, crusty bread, an assortment of olives and iced tea—no wine; they wanted high energy for their afternoon ride and certainly not the extra calories!

Thaddeus, their bartender, was helpful, offering information of local historical colour not usually found in the tourist brochures after they had introduced themselves. Smugglers Cove residents intended to keep their town off the map as a tourist destination except for a few *favoured* guests and semi-permanent residents.

Ombline seized on Thaddeus's knowledge of local lore and asked about the blue house as she was beginning to think of it.

"Call me Thad, most people here do—by the way I know your father. He's a regular here when he's in town." Thad continued. "The story of Dragons Roost as the structure is known in these parts has a history of mystery and strange goings-on, not haunted—just not lived in for a long time, strange purplish-blue lightening episodes now and again. A geologist passing the summer here believed that was caused by the building's location on the ridge, electrical activity of storms passing out to sea were likely attracted by the lightning rods and are the cause of these anomalies. No one here has actually ever investigated the phenomenon that I'm aware of. That's really all there is to the story. If you wish to know more you might inquire of Ms. Pendergast. She is the titled owner of Dragons Roost and most of the land out there—it's all posted—no hunting and no trespassing, strictly enforced. I'm sure you saw the sign on the gate of the drive." Thad excused himself when another customer drew his attention away from their conversation.

"Well," Georgianna said, still rattled from being almost run down from the night before, "who was the unconcerned passenger not stopping for a near miss at us if no one is supposed to be up there—very suspicious. As unexpected a vehicle as I would have anticipated coming down out of the woods in the dark from a deserted house—a chauffeured Bentley, would not have even been on my list—doesn't that seem more than a bit odd Ombline? The woman passenger was certainly *not* Serpentine, we could have been weeds for all she cared! Maybe we should inform Serpentine as to what happened."

"And maybe you're making much ado about nothing. Serpentine is a land owner here and into local real estate development. Consider that the woman in the Bentley was interested in purchasing Dragons Roost, someone in a hurry, maybe the driver really *didn't* see us, it *was* almost dark." Ombline rationalized in an attempt to keep Georgianna's feet adhered to the earth being very familiar with how her sister's creative imagination at times seemed to go flying off into other realms.

"In such a hurry as to almost run us down and not even stop? That driver had to see us—I don't buy that. Something strange is happening out there—I can feel it!"

"Here we go." Ombline mumbled under her breath taking her time in responding to Georgianna, knowing from past experience her sister was off and running and that it would most likely do no good to try and contain her enthusiasm with logic. "Listen, "Nancy Drew", that may be, but, we're here to relax and not get involved in a mystery that could be very dangerous to our good health—or worse—slinking around the countryside into something that we might be better off not knowing about."

"You mean druggers?" Georgianna narrowed her eyes at her sister in the excitement of a possible mystery. "That whole scenario did not speak to me of drugs Ombline. That woman in the Bentley didn't have the look of a drugger—too sophisticated, she reeked of money and power, and—something much more sinister needing the dark of night to be done. I almost feel as if it's our duty to let Serpentine know about this."

Ombline took a deep breath not ready to give in to Georgianna's quick draw suppositions; she had always been prone to an over active imagination since birth, Ombline was sure this was an attribute of a great actress which Georgianna was, acting was her life blood—the very substance of her life. "I don't know," Ombline said, then, quickly added. "Let's leave it alone for now unless something else untoward happens. Dad will be here tomorrow, we've looked forward to spending time with him, let's not allow something that's not any of our business to spoil it. He knows Serpentine well, let's see what he thinks."

Most of their family had long ago dropped all familial titles and used their given names, although living in England both young women had grown up vacillating between calling their father Dad, Daddy or Marc, circumstances seeming to dictate which. Usually it was Daddy. Marc instead of Daddy had only lasted in their early teen years as they had taken on pretentious affectations for a short period, Marc later related that he was thankful for its short duration, as he said it had always made him feel like the hired help.

Ombline was the one who thought things through with a more methodical and rational approach frustrating Georgianna, who was of a spontaneous temperament—often to her sister's exasperation, saying to Ombline on more than a few occasions. *You're putting way too much time in on this Ombline—just decide—do it—all it can do is kill you.* Ombline's more serious nature did not think this was humorous. Georgianna would only shake her head and walk away knowing she would never change her sister and if the truth be known, she didn't want to, for Ombline's more conservative nature, her attention to detail as a successful writer of fiction, gave a certain amount of grounding and a parameter of safety to Georgianna in her somewhat headlong attitude toward life. They had always been a balance to one another.

Georgianna, a successful stage actress in the London theatrical world was by nature a person of immediate spontaneity—always in a hurry. The two sisters seemed to complement one another in every aspect. Marc had commented on this explaining them as a lock and key—each different objects but necessary to a door—or—better yet as the co-dependency of Laurel and Hardy, an early twentieth century comedy team heralded by the film industry. Two opposite personalities but forever needful of each other—something no others could ever fill for them.

Ombline, made an offer she thought Georgianna could agree with for the present. "I say again, let's wait until Daddy gets here tomorrow and see what he thinks—or—we can get in touch with Serpentine right now. It's your call Georgianna."

Georgianna knew what Ombline was doing, making her appear paranoid and suspicious, embarrassed at her over eagerness at such titillation as she was perceived to be indulging in unnecessarily, so she would back down without a struggle—well she *would* wait till tomorrow and get their father's opinion. He would be a guest at Grey Hall himself instead of staying in Serpentine's guest house as they knew he usually did on his visits to Smugglers Cove. He loved spending time with his girls.

Georgianna relented. "Okay, you win, let's pay our bill and get out of here and on up the coast road and more of this never ending bike riding. By the way, why did we get that rental car anyway?"

Ombline smiled. "Don't you know? To get from the airport to here to the bikes."

Georgianna laughed. "We could have taken a shuttle and saved the fee."

"Come on Georgianna, I've never known you to be so frugal as all that—no car at your disposal?"

They left town and once again headed north past the Pendergast estate enjoying the afternoon sunshine and the sound of waves on the rocks below the cliffs. The scenery was as beautiful as they had been told and stopped occasionally to admire points of interest along the way. There was little traffic on the road being replaced decades ago by the interstate farther inland, bypassing the quaint coastal town of Smugglers Cove, leaving it almost, a place forgotten in time.

Ombline, always prepared, had brought bottled water and granola bars in her bicycle basket. They enjoyed these later in the afternoon while sitting on a tourist bench on a roadside pullover. As the day wore on, shadows quickly lengthened indicating it was time to turn around and head back before it got too late and darkness caught them on the road again.

The distance back to town was an easier ride than when they had left out as the coast road was an ever so slightly decreasing grade to Smugglers Cove, thus the increasing depression creating the inland cove for the sea to wash into long ago.

They had underestimated the time it would take getting back. It was going to be just as dark arriving back at Grey Hall today as it had yesterday. They pedaled furiously as dusk set in and were almost to Dragons Roost when from that very direction the sky lit up with the purple-blue light, so intense and lasting as to sear one's vision causing both to turn away with the brightness of the unexpectedness of such radiance.

Ombline's bike skidded to the side of the road, Georgianna following on her heels almost spilling them both onto the roadside gravel.

Ombline regained control of her bike pulling up abruptly in a sideways skid of gravel spraying the spokes of her sister's bike. She turned back to Georgianna. "Are you okay? What the hell was that—that soundless explosion of light?" Ombline passed her hands quickly over her eyes giving her head a little shake reassuring herself she could still see. Her biking partner was no better off than herself but did seem unfazed by their near collision and the blinding flash.

Georgianna saluted Ombline in sarcastic assurance. "Temporarily blinded, but still upright. Come on Ombline, I've had it—can't stand it anymore—we are going up there. I've got to see what is going on—with you or without you."

Georgianna took off in a spray of gravel sliding in to a purposeful sideways spin in front of the barred gate to Dragons Roost.

Ombline was vexed at Georgianna's irresponsible impatience and took her time pulling up behind her in a huff. "Are you crazy—what if that *was* some sort of radiation—or something far worse—maybe we're dying at this very moment?" She hissed, unbelieving at the dark haired outline's naïveté in front of her.

Georgianna wanted her sister's compliance and explained in her view how innocent this little hike up the hill would be, for in reality she knew she would be a lot braver if Ombline went with her. "Listen, Ombline, since almost being road kill last night I've been bursting with curiosity. We'll stash the bikes here in the bushes beside the gate, climb up the ridge and peek in the windows then leave. That's all—just a peek. You know you're just as curious as I am!"

C h a p t e r   F i v e

Ombline was stubbornly quiet for a moment, then grudgingly relented whispering under her breath. "Alright. Alright. The flashlight that we don't have by the way, would have been helpful if we're going to be stumbling around out here clawing our way uphill through underbrush in the dark, but I'm sure that's okay too, as most likely we'll soon be glowing in the dark anyway from whatever that blue flash was! Just a peek in the windows, that's all, then leave Georgianna, *that*, is—all! Oh… and another thing you haven't considered, what if that Bentley woman is up there tonight, as last night, I don't think it would be wise to run into her in person, have you even considered that a possibility?"

"Yes—I have! It rained last night—a lot. Even in the encroaching darkness *Watson*, (Georgianna made it plain Ombline was Watson—not Holmes, since Ombline was a very reluctant participant) you can see there are no tire tracks in the mud— earth as smooth as a baby's bottom. No one is up there."

Ombline still looked for a way out. "What if there's a back way up from the other side of the ridge. Have you considered that?"

"Look, you can wait here if you want." Georgianna proceeded to drag her bike into the proverbial bushes *pretty* sure Ombline would come with her considering the curious nature they both possessed, and, Georgianna did not intend to go up there alone.

Ombline, against her better judgment did the same. They squeezed around the sides of the gate and ducked under the shrubbery overhanging each end of it and made their way up the lengthy overgrown drive to the dark Dragons Roost as if it waited for them. There was no evidence of the explosive light they had just witnessed. All was quiet, still—and yes—even darker.

Ombline thought to herself why in the spookiest situations did everything always get completely quiet—no sound—just to more so scare the pants off you at the slightest nudge of abnormality when all you can hear is your own heart beating. She tried to fight off visions of every slasher movie she had ever seen, but such mental pictures certainly fit this outing, two brainless twits out in the dark woods trying to break into the crazed killer's home!

At the top of the drive they softly scuttled through years of dried dead leaves and on across to the dark building surrounded by those spooky gnarled leafless trees seemingly just waiting to grab them when they weren't looking. They cautiously peeked in the windows—actually several—only a few had the inside shutters opened to let in light which had become almost nonexistent with the final setting of the sun.

Ombline intently gazed through one of the windows to the dark interior trying to determine what, if anything, she could see inside the building and didn't notice Georgianna wasn't with her anymore until she turned around to ask if she'd had enough and was ready to go. She didn't see her anywhere. "Georgianna—Georgianna, are you satisfied?" She called out into the dark, lowering her voice as much as she could and still be heard. "There's nothing to see—let's go—I have to believe we saw some sort of unusual freak lightening. That's all—come on!" Ombline turned to start down the drive when a strong hand grabbed her by the back of the neck. "Oh God!" Ombline's knees almost deserted her until she whipped around recognizing her grabber with great relief. "What the hell are you doing sneaking up behind me like that after taking off without telling me? This is the last time I go breaking and entering with you Georgianna!—I'm so-o-o ready to get out of here and back to Grey Hall! Freddy Kruger is all I've been able to think about since we came up here!"

Georgianna laughed at the reaction she had elicited from Ombline by grabbing her by the back of the neck again, not expecting her sister to completely freak out like she had. "Sorry." She whispered. "But I just couldn't resist. You won't feel that way when you see what I found—an open door around back. Georgianna didn't wait but disappeared around the corner of the building.

Ombline, against her better judgment followed her sister around back and up a wide set of stone steps to a weighty wooden door attached with iron fittings and hardware. "Georgianna, you wouldn't be so brave if I weren't with you"

"You're right, I admit it, you're very kind to humour me even though I know what a curious bent you're possessed of yourself, though, of a more conventional academic nature."

"I too am puzzled, and knew in the back of my mind we were going to find ourselves up here sooner or later—which we both know without a doubt is most likely dangerous and none of our business, but, here we are. Come on, let's go in and get this over with and back to Grey Hall."

Georgianna pressed the handle and the door swung inward leaving them standing on the stoop. With the absence of almost any light inside they could see only the barest of furnishings still occupied the abandoned dark interior; the room they first entered was centered with a fireplace bracketed with floor to ceiling shelves now vacant of books or decorative items.

They went throughout the house similarly bare and containing only a few major pieces of furniture most likely too heavy to have been easily transported, giving rise to the feeling that Dragons Roost's former occupants had the intention of one day returning.

They moved to the center-most room, much larger than the others, it too contained a fireplace, almost filling one central wall—likely backing the fireplace in the room they had first entered. A tiny closet flanked one side, bookshelves on the other.

The room contained sparse laboratory equipment and high long tables evoking a deserted laboratory setting. The lofty ceiling's wooden beams were draped with the remnants of pulleys and chains hanging in the open space above—and—so out of place as to be in a Salvador Dali painting—a massive ornate blue metal frame—a floor to ceiling piece one would expect to contain mirrored glass, but empty. Much taller than wide, it stood positioned on a four-legged stand in the middle of the room.

"Why would such a thing be in a laboratory?" Georgianna looked to Ombline.

Ombline moved closer to the blue monstrosity slowly moving her hand along it as if reassuring herself it was real. "Holy Alice! What could this possibly be used for in a laboratory—I've never seen anything like it!" She said this to no one in particular walking around behind the giant frame as if it would somehow be different on the other side.

Their speculation was abruptly brought to a halt by the slamming of a car door. They froze for just a brief moment not doubting who it would be.

Georgianna rose to swift action, frantically dragging Ombline by the arm across the room shoving her into the little closet and squeezing into it with her. A hushed urgency prompted the two to cram themselves side by side into the small space fearful of even hearing their own breath—one peering out through the hinged side of the slightly ajar door while the crack of the doors handle side provided an equally good place to observe the room.

The dark of the room's interior helped to conceal the obviousness of such a choice of concealment, but then, no one could have suspected their presence.

They heard her footsteps before they saw her. As last night, a dark odious presence preceded the woman in the expensive designer suit and thick coronet braid around the top of her head as if in a self coronation.

Both Patrones were frozen in place and made not a sound. They were in the perfect spot to observe what she did.

The woman turned, scanning the room, believing she was alone. She had brought no source of light so as not to draw any attention to Dragons Roost and what she was attempting. She carried a black box emitting a greenish glow from the technology engaged in its interior. Lights flowed in coloured sequence on its top as she made adjustments in hurried movements standing expectant before the blue metal frame. A glow started around the interior of the frames edges and quickly spread to the center filling the frame with a blue swirling surface. Fog drifted outward as the surface began to shift and pulse in intensity.

Both closet dwellers were spellbound by what they were witnessing.

The woman adjusted the black box once more as freezing cold accompanied by a nausea inducing vibration filled the room. She stepped forward and attempted to enter through the frames blue pulsating surface. Straightaway she was jettisoned from her attempt and thrown back against the wall opposite the mirror and lay momentarily unmoving on the floor as if she had been spit out.

Georgianna was afraid to move fearing disclosure, but to reassure herself that Ombline was seeing what she saw, cautiously nudged Ombline's arm where they touched. Ombline nodded in agreement looking only straight ahead, afraid she would miss what would come next.

The woman raised up on one elbow and hissed in anger as she got to her feet, then gracefully maneuvered out of the way as she was unexpectedly pummeled with objects coming through the mirror. She screamed in a fit of rage and ran from the house still clutching the black box. Her hurried exit ended with a car door slamming and the quiet motor of the car descending the drive.

Georgianna and Ombline exited the closet and for just an instant leaned back against the wall on each side of its door in adrenalin-induced exhaustion. The interior glow of the blue frame had blinked out. They were now in darkness and moved ever so slowly away from the presumed safety of the closet.

"Ombline," Georgianna began, knowing her sister knew no more than she did. "What the Hell was that—*what* just happened? Is that woman an alien? Are we in some secret alien outpost where they come and go?"

"I—do not—know, but I do know we have to get out of here now!"

They felt their way across the floor in the dark with Georgianna summarily stepping on something squishy and sliding almost to the floor before Ombline grabbed her arm in mid fall. Ombline stooped to pick up one of the lumps on the floor that Georgianna had slipped on and could tell even in the dark it was some sort of fruit. She began stuffing the pockets and inside of her sweatshirt with as many as she could.

Georgianna hissed in eagerness to be on their way. "Why are you taking time to do that—what if they're poison or something, she could return any moment?"

Ombline continued stuffing her bulging pockets answering while she did so. "Since it seemed to be the eruption through the mirror that so traumatized our *dark Alice*, who, after trying unsuccessfully to walk through that—that—portal—or whatever it was she conjured up with that little jewel of technology she carried, I would like to know why she was so frightened into giving up so easily by a bunch of fruit—but, as you say she could return at any moment for another go at it—let's get out of here!" She started for the door not looking back to see if Georgianna was behind her or not but paused briefly as both took one last look at the inactive frame and then navigated out and down the drive to their bikes and back to the sane safety of Grey Hall.

They were so tired they left the bikes outside by the garage doors. Inside, Ombline emptied the contents of her scavaging into the vegetable drawers of the fridge. Georgianna stared at what Ombline held in her hands, turquoise, bright blue and purple fruit similar in appearance to apples or maybe nectarines. Small nicks on some evidenced a bright orange interior along with a scintillating aroma. Ombline finished stashing her booty from Dragons Roost and plopped into one of the kitchen chairs as Georgianna had for herself.

Georgianna looked to her twin. "Are we in Oz yet?"

"I would *say* so!"

Chapter Six

Georgianna had slept late. It was almost nine and she had just finished showering and dressing in jeans, white sweater and short brown boots when she heard a vehicle in the drive of Grey Hall. Ombline was in back on the second floor. She could easily see the driver from her window as he cut the engine of a black SUV. She recognized the disembarking figure as that of her father, Marc Patrone, who had begun removing luggage from the back of the tailgate. Tall, like all the Patrones and Steffingtons, Marc had a lean well structured physique that had endured through his life without much effort; he had the blue-black hair that Georgianna had inherited from him, the only difference in their coloring was his deep *blue* eyes, so different from hers.

Marc had been a widower since early September and had seemed to recover surprisingly well in so short a time, not quite two months; but then he had been married to his sixth wife such a short time and knew her before their marriage an even briefer time. He was looking forward to this quiet, laid-back respite with Georgianna and Ombline.

He had always been there for his twin daughters, even though he and their mother had been divorced since they were very little girls. Their mother Octavia had remarried Sir Gregory Prichard. Georgianna and Ombline had grown up in Octavia's London town home and Sir Gregory's English country estate.

It had been said of Marc Patrone, that he was a financial wizard with all his accrued wealth, not withstanding, he had always exuded a magnetic appeal to the opposite sex, it had seemed to ooze from his very DNA. The epitome of a man of the world imbued with initiative of spirit, foresight and a respect for reality that had proved a formidable combination on the world stage. His name appeared in the gossip columns of the world's most glamorous cities. Never having been one to settle in one place for long, he had homes in the states, (the Virginia mountains, Montana and San Francisco) Sweden and Monaco.

And with his appreciation of the female species, neither could he seem to *light* in just one relationship and call *it* home— even so, the love of his life had and always would be his adored daughters. He had looked forward to a week or so in this tucked away autumn paradise with Georgianna and Ombline, his old friend Serpentine Pendergast and the quiet solitude of nature.

After the abrupt and unexpected accidental death of his sixth wife Ursula, he had felt the need to revaluate his life, he had planned to be unencumbered by any serious romantic entanglements for a bit—even though he knew this would not last, acknowledging his own nature. Maybe he had just not yet met *the* woman—then again, maybe it was futile to ignore his roaming nature.

His two most recent trips to Smugglers Cove had opened to him an aspect of life he had not expected, and he wanted to this time make introductions to his daughters before making further decisions. He had known before the lab accident that killed Ursula on the Steffington estate in Michigan, that their hasty marriage had been a mistake and knew it would have to be dissolved quickly. With the prenuptial agreement, his regrettable state could have been resolved with an expediency that would have freed both parties to resume their lives if the accident had not happened.

Ursula's cruel nature and her prying into privileged technologies had caused her death to be complete in a laboratory experiment she had forced her way into, resulting in the annihilation of her physical body—no funeral or memorial service as she had no family or friends Marc knew of. He believed her to have been a creature of her own creation—a loner—a predator of sorts; and for all his worldliness he had been taken in by her allure. Now he wasn't sure if it had been even that. In the beginning after her death, only a passing guilt stayed with him for a brief time at feeling nothing for such a tragedy—but, he didn't— only a kind of relief as in her last days a coldness of nature seemed to erupt from her that was disturbing, he had wondered after her death if she wasn't a psychopath. This was a mistake he would *not* make again. The sunlight of life was what he now sought.

"Daddy…!" Both daughters ran out to help with his bags. They hugged Marc. Even if he had not been their father he was a man people gravitated to as he seemed to bring people together in a spirited enjoyment of life. They walked back to Grey Hall each carrying a bag while talking over one another eager to catch up with all that their recent lives had been about and their plans for the future.

"Dad," Ombline asked, "did you drive all the way up from Virginia?" As a general rule she was a Dad person while with Georgianna it was usually Daddy. Even with that they were different.

"Yes I did, it's a beautiful drive this time of year if you take all the back routes instead of the interstates, gives one time to take stock of things—very enjoyable."

Neither Georgianna nor Ombline had met his sixth wife Ursula before her tragic death, but, had known of the hasty marriage's strain and that it had been a great mistake from phone conversations with their cousin Chloe in Michigan. A number of family gatherings had been disastrous when Marc had introduced Ursula to family there—it had been a difficult time. They understood what a sour taste the woman had left their family with, so her name was not brought up. The details of her death had never been fully explained to Ombline or Georgianna. They wanted their father to be happy and put all that behind him helping to get him settled in upstairs in a suite of his own. Afterward the three sat down to coffee and some breakfast nibbles as it was getting on toward lunch. Ombline brought a tray out on the big half round porch on the east end of the house so they could discuss their plans for the day—and—they needed desperately to talk about last night.

Chapter Seven

Marc enjoyed the dark aromatic coffee and brisk air in the company of the two people he loved most in the world—and yes—he instinctively knew something was up with them. They had seemed happy at his arrival but they were conversationally antsy and he could see they needed to dive into something they felt awkward about. He began a second cup of the dark brew. Peering over it he simply said. "So—what is it girls—what's up?"

They looked to one another as to who would begin their tale of Dragons Roost. Georgianna nodded to Ombline. "You tell it, you've always been the more rational and conventional of the two of us."

Ombline licked her lips and took a deep breath. "Dad, we have something so strange to relate, it's hard even to begin. I'm just going to lay it out." She continued with all that had transpired concerning Dragons Roost since that first day culminating with their break-in and the strangeness of last night's developments. There was no immediate response from their father after Ombline finished. They didn't know what to expect—ridicule, pharmaceutical drugging or just what his reaction might be. Not surprising, they could tell he had been taken aback by the description of such fantastic events. Whatever the outcome, they knew he was the one person they must convince with the seriousness of their experience, and, what were the implications of such bizarre happenings?

Seconds passed. He gave no comment, then stood, tossed his napkin on the table and hurried inside and up the stairs yelling back to them that he had to make a most urgent phone call and to stay put, he would return shortly.

Georgianna looked to Ombline. "Strange reaction—how are we supposed to take that—he just walks away?"

Ombline concealed her concern at Marc's turn but said nothing. Ten minutes later he returned certainly preoccupied. He offered reassurances that both young women were unconvinced of. They were concerned with the gravity evident on his face. Was it from their related events or some other urgency of his own from the phone call? What had so affected him that he had made not one comment before running upstairs to phone *who*? A cloistered seriousness so unlike their father now clouded his previously jovial nature.

He sat down at the table choosing his words carefully. He knew he need be selective with what he said next. "I just spoke with Peter Steffington about your experiences."

Peter Steffington, the grandfather of their cousin Chloe, was a long time friend and confidant of their father. They knew the two men had a history of sheltered secrecy hidden in international intrigue which their father had never disclosed the details of; it was just something they had lived with, the knowledge of—an accepted given, never questioning.

Marc related the basics of his phone conversation. "The original owner of Dragons Roost is an unconventional colleague and very old friend of Peters. I'm familiar with the man, being acquainted with him off and on through the years and know him simply as Zorloff. He's a physicist like Peter. Dragons Roost was closed by Zorloff, locked and boarded up for the years he has been in Europe. Earlier in his life he did research up there. After he left for Europe Serpentine bought the property from him leaving everything as it had been. No one should have been up there. He has some concern. Old laboratory equipment can be dangerous." That sounded weak even to Marc.

Georgianna blurted out her incredulity. "There's not much else up there in the way of lab equipment to be concerned about Dad. What kind of research was this Zorloff doing that he needed that big blue frame in a laboratory?...What is that for—that woman last night sure seemed to think she was going through it to somewhere! Come on Daddy, this is more than weird—what is it you're not telling us?"

Marc ignored her attempt at pinning him down with her questions knowing full well anything he might say would be suspect. "Peter and Zorloff are involved in a project of great consequence without the involvement of others. Peter and I believe what the two of you witnessed is somehow related to what they are trying to achieve. The two of them will be here tomorrow."

Georgianna looked to Ombline, both knew their father was being careful with words and yes—something serious was a-brewing here but didn't voice this not knowing any more than they did for now. Their concerns seemed to be completely unaddressed—certainly not satisfying answers for such high strangeness.

"Daddy." Georgianna began, knowing it was time to bring up the subject of the fruit. "We brought back some of the fruit catapulted through the vortex of the frame that convinced that woman into leaving in such a hurry. We have it stored in the pantry fridge. It looks like no fruit we've ever seen. Come take a look."

The three left the porch for the fridge's strange contents.

Marc stared into the drawer saying nothing.

"Unearthly edibles huh?" Ombline said, not expecting an answer. "And no, we haven't taken a bite or put any on our cereal just to ease your mind Dad. Smells really good though, and they seem to be as fresh and robust looking as if they were just picked."

Georgianna wondered why her father didn't seem to be as impressed as they both had been with the drawer's contents and its effect on the dark woman, maybe you just had to have been there and seen her response. "We should duct tape the drawer shut till Peter and his friend check them out."

"I have a better idea." Marc said. "It's a little remote out here and considering all that's going on just down the road I think I would feel better if you girls moved over to Serpentine's estate. She certainly has room—maybe even the guest house."

They looked to one another saying nothing yet.

He began searching through the pantry and came up with a white cooler filling it with the fruit and crushed ice. "First we need to take these over to Serpentine's. Her pantry is equipped for the long-term storing of produce. I'm sure her cook will guard them well."

Georgianna said. "Sounds like a plan for the fruit Daddy, but for us (she looked to Ombline) we've enjoyed the seclusion of Grey Hall—and," she smiled, "we've started to really get into this biking business. I don't think there's any danger to us as we were never seen in Dragons Roost."

"We'll discuss this later." Marc said with the finality that only a concerned father can relay no matter how old his daughters are.

With the suddenness of a click, that rascally persona returned that they were most familiar with—as if the sun had come out from the clouds.

"That's done." Mark said dusting his hands as if finished with a burdensome chore. "Let's go to lunch in wheels—*not* bicycles." He cajoled his daughters. "There's someone I'd like you to meet." His old roguish sparkle had returned as a twinkle evidenced itself. He had a surprise.

Ombline and Georgianna were not fooled. They knew what this would be about. "Right Dad, sup-rise—sup-rise—surprise!" They giggled and voiced in unison hi-fiving one another after Marc went inside to freshen up before they went to lunch.

Chapter   Eight

They dropped off the fruit to Serpentine's cook Delia with the story and instructions as how to preserve the fruit, that it was not to be disturbed for it was a rare tropical fruit needed for seed propagation being held for a friend of Serpentine's. They then went on their way to lunch at Contraband.

At the restaurant the hostess seemed pleased to have Marc once again on the premises as a regular. Georgianna looked knowingly at Ombline as once more their father had a home away from home. They too, being his offspring had been welcomed at Contraband. They sat in a private alcove in back of the restaurant containing five cozy tables. This seemed to be familiar seating for Marc as their hostess knew just where to put them—at what particular table.

This made Georgianna immediately suspicious and amused. *It's a pretty sure bet that he, a recent widower, is already on the prowl.* It didn't take long for her suspicions to be verified. Marc lit up as he spotted a familiar face across the way just entering the dining room.

He stood, excusing himself, explaining that they would be joined for lunch with a friend of his. He walked across the room to a smartly dressed Esmeralda Marrs, escorted her to their table then introduced the three women to one another saying they had probably met at Grey Hall but because of his intervention they were now officially, socially introduced. Everyone laughed.

They shared a bottle of wine and an assortment of appetizers during a lunch of unexpected camaraderie between the four people.

They had never seen their father so engaged with another woman intellectually—actually sharing friendship. The two seemed in complete harmony—very comfortable and yet the affection between the two was obvious. This was new for Marc.

Ombline commented to Georgianna later. "Seems to be one of those *I finally got it right matches*, seeing as how she's finished four marriages and he six."

"We'll see." Georgianna just smiled and said nothing more knowing her father's history. Or, she thought, maybe he's just met his match.

Ombline said. "My guess is, they've both had enough of experiencing all that can go wrong—wouldn't you think?"

Georgianna shook her head. "I wouldn't bet on it. They're both unique individuals. Esmeralda seems out of type for Daddy though—extremely independent—actually wealthy from her landscaping business. I understand eleven stores in three surrounding states plus all the projects she travels to overseeing the progress. How would she have time for him?"

Ombline rolled her eyes. "Don't you know by now there's always time for romance? You know our father, if there had been a memorial service for Ursula, he would most likely have brought a date!"

Georgianna just smiled and shook her head. "No doubt."

Before lunch was over Mark got a call from Serpentine to remind them that they should stop by the South Moon House if they didn't already have costumes for the Harvest Moon Ball. If they delayed, all the best costumes would be gone.

Marc dropped the two off at Grey Hall and headed back toward town not disclosing his destination but admonishing both young women to be careful knowing they had an afternoon of biking and costume hunting planned so as to be ready for tomorrow night's festivities.

He informed them Esmeralda would be his date for the event and added with a twinkle in his eye, "I'm sure there will be some single young men there—lawyers, surgeons and astronauts—you know the type—just what every girl is looking for." He laughed at his own cuteness. They did not.

"You two have no sense of humour ladies. Go—go, get out and get on with your bicycling." He shooed them in good humour, both giving him a peck on the cheek.

"See you at dinner Dad—lots of goodies in the pantry freezer." Georgianna said.

"We'll see about dinner—anyway I'll be back at Grey Hall early. If there's anything, and I do mean *any* trouble, call 911 immediately and then me. Okay?"

"Okay." They both drawled in unison as if they were teenagers whose good times were being trod upon. Old habits die hard.

Mark pulled the black SUV out of the drive and onto the road to town. The afternoon was unnaturally warm and still holding as Georgianna and Ombline once more pedaled to town. They had grown to love these outdoor excursions, their rental car still in Grey Hall's garage untouched since they had arrived.

The weather hopefully would hold for the Harvest Moon Ball. The moon would be full and ready in all its glory, seeming to be at its largest this time of year only because of the tilt of the earth.

The two costume shoppers parked their bikes in front of South Moon House (where, if you were a local going to the ball, Serpentine had said, this was the place to find your costume) and entered a barn-like interior containing racks of costumes lining the walls in back of the store. Every sort of gift item imaginable covered the rest of the store's considerable space. Smaller antiques rested atop large ones. No inch of space had been neglected— something for every size wallet or credit card—truly a Shopper's Mart.

Ombline remarked, taking in the crowded inventory contained in the building, that there were more than enough customers milling about to make getting to the costumes difficult; and, like Serpentine had advised, the choices were dwindling.

"I'm surprised she didn't mention this earlier." Ombline said.

"I guess it just slipped her mind. Maybe she thought Daddy told us to get costumes. She seemed awfully busy the day we had lunch with her."

Georgianna held up what looked like a Morning Glory flower petal hat and purple leotards with a green leaf tunic. Twinkle toe shoes with little gold bells completed the costume.

"I love it! I'll look no further." She laughed, still holding the outfit up for her sister to admire.

Ombline's look of condescending amusement said enough. "Suit yourself." She turned and moved on down the racks, finding nothing that appealed to her.

Georgianna spotted what looked to be a giant skunk suit with a white Mohawk hat that tied under the chin. She put the hat on turning sideways for Ombline to see the resulting profile. "This is just what you need to get that astronaut Daddy was talking about."

This broke Ombline's above it all composure and brought her into the spirit of things. "Definitely an Astronaut magnet Georgianna, black, white and fuzzy all over! Are you sure you don't want it for yourself?" She smugly turned back to the costumes and finally settled on a queen of the barbarians' costume—all faux fur, miniskirt, shield, pole axe and lace up boots.

"Well, won't we be attractive—the Woolly Mammoth Queen and her purple and green associate—suits you perfectly Ombline, woman Amazon that you are most times!"

Ombline smiled. "I get the message little *flower thing*-you can leave off now."

They paid for their rentals and left the store intending to pick them up the next day only to find their bikes lying out in the middle of the street replaced by two Harley motorcycles.

"What the…" Ombline looked up and down the street seeing no for sure motorcycle owners around.

An older man walked up to them. "It's those biker girls, Pearl and Arnell. They have no respect for anything. Nothing will come of this, just take your bicycles and go is my advice."

They did just that for the afternoon was getting on and arrived back at Grey Hall without incident as they rode by Dragons Roost arriving just in time for *Tea* as they were used to calling that time of day. They saw Marc's SUV parked out front beside Esmeralda's company vehicle.

"This might be her final inspection of Grey Hall's landscaping." Ombline commented as they came up the steps.

Inside, Georgianna tried her hand with the espresso maker in the pantry.

She called out to Ombline in the kitchen preparing a plate of treats to accompany the expresso. "Ombline, would you mind checking with Daddy upstairs and see what he would prefer for Tea; we should see where Esmeralda is too—she might like to take a break—what each would like, tea or coffee, would you please?"

"Right, back in a jiffy—then I'll help you move the tray table in front of the fireplace."

Ombline didn't return in a jiffy at all.

Georgianna decided to go see what the holdup was. At the top of the stairs her heart stopped for Ombline stood leaning back against the wall beside their father's door. She thought her sister was crying.

"Oh my God!" Georgianna grabbed Ombline by the shoulder. "What's wrong?" She could only imagine their father dead of a heart attack lying cold and inert on the floor—gone from them forever. She started to grab the doorknob only to have her hand stayed by Ombline.

"You don't want to do that—trust me, you don't want to do that, it's not a picture you want to have forever in your head."

"What do you mean," Georgianna asked her heart racing, still not understanding. "What's wrong—what's wrong, do we need to call an ambulance...?" She was frozen in mortal fear as her heart thumped with wild anxiety. Realization finally struck her as vibrations emanating through her fathers door revealed the heavy rhythm she now recognized as that of the pumping strains of Barry White coming from Marc's bedroom—*love* music as their father's generation knew it.

Georgianna blinked and looked questioningly at Ombline. "Not dead?"

No longer able to contain her laughter, Ombline held her hand up to her mouth. "*Definitely*, not dead!" She squeaked out between her fingers and could not stop laughing. "I knocked softly but I got no response so I peeked in to see if he was asleep. *They*, still didn't know I was about. I guess they're auditioning each other. He has *company*, Georgianna—Esmeralda!" Again, she put her hand to her mouth to stifle herself.

They tried to muffle their laughter as they crept softly away to the still pumping strains of Barry White and back to Tea-Time as they knew it. Their father had certainly regained his sea legs so-to-speak!

Chapter Nine

Esmeralda had not spent the night, but snuck down the back
stairs and left. Marc showed up for dinner giving no indication that
he had had company earlier. Again, they raided the frozen food
pantry putting to use Delia's frozen California style entrées easily
warmed up in the microwave along with croissants crisped in the
oven.

Marc chose an appropriate wine to complement their first
dinner together in Smugglers Cove. Afterward, he gave Peter
another call confirming his and Zorloff's arrival the next morning. The evening was a short one.

After retiring early the night before, the morning found all
three of Grey Hall's guests up early. Marc explained that Peter
and Zorloff would be flown to Boston by John Steffington,

Peter's archaeologist son and that he and Zorloff would be driving up from Boston and should arrive before ten in the morning.

Grey Hall would have two more guests. It was Peter's intention upon arrival to go right away to Dragons Roost accompanied by Georgianna and Ombline to ascertain just what they had witnessed. Marc didn't offer further details and kept to himself the fact that Peter seemed very concerned but had given him no further explanation. Marc was subdued and quiet, so unlike himself. This left Georgianna and Ombline concerned—even somewhat fearful—what could their experiences have conveyed to Peter as being of such importance to bring the two men back east on such short notice. They felt uneasy with such urgency. Georgianna once again voiced her concern to Ombline that maybe this was about aliens—Ombline just smiled and shook her head causing Georgianna to shake *her* head in disbelief at her sister's stubborn conservative view of life—always calculating every step—so very comfortable in her own personal square box. *Why*, Georgianna thought, *shouldn't there be aliens?! What's wrong with that?*

The Patrones sat on the half round porch of Grey Hall sipping strong coffee in the brisk morning air when a dark blue SUV pulled up. Marc set his coffee down and went down the steps to the drive welcoming the two men exiting the vehicle. Marc hugged Peter and shook hands with Zorloff the man accompanying Peter. Marc and Peter were briefly in conversation as they came round from the back of the tailgate of the SUV each carrying boxes. The twins could not hear what was said, but both men seemed genuinely glad to see one another. Marc seemed to have perked up somewhat with Peter's arrival.

The three came up to the porch where Ombline and Georgianna stood by the railing. Zorloff was introduced to them after they hugged Peter. They treasured the summers and holidays they had spent on the Steffington estate along with their father and looked upon Peter as a beloved uncle. Time had treated Peter well. Tall, lean and angularly handsome he still retained his thick dark hair, only greying temples had given way to the march of time. The sparkle of his blue eyes denoted an intensity for life fuelled by the ferocity of an intellectual mind—all guided by a strength of spirit—rare in combination for many. Both twins had very fond memories of the times spent with the Steffingtons and Peter and Mona's kindnesses, the interest they had showed in the twins as children. Georgianna recalled many times the summers they had spent with Chloe and had slept in a tree house on the estate grounds with several adopted cats up there with them; the rest of the time the girls included the Steffingtons seven dogs in their games and with several of those sleeping with them at night when they did sleep upstairs in Chloe's room. Chloe woke up one morning on one of their summer visits swiping furry fuzz from her face saying. "If you haven't noticed yet we're a hairy bunch here!" The three pseudo sisters laughed finding this funny as little ones do in their innocence. No one in their family had ever minded a little *hairiness*. Certainly not the Steffingtons or the three girls. The Steffingtons had always adopted the unadoptable, refusing no one, each becoming a loved family member for life. Those were some of Ombline and Georgianna's most treasured magical childhood memories. They would always love the Steffingtons, they were all part of the same heart.

Georgianna thought to see Peter and Zorloff together they could easily be mistaken for brothers—but maybe they were—no one had said, but surely, if they were, it would have been mentioned. In all the time she had known the Steffingtons, Zorloff's name had never come up that she could remember. *What*—she wondered, was their relationship? She was brought out of such conjecture by Ombline asking if she wanted a second cup of coffee as she poured for the new arrivals. A tray of muffins, cream cheese and jam gave them all a chance to get reacquainted and for the twins to begin their story of Dragons Roost.

The new arrivals seemed riveted with the girls description of what had taken place from the first flash of blue lightning to the dark woman being spit out of the blue portal, and, especially, the black box of technology she used to transform the empty frame into a containment field of roiling unknown quantum activity. They agreed amongst themselves that what ever she had attempted it was not yet fully attuned to her needs—or was the portal (as they now referred to the blue frame when operable) she had engaged, not accessible on the other side—possibly blocked—or—was it only the fruit preventing a further attempt as it had seemed? Who was she? What was she doing in Zorloff's old laboratory—how did she did become familiar with such technology attempting to engage it for her purposes? So many questions.

Georgianna and Ombline looked to each other with that knowing which only twins seem to have, that Peter, Zorloff and yes, their father, knew a lot more about the mystery of Dragons Roost than they were willing to reveal. Both scientists asked questions so detailed that neither twin had answers for them, only able to relate what their individual observations were—no different than accident observers seeing the same accident from different street corners.

Ombline knew from the questioning she and Georgianna received that something of Earth shattering importance was taking place and she suspicioned that Peter and Zorloff knew exactly what had happened—and likely their father too—or at least he had some understanding. It was Ombline's opinion that she, with the unrelenting curiosity and encouragement of Georgianna, had stumbled upon something of incomprehensible consequence. Why did Marc know to call only Peter right away and not some sort of authority—but then what sort of authority? It was all so strange. Since the summers spent on the Steffington estate with Chloe, Ombline and Georgianna had instinctively known there was a lot more to Peter's below stairs laboratory, the cave, (as the three little girls had begun to call it even back then) than they had a clue about. It was an underground cavernous area that rivaled the footage of the estate home above it. They had at times been in Peter's study and outer lab area as children when upon occasion Peter would demonstrate a scientific principal he made interesting and understandable to a child's stage of development.

Once though, during those times, Georgianna had had an unexpected experience when looking for Chloe, thinking she might be in the lab with Peter. She had wandered in to find her cousin nowhere around. Just as she turned to leave, a bright flash caused her to turn around facing the back of the lab. A section of the wall opened allowing Peter to come through from beyond. Till then, she had never known there was more to the lab; the brief glimpse through the wall conveyed a sci-fi scene beyond anything that a child could have understood the magnitude of at the time. Peter never mentioned this and somehow Georgianna knew at the time it was something to turn a blind eye to—that is—until now when she recalled the scene from childhood.

The fruit was the strangest unknown of all, to see the alarm it had produced in the mystery woman—so many questions. All sorts of theories filled her mind, everything from a secret new form of energy used to travel to and from somewhere very far far away, inter-dimensional portals, or even time-travel; and yet, considering how scientific theory of the moment seemed to be on the verge of connecting all such subjects, any answer could suffice—one, or all!

They left things for the maid later in the day as Peter and Zorloff were anxious to investigate Dragons Roost.

They all rode in Peter's SUV the short distance down the road and up to the ridge top. Ombline jumped out and swung the gate open. She related how the gate had swung open automatically for the Bentley that first night and that she and Georgianna *had* been able to manually open and close it themselves they found out later.

She climbed back in after swinging the gate closed as they had no automatic access to it yet—at least as far as she knew. She was beginning to wonder what she did know, if anything at all. They drove slowly up the ridge and parked around back entering through the same unlocked door that she and Georgianna had used in their break-in. Whoever had unlocked the door in the first place had intended to come and go expecting no interference since it had not been relocked and showed no signs of forced entry.

Their group walked the outside perimeter of the building and saw nothing unusual. The dried grasses embedded with last year's leaves gave no clues—all else seemed undisturbed too. A mustiness permeated the air from years of decaying foliage.

They went through Dragons Roost room by room finding nothing of note other than the solitude of time upon its walls. They entered the great central room the girls had correctly assumed had been a laboratory. The monstrosity of a blue frame still stood on its stand, the central piece of the room not revealing a clue as to its possibilities if one did not possess the little black box that the woman from the Bentley had brought with her.

Ombline held off questioning just what was going on yet as both Peter and Zorloff seemed puzzled, but connected by something only the two of them and Marc had a clue about. For a fact she intended to ask her own questions soon. She and Georgianna deserved to know what was happening, experiences such as they had had and be kept in the dark was not going to work. Some very high strangeness was now a part of their lives.

On the way back to Grey Hall little was said. The SUV was pulled up to the steps of the porch to unload the rest of their luggage, laptops and other larger scientific equipment. Much of it was unrecognizable new forms of technology obviously known only to the two scientists and so unlike anything the two young women had ever seen or could conceive of even existing. They said nothing about this knowing for now it would net them no answers.

Marc made no comment as he helped carry in several pieces that needed help setting up. He seemed at least familiar with what was about to be done and could be of some assistance.

Georgianna and Ombline offered to help but their help was declined. It was obvious they were being encouraged to get out of the way so they decided to lunch in town on their own and afterward pick up their costumes. Georgianna asked before leaving if Peter and Zorloff would be going to the ball.

"No." Marc said as Peter entered the hall.

"We have a lot to do in a short time." Peter said. "Have a good time tonight, Serpentine is a great hostess, you're sure to have fun." He went back the way he had come saying nothing more.

Peter seemed to be in a rush, as polite as he could afford to be without drawing attention to his urgency. It was hard to ignore. Georgianna felt like she was on the outside of something fantastically illusive going on right in front of her—what, she didn't have a clue about and no one who *did*, was offering explanations. That elephant in the room thing she and Ombline were supposed to ignore was growing by the hour. There seemed to be something in the background of Marc's familiars that shared a connection, an undercurrent of commonality that they believed they owed no answers for. Any questions from the twins had been met with a change of subject or completely ignored. A clandestine aura now surrounded their visit here!

This was not turning out to be the simple quaint getaway that Smugglers Cove had been supposed to be.

Chapter   Ten

The costume rack of South Moon House was almost bare when the Patrones stopped by to pick up their rental costumes. It would seem most of Smugglers Cove intended to be at the ball tonight. It was definitely a big social event for the town—and, as Marc had insinuated, many prominent people of importance would be attending this well-known event as well.

They were lucky in finding a parking space up the street at the end of the block from Contraband. They locked their costumes in the car and went on to lunch. Again they ate at the bar for faster service. Thad seemed happy to see them, remembering them and their conversation, expediting their menu choices—and yes, he too would be at the ball, as Robin Hood, not, he laughed, as Master Friar Tuck, a wine master of another time!

Georgianna smiled askance at Ombline while Thad attended to other patrons. "He's too hot to be Friar Tuck."

Ombline raised her hand in a mock salute of perfect agreement with her sister's observation. "He was definitely *not* created for celibacy." She smiled watching Thad attend to his duties down at the other end of the bar. "I'll bet there's a long line outside to get in here on ladies night."

They took their time with lunch leaving a generous tip for Thad and intended to take a ride farther on up the Old Coast Road than they had ridden on the bikes, but that was not to be.

Their car had been last in line on the corner-somehow it had been pushed up and out into the street to make room for two motorcycles—again they were being messed with—why?—Why them in particular?—They knew no one here.

Ombline angrily circled the two Harleys. "Well, well, well— looks like we've had another visit from Pearl and Arnell. We let that bicycle thing with them go, but this could cause an accident. I'm calling 911."

Before she could get her cell out Georgianna smiled mischievously. "Not—just—yet. I'm not through with those two." She kicked up the stand on one bike and shoved it over on its side as heavy as it was. She jumped back out of the way as it hit the pavement—then repeated with the other one. Both bikes lay on the ground at angles on their sides. That had not been easy.

Ombline did not attempt to conceal her satisfaction with what her sister had done. "Georgianna, I don't think 911 is a credible call now since I'm sure you broke some sort of law in doing that." Even so, she smiled in wicked satisfaction with her sister's vandalism.

"We had better get out of here pronto!" She shoved her cell phone back in her pocket.

All was going well in the retribution department until the two hulking bikers saw from their perches inside the pool hall window their pride and joys being dumped to the ground.

Beady eyes in red puffy faces zeroed in on the two young women as both bikers snorted venom and mutilation upon any brave or stupid enough to touch their bikes—sacrilege had just been committed. They burst out of the pool hall dressed in leather and chains bent on a kill!

Ombline saw them first. They were cut off from the car.

Pearl caught Georgianna by the back of her jacket ripping it down the middle into two halves. Georgianna screamed out. "Get off me, you slimy, green finger-nailed wart-hog! Get off me!" She broke free and whipped around to face Pearl, kicking her hard in the knee further enraging her if that was possible.

Not thwarted by Georgianna's attempt at self-defense, Pearl roared. "What the two of you *are* is dead—okay Arnell, let's show these two wusses what happens to people who touch our bikes!"

Arnell, who seemed to be Pearl's follower, not her equal, went for Ombline with hands outstretched for vengeance. They both seemed to puff up even more massive from the adrenalin rush they were experiencing due to playing the role of brutes; the dark red of their raging anger intensifying.

Georgianna hoped being leaner they could out run them for that was all that was left to do.

Just when things seemed the darkest for the Patrones, Esmeralda Marrs showed up with a tazer the size of an automatic weapon. "Stay cool ladies!" Was all she said as she calmly held the Swinsters at bay and recommended the Patrones move over to where she stood. "Hurry up." She urged. All the while facing and threatening Pearl and Arnell with the tazer to stay put while Georgianna and Ombline were to back into the pool hall ahead of her.

The Swinster sisters as Pearl and Arnell were known by the townspeople held back until Esmeralda disappeared inside the darkness of the pool hall with her rescuees.

"Quick, this way!" Esmeralda led them toward the back of the dingy building to the ladies room. None of the pool hall patrons took notice of what was happening—or—maybe they didn't want to be part of anything that would put themselves in trouble with the Swinsters.

"In here—hurry!" Esmeralda ushered them all into what was labeled the ladies room—small, smelly and dark with only a toilet, a filthy sink and one grimy window. Esmeralda pushed both Patrones to the window. "Raise it or break it," she instructed. "Hurry up! Climb out as fast as you can!" All the while she squatted on the floor under the sink mixing the contents of two containers into a filthy bucket. A battering started on the other side of the door with their pursuers screaming obscenities, their break through eminent at any moment as the door began to splinter.

Esmeralda shot up from the poisonous potion she had just mixed holding her breath and followed like a laser shot on the heels of Georgianna and Ombline out the window to the fresh air of the alley, her eyes tearing, her lungs desperate for clean air free of the poison gas she had concocted. As they escaped down the alley they could barely hear the choking and hacking sounds of the Swinsters as they broke into the filthy gassed little room overcome with toxic fumes.

At the end of the alley Esmeralda gasped. "This way, my company van is in back of Contraband." They ran as fast as they could expecting the two enraged women to come pouring out the window after them any second. They jumped into the vehicle locking the doors in relief.

The two halves of Georgianna's jacket had fallen forward and slid down over her arms. "I'm just glad we don't need casts, stitches or coffins." She breathed. "What the hell is wrong with those two anyway?—and—Esmeralda, what *was* that concoction you mixed up in such a hurry?"

Esmeralda smiled. "Just something my housekeeper told me never to mix together—bleach and ammonia—it can be deadly—two cleaning products obviously never put to use in *that* ladies room. If the Swinsters broke down the door they won't be coming out the window after us." A smile of satisfaction crossed Esmeralda's face as she dialed 911, pulled out from the parking space and around the corner to the rental car still out in the street. The biker *ladies* and their Harleys were nowhere in sight.

The flashing lights of a police car gave comfort to the three escapees as they related their tale and reclaimed the rental car. The officer commiserated with them but no one was injured so once again nothing would be done. Georgianna's vengeful action wasn't mentioned to the officer either. They thought for now they had best leave it all alone.

Esmeralda followed Ombline and Georgianna back to Grey Hall just to make sure they weren't followed. They were sure this wasn't over though. At least for now, law enforcement had a record of it.

Mark heard them come in the hall and ran down the stairs to meet them. The disheveled three before him gave rise to the fear they had been involved in some horrific accident or attack. "My God! What happened to you people?" (He included Esmeralda in his concerns).

His daughters were silent, each deciding just how to tell this story seeing as how, since their arrival in Smugglers Cove, all the action had seemed to converge on them. With Marc's tendency to over-protectiveness it just seemed prudent to filter their version of events until Esmeralda spoke up first.

On their behalf she alleviated some of Mark's concern. "They had a run in with the town bullies Marc, just a *petite* brawl if you will, but all is well for now."

Marc looked to Esmeralda questioningly and then back to the two bedraggled young women in front of him. "First." He asked. "Are you okay—you don't look okay?" He put a hand on each of their shoulders scrutinizing their appearance. "What happened—do we need to call the police—take you to the hospital?"

Ombline reassured him. "We are positively fine Dad. We've talked to an officer and all is square. All our thanks go to Esmeralda, her taser, her knowledge of chemistry and her get-away vehicle close by saved our butts."

Marc was wide-eyed. "But your jacket." He started.

Georgianna said. "Collateral damage. That was just a preview of things to come if Esmeralda hadn't come along when she did. She's a true heroine, armed impromptu improvisation—just magnificent—you should have seen her Dad—just like in the movies, a chemical, electrical super heroine!"

Marc hugged his daughters and then Esmeralda thanking her profusely. He ushered them all to seats in front of the fire where they related a more detailed version of what had transpired.

Marc was finally satisfied with their story and made hot toddies for all of them. They felt good to be back *and* whole as Georgianna had put it back in the van. They thanked Esmeralda repeatedly before going upstairs for calming soaks in the tub before the ball later in the evening.

Esmeralda said to Marc. "I need to be on my way." She gave him a peck on the cheek. "I'll see you about 8:30?" She smiled up at him. *"After it's very dark."* She narrowed her eyes in promise. He smiled knowingly at her little jibe as she exited the front door of Grey Hall.

A ball was just what they all needed.

Chapter Eleven

Peter and Zorloff hadn't been seen since earlier in the day; they were locked away with the technology they had brought with them in one of the meeting rooms. They would fend for themselves while the Patrones' were at the ball.

Marc had been to several of Serpentine's previous entertainments and raved about the magnificent buffets at all her events; the affair was promising to be more than just a local Halloween party. After short naps and long soaks it was time for costumes. Ombline descended the stairs thumping her pole axe on the way down. She epitomized the wild barbaric beauty of a Viking Queen. Georgianna followed along behind in the purple and green Morning Glory get-up erupting in strange chanting sounds she referred to as spirit songs, purposefully tinkling the bells on her curly toed green shoes.

At the foot of the stairs Georgianna gave a low curtsey, turned away from her audience, bent over and gave her booty a little shake, stood up and said. "That's all for tonight folks," laughing at her own silly theatrics—always the actress.

Everyone was in a good mood. Marc had taken pictures from the time they had come down the stairs. "How often does one get costumed up—I want a good pictorial memory of this." He continued checking the shots he had taken deleting none.

Ombline said. "We should say good night to our two embedded scientists before we leave for the ball, don't you think?"

"No." Marc said in a rush, leaving no room to question why. "I would just leave them for now." He seemed heedful, but quickly changed demeanour. He wanted tonight to be a memorable occasion for himself and his daughters, no new unanswered weirdness need intrude on that.

"Well ladies, to the ball we go." He took each on an arm and out the door and down the steps to their respective vehicles they went.

It was fully dark now and if it hadn't been for the motion detector lights on the garage Mark would have disappeared into the night considering his all black attire and blue-black hair blending into the night.

After they were seated in the rental car with Georgianna as driver, she asked Ombline. "Daddy's all in black, what is he, his costume I mean—what's he supposed to be—black shirt, black pants and a black cape with a black mask dangling from around his neck?"

"I think his intention is to look good for Esmeralda—it's whatever she romantically perceives him to be—you know, Zorro—Dracula—just plain hot stuff!"

They laughed as Georgianna started the car and drove down the drive and along the road on the way to the Harvest Moon ball. Light from the full moon inched its way up the eastern horizon over the Atlantic and would be the belle of the night sky. The autumn moons always seemed larger-more prominent not only because of the tilt of the earth this time of the year but also from the point of observation, another of the seasons gifts of beauty free to all.

As they drove by, they glanced up the ridge in the direction of Dragons Roost now in darkness, unobservable at night to anyone not aware of its existence. No blue lightning tonight.

Chapter Twelve

The hilltop of the Pendergast estate did appear to be under the spell of the moon itself. All the trees and grounds foliage, including the drive up to the estate home were illuminated with small pearlescent lights, reminiscent of moonglow. *Enchanting* was the only word Ombline could think of to describe the scene. The moon now glistened off the ocean far out in the Atlantic creating almost a light path through the dark water.

Attendants parked both limos and vehicles of the locals. The drive disappeared on around the back of the estate indicating parking some distance beyond the stables closer to the property's forested foothills.

Georgianna pulled into the line of waiting cars, third in line behind two black limousines.

A well-known senator and his date exited the first limo, a national news anchor and his date from the next. Clearly, the two men didn't think it necessary to costume themselves as both wore tuxedos; the women wore very chic evening attire accessorized by exquisite Venetian masks—this, Georgianna recognized having studied theatre arts one summer in Venice.

"Compared to those disembarking *elite* we look like the local yokels idea of a costume party," Georgianna said. "It wasn't mentioned as I remember, that we had a choice to *dress* or wear a costume."

"Oh well, you know how politicians and the news media are, anything to draw attention to themselves—I don't care, I'm having fun tonight."

The attendant claimed their car under the porchere. They went up the steps and down the entry hall to the solarium packed with dancers. A scene reminiscent of a celestial fertility rite, here the moonglow theme was more a paganistic pageant than ball, the focal point being the powerfully executed horned sculpture of the male nature spirit they had admired on their first visit. Its subtly lit magnificence surely captured the theme of the ball— the overlord Phantom of the autumn night.

Georgianna still wondered why Serpentine had been so dismissive of such a work of art, not at all interested in divulging the artist, or its origin.

They had not anticipated such grandiosity. The mixed crowd was surely a successful plan that had worked here. It was hard to navigate through the dancers. All the French doors stood open to the terrace beyond. It would not be unexpected for there to be paparazzi at such a grand affair and now they both felt silly in their dippy rentals.

Many in costume wore works of art, cunning enough to be envied by a theatrical company. The music had been chosen for a dancing crowd. One of two buffets had been set up, one in the solarium, the other outside on the curving terrace surrounding the solarium strung sparingly with the pearlescent lights so as not to distract from the night sky. Two open bars were manned by white coated bartenders.

Both Patrones took champagne from the tray of a passing waiter giving them time to size up the crowd. A tap on the shoulder brought Ombline around to face Thad from Contraband sporting a tux and looking every bit a Hollywood leading man. "Thad," she exclaimed, "I thought you were going to be Robin Hood!"

"Not tonight," he laughed. "South Moon House double-rented the costume and the other renter got there first."

A pretty young green-eyed brunette came up behind him placing her hand on his shoulder. "Wonderful party, is it not?" She said, extending her hand to both women.

Thad turned, putting his arm around the brunette's shoulders drawing her affectionately to him. "Georgianna, Ombline, I'd like you to meet my fiancé, Prudence Farthington. We met while working on mutual PhD programs in the field of paleobiology."

Georgianna was surprised as Thad had never spoken of his private life. She had just assumed his life was connected with his job at Contraband.

Prudence said. "After the holidays Thad and I will be part of a six-month expedition to the Amazon rain forest. There's the possibility of so many new pharmaceutical plants being discovered. We are very excited to be part of the group. We'll be accompanying a mutual professor from our past academic studies." She smiled at Thad explaining that they had taken off six months to help Thad's father out at Contraband—it had gotten so busy—grown so much. "Thad tends bar and I help in the office." Prudence exuded an Ivy League sort of natural beauty— an authoritative self-confidence. Putting her hand up to his face she said. "Okay *Fred*—let's dance!"

He smiled down at her. She turned to Ombline and Georgianna. "So very nice to meet you both. I hope to see you again." Off the two went, dancing to the rhythms of the latest Latin music.

Marc and Esmeralda hadn't shown up yet. Ombline was beginning to wonder what had happened to them. "Looks like Dad and Esmeralda have been *delayed*." She put an emphasis on delayed.

Georgianna just smiled. "Got your drift sis."

They worked the room making small talk with the occasional townsfolk they were familiar with—dancing with a few. It flashed across Georgianna's mind that the Swinsters might attempt to crash the ball. She had noticed what she knew to be security and was sure Serpentine would have apprised such of the Swinsters and the trouble that could be expected from those two.

Georgianna set her half empty champagne glass on a passing waiter's tray. "Let's go graze the buffet, I, like Chloe, will be tipsy if I don't eat something." Their cousin was one of those cork-sniffer champagne drinkers—a little went a long way.

"Good idea." Ombline agreed. "Let's try the one on the terrace just as soon as I stash this battle axe somewhere." Outside she found a potted palm and placed it behind the plant. The buffet was as elaborate as the rest of the evening. They both nibbled at the many varied gourmet offerings eventually making their way back inside.

Still, Marc and Esmeralda had not shown up. "They're awfully late." Georgianna said, glancing around the room, "as a matter of fact I haven't seen Serpentine—have you?"

No sooner had she said this than a voice behind them caused both to turn facing the subject of their conversation.

Serpentine stood with a guest, one that brought instant recognition—one of finally meeting the *beast* face to face.

"Good evening Georgianna, Ombline. It's so good to see you could make it." Serpentine paused momentarily, purposefully looking askance at their costumes, not commenting on their choices. "I would like to introduce a newcomer to our community, Madame Seurat, a native of—of—which European country? I'm so sorry, I believe I forgot your country of origin…"

Serpentine was left hanging with no answer forthcoming from her non-costumed guest wearing a dark austere militaristic seeming designer suit.

Madame Seurat only smiled, slowly—slyly. "I didn't say, I'm sure." She brushed this little question aside. "I'm charmed, such lovely young women." She held out her hand to each, lingering too long with the clasp of their hands, allowing her hand to slowly slide through theirs.

Georgianna felt as if a snake had just slithered through her palm raising the hair on the back of her neck. She was shaken and wondered what had just happened. Did Madame Seurat have the same effect on Ombline she wondered. She felt defiled and corrupted by a kind of passing darkness. Why would this be? The woman had the persona of some sort of European aristocrat, elegant, well groomed and to be blunt, damned scary! Her very touch had made Georgianna want to turn away from her—like chalk on a blackboard, only worse—much worse! Thankfully Serpentine did not leave them alone with the woman as she quickly maneuvered her to a new group of introductions.

Ombline tilted her head back and breathed deeply. "I think I'm going to hyperventilate. I thought we were both going to be swallowed whole."

"You first." Georgianna snickered. "I was getting ready to make a run for it! How disgustingly disgusting! What tomb did she crawl out of?! I feel like I need to wash my hands—gargle!"

They got a grip on themselves. "The—Bentley—woman!" They silently mouthed to one another in sync. They had known this the moment they set eyes on Serpentine's guest. The first night when they were almost run down by her chauffeured car there was only the fleeting impression of the moment, one of patrician arrogance, but the night of her failed attempt in the abandoned lab they got a good look at Madame—not full face on as now, but enough to surely recognize her.

"Oh—yes!" Ombline said. "What is *she* doing here? There's got to be a daylight explanation—something that makes sense. But then there's all this Peter and Zorloff stuff—we both know Georgianna, it's just as weird as it seems!"

"Whatever the truth of it," Georgianna said, "this Seurat woman creeps the hell out of me."

"No kidding! When she shook my hand I felt like a black serpent had just slithered across my palm—such a strange sensation. Wouldn't Serpentine have noticed anything with her? It can't be just us."

Momentarily fazed and wondering what had just happened, they both sipped on fresh glasses of champagne snatched from a passing waiter's tray.

"I could maybe consider her looking at real estate late in the day Ombline, but not that little black box thing and the blue mirror—the fruit. I guess I was still holding out hope for an easy answer as strange as that would seem now."

"How could you *possibly* still have any expectation that she's just looking for a house—get used to it, we have landed squat down in the middle of weird, and, if you remember, it was you who just had to go up to Dragons Roost in the dark to see what was going on. I would have been happy to have left it all alone."

Georgianna drew an imaginary halo over her sister's head. "What must it feel like to be so perfectly, sanctimoniously rational, every moment—so justified! I envy you!"

"You should!"

Abruptly, the who was to blame spat was put aside for both felt the fingers of a watcher—what Ombline had once called it when you actually feel the eyes of another on your person, and this they surely did, for across the far side of the room a dark well-dressed man wearing an old-fashioned monocle glared at them. His dark slicked back hair and dress made him look like something from an old horror film. He never touched the martini he held, just continued his laser-like scrutiny of them. What had they done to elicit such attention. Now they were going to be honoured with meeting the *next* weirdest person at the ball. For once again Serpentine swooped down seemingly unnoticed till she was right there with them.

"I must introduce you to another of our newcomers." She took them by the arm escorting them to where the shadowy figure stood. "Ombline, Georgianna Patrone, meet Dr. Zachary Frank, Dr. Frank is an associate of Madame Seurat, both, soon-to-be residents of Smugglers Cove."

"Of course they are," Georgianna said under her breath to Ombline, "weird attracts weird."

It was obvious the introduction was an imposition not relished by Dr. Frank but relented to by clicking his heels and nodding to each as he lightly touched his monocle saying only. "Charmed, so charmed." He clearly had no interest in socialization—at least not in the twenty-first century!

Serpentine came to the rescue. "We're delighted you could come tonight Dr. Frank. We'll leave you to the evening, if there is anything you wish, I'll see to it."

Dr. Frank nodded looking up and away into the crowd making it plain he wanted no further discourse.

Serpentine steered them away and out into the crowd for which they were grateful. She left them as hastily as she had appeared.

"What do you make of this," Georgianna asked Ombline, "it seems as if we are being purposefully subjected to these strange people, to what end?"

"*I* do *not* know, but I'm ready to get out of here.

"Me too, but, I have to stop at the ladies room first, one complete glass of champagne for the whole evening equals two trips to the john for me you know." They got rid of their unfinished glasses of champagne as it had lost its charm after their nauseating introductions to the crypt-couple.

Ombline smiled, remembering when they were little girls visiting their cousin Chloe and her grandparents for the summer and one big glass of lemonade while playing outside had prevented Georgianna from making it back to the bathroom in time so she squatted in one of Mona's herb gardens causing Mona to wonder days later what had happened to such a healthy plant.

"I'll wait for you out on the terrace, check out the moon or something." Ombline said this not needing to make the trip herself.

Chapter   Thirteen

Ombline stood propped against the perimeter of the chilly terrace surround admiring the night sky and grounds while she waited for Georgianna. It seemed she was taking an awfully long time. Ombline was thinking she might search out the ladies room herself and remove the hot cumbersome faux-fur vest of her costume when a flower clad figure appeared in one of the terrace French doors. Georgianna pushed her way through the crowd making a dash for her sister. Her seeming determination filled Ombline with unease.

"What's wrong—what's wrong—is it Dad?"

"No, why do you always expect the worst?" Georgianna asked breathlessly. "It's those two fiends we met tonight—we've got to get out of here now!"

"What do you mean?"

She pulled Ombline by the arm back inside and on out to the porchere whispering on the way, "just hold on till we get in the car."

While they waited for the attendant to bring their car around, Ombline couldn't wait any longer. "Tell me now Georgianna, what's wrong? Just tell me!"

"All right!" She lowered her voice. "When I came out of the ladies room, which was not all that easy to find, who did I almost run into but the two associate weirdoes of the evening discussing what is coming next tonight, a retry to *this time* send *Mr.* Weirdo, our Dr. Frank, through the portal, because, apparently Ms. Weirdo—Madame Seurat is not, for whatever reason, accepted by this science as a participant, as if that's news to us!"

"Stop for air Georgianna. We've got to get hold of Peter."

"I tried on my way out, there's only answering. I left a message."

"Did you try dad?"

"Same deal. Left a message. It's up to us."

"I can't believe you're saying this, what can we do? We don't know squat about what's really going on. At the very least Peter needs to know; we should go to Grey Hall first, keep trying the cell on the way back."

Georgianna huffed. "Maybe we should just notify 911 two strange people are attempting inter-dimensional travel in an abandoned house through a blue mirror tonight—huh sis? Just how do you think that's going to go down?"

"Well, what are we going to do—all we *can* do is again hide in the closet and be observers. That accomplishes nothing!" Ombline was embarrassed at even bringing up such a juvenile campy thought of again hiding in a closet. It seemed imbecilic, but what other choice was there? She heaved a great sigh. Reluctance still filled her very being knowing how dangerous, irresponsible—and, yes—moronic, such a stunt could prove to be.

Georgianna too, felt a slight tinge of dread at considering this but felt it was destined—under the circumstances, what else could they do? "We can report to Peter exactly what happens and hope he gets the message in time—and, that Serpentine knows these people for whatever good that does."

Ombline looked at her sister with apprehension knowing full well their only recourse was the closet.

Their car came around just in time to halt their discussion. Georgianna jumped in on the driver's side following another partygoer down the drive to the dark highway. Ombline kept trying the cells of Marc and Peter with no luck, but leaving brief details as to why and where they were headed.

Ombline said. "How do you know Frank and Seurat are not already there and in the middle of the process by now?"

"*Because*, they said they intended to first say goodnight to Serpentine. That's when I found a different route away from the restroom. We've got to beat them there and hide the car."

Ombline, with the greatest of reluctance gave in for good. "Since there's no talking you out of this, I saw the tracks of an unused dirt road into the woods on the opposite side of the road from the ridge. We can pull the car in there and hike up the rest of the way." Ombline couldn't believe she was saying this, even assisting with this foolhardy and dangerous plan. She scowled out the side window of the car saying under her breath, "shades of Nancy Drew here we two fools come again!"

They arrived to an almost deserted Smugglers Cove and turned west toward their destination. "Slow down Georgianna, it's hard to spot the tracks in the moonlight. There! Stop—that's it! Pull in slowly, no telling what it's like, unused deep ruts filled in with dried grasses and leaves likely obliterating any evidence of the roads condition even in daylight. One thing we don't need right now is to get stuck out here where we can be seen!"

They pulled in slowly around and behind a copse of trees hiding the car from the road.

"Okay!" Ombline finally accepted that they were here and she was going to be a partner in *stupid* once again against her better judgment. "If we're doing this we've got to hurry no telling how soon they'll be here."

They made a dash out to the road and across it to Dragons Roost's drive. The full moon provided just enough light to make their way up to the ridge. There was no sign of anyone having been there yet. But relief was short-lived as headlights stopped at the gate down at the road. It swung inward allowing the Bentley admission. They ran in the back door of the building, on through the house and back into the closet refuge.

They were tenuously secure in their vantage point and none too soon, for the sound of car doors being shut fixed the closet dwellers into position. Georgianna whispered. "I feel more and more like I'm in a Nancy Drew mystery—The secret of the old closet!"

Ombline shushed her as she glared at her in the dark.

The recognizable figures of Frank and Seurat entered the darkened lab and promptly brought out the black box that had engaged the blue mirror before. Again its lights flashed repetitiously in the dark room with only moonlight filtering through the window panes onto the wooden floor. The blue mirror came to life with an even stronger pulsing vibration than before. It could be felt in the very floorboards. The intense blue radiance snaked and crackled its way around the edges of the frame, finally filling the surface with roiling shades of blue.

Dr. Frank spoke something indistinguishable to Madame Seurat and then without pause stepped into the blue essence disappearing completely. Even in the eerie blue light illuminating the lab contemptuous victory was evident in the very stance of Madame Seurat.

The unhinging of it all happened with the ringing of Ombline's cell. She had forgotten in their haste to turn it off. Fury erupted on the face of the arrogant woman as she whipped around to face the closet, simultaneously pulling a pistol from her jacket as she set down the black box. "Out!" Seurat shouted barely containing the rage in her voice. "Turn—that—off!"

They edged out of the closet fronting the enraged woman. Ombline slowly pulled the phone from the jacket she had put on back in the car, then, defiantly tossed it into the blue portal hoping for a distraction.

"Aaah—the two young Patrones." Seurat smiled evilly, as she held them at gunpoint not distracted by Ombline's hoped-for diversion. Waving the gun she backed them away from the closet to stand in front of the roiling energy contained in the blue frame. "The two of you are going on a one-way trip." She gloated, as she, without warning, violently shoved Georgianna into the blue swirling vortex backward.

Terror coursed through Georgianna grasping the frame's rim with such bare-knuckled strength as only the fear of death can put in one, her butt already immersed in the frothing blue, her heels and hands in a death-grip on the outer rim of the frame preventing her immediate absorption by the swirling blue portal. She tried with all her might not to be pulled in. Hopeless horror filled her very being as she felt herself losing the battle, sinking ever deeper within the portals pull.

Ombline disregarded the evil woman coming at her next and leaped to grab Georgianna's foot holding with all that was in her to save her sister's life. No sound issued from Georgianna, silent in the grip of fear. The only sound was the tinkle of a golden jingle bell scuttling across the floor where it had been ripped loose and fallen from the curly toed shoe of Georgianna's costume in her struggle to pull herself free of the portal's draw. This small round bell proved the undoing of Madame Seurat, for as she moved toward Ombline to shove her in the portal with Georgianna, she slipped on the little gold ornament falling hard onto the floor backward, her head making a hard ker-thunking sound as it connected with the edge of the fireplace. She lay unmoving, the gun on the floor beside her.

Ombline screamed. "Hold on—hold on!" Georgianna sank inescapably—hopelessly further and further into the blue of the swirling portal.

Ombline could no longer keep hold as Georgianna's hands slipped off the frame engulfing her head and upper torso. Ombline, till the last, held to her by one foot until her own hands were immersed in blue. She could feel its unrelenting pull. Finally no worldly strength could save Georgianna—she was sucked into the blue void disappearing into its depths. Ombline was on hands and knees when sharply the blue blinked out leaving her sobbing on the floor.

The back door burst open revealing a silhouette backlit by moonlight. In a flash Madame Seurat's chauffeur scooped up the unconscious woman and her gun carrying her away to the Bentley. Ombline could hear it leave, but down the other side of the ridge—so—there *had* been a back road.

Ombline crawled around on the floor not realizing why she did such a thing. She bumped into an object only to discover the black box lying on the floor where Madame Seurat had dropped it. Could she save Georgianna with it? She had no idea how to even use such a thing—Peter or Zorloff, if anyone could, it would be them—if Georgianna was still alive—no, she couldn't even think that, after all, Dr. Frank had willingly walked in.

She staggered out the back door and around to the drive in front carrying the box and heard herself sobbing not realizing she was doing so, it was like hearing someone else. She couldn't seem to stop and started down the drive only to stop in her tracks and hide behind a tree as the lights of a dark SUV came up the drive. She recognized her Dad's vehicle and leaped out in front to stop him.

Marc jumped out the driver's door grabbing his daughter to him followed by Peter and Zorloff. Ombline told them what had happened as best she could and turned over her technological find to them. The last thing she remembered was the smell of decaying autumn leaves as she fainted dead away, her head settling in the musty earth's comfort.

Chapter Fourteen

Peter and Zorloff, were once again in alliance to defeat at last, the same ancient enemy they had assisted in conquering in their youth—ever vigilant in their adopted world against such a darkness of nature. Because of the fruits premature introduction and Seurat's problematic prying—coming all too close to the shrouded nature of their work, all they had secretly strived toward for decades had to now be on the fast track and would have to be put to use. The long awaited time had come sooner than they would have liked.

The two had been instrumental in the finalization of such a victory as young physicists. It had changed the very existence of the humankind they had been part of. A new age of enlightenment, a miracle of peace, global cooperation and scientific advancement had propelled their world into a golden age never before experienced by its people. Things were somewhat different here, so it had been necessary to take a different route to arrive at the same end and remain inconspicuous in the process.

When young, both were slaves to their science as now. In those early days of adrenalin-surged exuberance, the eruption of a volatile disagreement in the secret lab where they worked together on a project outside the confines of the scientific community resulted in the two brothers being dispatched to a parallel world, not unlike their own, but initially arriving in different time periods and continents from one another.

Zorloff arrived in the Gobi Desert of Earth's eighteenth century. He eventually made his way by caravan to France, surviving by his own wits as an alchemist of that time under the auspices of a Courtesan of the French Court living in a Château in the French countryside.

With the protection of her patronage away from the prying eyes of city life he was able to crudely reconfigure the time travel technology he and Peter had devised and disagreed upon the useful purpose of. Only—barely, after several failures in a time so vacant of any and all technology was he able to arrive in the latter half of twentieth century Europe with secret trips to America, finally locating and joining up once again with his brother Peter. Each had, after their disbursal to this world, been able to mathematically calculate the time period and location where the other had arrived, both thriving by their wits but in very different circumstances. They were both ecstatic to have found one another and be able to proceed with their science once more in this world they were temporarily stranded in. They were able to secretly confer scientifically in an atmosphere of grand adventure so appealing to young men such as themselves. Both had quickly recognized the familiar form of Earth's enslavement and made a moral decision to free mankind here as they had helped to finalize such undertakings on their own world knowing that because of their scientific technology being so far in advance of Earth they would be able to return home when all they had formed oath upon was accomplished—they were committed to changing the state of Earth's people—give them the same chance they had had. It would take time and much preparation since this world was not as advanced or free as the one they had come from—it would all have to be done in secret—out of the notice of those dark ones they were so very familiar with—the former enslavers of their own world. All these years their pact had endured for their commitment was no small thing.

Zorloff had been able to maintain for decades his anonymity. After being consulted by an elderly friend's grand nephew concerning strange documents the uncle had requested on his death bed be dispatched to Peter, Zorloff knew the game was afoot—it could be postponed no longer, and, with Marc's daughters' discovery of the fruit there could not be the option of waiting. Time and events had intruded. Their time-table was being stepped up by fate alone. He only hoped fate was on their side. Peter had contacted him right after learning from Marc of the events at Dragons Roost through a code known and used only by the two of them through the years.

They had worked together in secret denying themselves little close contact of friendship or family so as not to come under scrutiny with what they were about. And now, together once more after these many years of secrecy in the science they conspired to and perfected beyond anything the scientists of this world could imagine even existed, they would now finally liberate this parallel world's civilization from that most hideous of human species—the Vraang!

The brothers carried in lab equipment with the early morning sun shining through the trees on the ridge surrounding Dragons Roost. They were putting into place *certain components* of a science designed for specific results into the old lab. Both were elated to be able to actually work together once more as they had in the old days—it gave renewed energy and zest for what life here could be, the culmination of a sense of purpose.

New locks and alarm systems were due to be installed by afternoon, those of Peter's own contriving. Serpentine was shocked and filled with sorrow at Georgianna's loss and eager to do whatever was necessary to assist in her recovery. Their little group, Peter, Zorloff, Serpentine—even Marc and others— some little known, but in the background, had long prepared for this day of reckoning. The time could no longer be delayed. Everything was developing at light-speed!

Cleaning and necessary home goods were being recruited and by the end of the day the premises would again after so long, be livable—even comfortable. Serpentine had the means to see to all that. She had been paramount through the years in their being able to exist and work without notice. She had borrowed one of Esmeralda's paneled company trucks proclaiming such by the lettering on its side to deliver all they needed under cover of a fall cleanup around Dragons Roost after so many years of neglect. Everyone wore work clothes and caps so as to appear as workmen coming and going around the grounds if anyone became curious as to what was going on with a property so long vacant.

The two scientists worked feverishly aligning the technology only they had. Both being so of like mind and talent had, through the years, so surpassed this world's science that it would not be understood by most of Earth's scientific community. Now it would also be used to return their dear friend Marc's beloved Georgianna to them.

They had to be cloistered with what they had to achieve besides the problem of Georgianna. Serpentine would see to whatever needs arose necessary from the outside while they discerned the particular circumstances of Georgianna's situation and returned her safely home.

This was not as difficult as it might at first seem, since in all the ensuing years their scientific advancements had taken them in many directions. Initially in their youth, time travel and parallel worlds were the very sciences they delved into until the hasty hot-blood personalities of their youth kicked in resulting in the unexpected engaging and duplication of their inter-dimensional time-travel conveyance, depositing them in this world. They had made fantastic advances since then—advances that could not be allowed in the hands of a humanity that in this stage of their Vraang controlled existence turned every advancement into a weapon when such were designed for enlightenment, not destruction. That would come later—post Vraang.

Early on Dragons Roost had been ascertained by them as a place of power conveyance on Earth, such concepts being of scientific understanding and used as worldwide free energy on the home world of Peter and Zorloff.

This could never be on the world they now were part of until things were changed. Humanity here had never known freedom from the Vraang to reach for all it could be—not even realizing it was enslaved all these eons—just accepting life as it was. Somehow humanity had never guessed life could be better—had never even suspicioned they were not in control of their own destiny, unknowingly used as suppliers of Sesca—a molecular component of human adrenaline.

Adrenaline did not need to be physically collected to remove a molecular peculiarity found only in the trunk species of humanity, the component that the Vraang so coveted—Sesca—it's life enhancing properties so compelling to the Vraang that no moral implication could stand in the way of their obtaining it from any sort of cruelty coerced upon humanity. Through constant war and mass trauma encouraged through background manipulation in all aspects of human life by the ancient Vraang species of human, it was in the very atmosphere, only to be removed by cloaked collectors in high Earth orbit on the edge of space. Not even NASA or any of the Earth's military had ever discovered such devices. The collectors worked well, and had for much of man's history—Earth was what was known as a feeder world—one of the Vraang's gardens.

Many civilizations over the centuries including the Vraang themselves had searched for an alternative to the harvesting of Sesca—not that they really cared for the unsuspecting humans—just curious. No drug could do for this particular human species—the Vraang (different from all other humans in their genetic makeup) what Sesca could.

Sesca had no positive effect at all on other humans—only the Vraang—it was truly their drug alone. Experimentation done on captive human subjects by the Vraang revealed Sesca could have a most deadly effect—causing depression so deep that the subjects became suicidal. The Vraang needed humans—help build up their civilizations and populations to self-destruct at certain points along the way—collect the Sesca and help them rebuild civilization, again and again this scenario repeated throughout human history. Humanity had never guessed they had always been groomed to failure—fearing that beneath it all they were a truly, deservedly failed and inept species with very little hope of ever overcoming their self-destructive tendencies.

Only a handful on Earth realized what was going on and always had; but who among their fellow humans would believe such. A secret organization had long ago been formed to preserve this esoteric secret knowledge in the hope that one day a solution could be found for Earth's liberation—those efforts had been futile and hopeless for long and long, for there had been no way to combat the advanced Vraang and so lived with and kept to themselves a knowledge so dark it could destroy all hope.

Misery and sorrow were and always had been the portion of human life—they knew no other, this was just how life was—*wasn't it?* The Vraang of Earth, were safe.

* * *

By nightfall thanks to Serpentine's enterprise, Dragons Roost was livable. It had been a beehive of activity all day—everything had finally fallen into place; a fire in the labs fireplace flanked by two wing chairs and fronted by a big heavy sofa gave the laboratory space an area of respite from the intensity Peter and Zorloff were submerged in.

They could exist and work together as they needed to on these last preparations without being disturbed. Even so—both men carried pistols having dealt knowingly in their youth with the Vraang on this world, they would leave nothing to chance.

Marc and Serpentine had begged Ombline to move her things to Serpentine's as it was more protected than Grey

Hall, but she refused. "What would it matter?" Ombline asked. "Seurat knows she's been discovered, she can no longer come here to use this portal—surely there are others, and don't think for a moment I don't realize you're not telling all. It's not me she's interested in, it's what you guys are doing, Georgianna and I were just in her way. She strikes me as someone who operates out of anger and arrogance, a kind of sociopath."

Peter and Zorloff looked to one another hearing this from Ombline, saying nothing, but in the nothing—much.

She had felt comfortable at Grey Hall and refused to move.

They gave up and left the issue alone for the time being.

Ombline had been consumed with guilt at not having been able to save Georgianna. Everyone assured her no one could have done more. Georgianna had always been self-determined, there was never any stopping her when her mind was made up and last night would have been no different.

For now, there was only the waiting while Georgianna's destination was determined—and, Ombline considered, once this was accomplished, how would they find her on the other side and bring her home? She believed without knowing, someone would have to go through to locate her, because knowing her sister, after getting over the shock of where she was transported to, she was sure Georgianna was not about to hang around where ever she had first appeared; but then why would she—maybe check back occasionally if she could. Regardless, she was sure someone would have to go in search of her—she wanted to be that someone.

Chapter   Fifteen

Whoosh! Bump! Whoomp! Georgianna rolled across the ground backward at first, entangling in vines and bumping into what appeared to be in the moonlight, pumpkins, and finally came to a stop. She knew she had been discharged with finality, there was no going back, at least for now. Where she had come through to, wherever this was, there was no evidence of the conduit of her transference—no portal. She came to rest sitting upright propped against one of the large orange globes of the gordy fruit, stunned by her transit, but not immobile. Wherever it was she had been sucked into and shot out of, it had geological similarities to the ridge of Dragons Roost, the same night sky with a full moon, only here the hillside was larger and planted completely in pumpkins. Even in the moonlight she could see they grew and prospered around and under the lofty trees of a forest—*the trees—the trees*, such mighty trees. She said this aloud to herself in awe of such magnificent trees—monuments of trees, the like of which she had never seen. She could see twinkling stars between their mighty branches above.

Bit by bit she regained a grip on herself, standing and attempting to assess her situation. *Just where was she, her mind roared with possibilities?* It had not been long after Dr. Frank had walked through the blue portal before she had been shoved in. Surely he could not be too far ahead of her. He would not be a companion to search for, no matter what she encountered in this place. What was his purpose in being here willingly? She couldn't imagine, but was sure neither of them would have any commonality.

She saw no roads, nothing that indicated anyone lived nearby, but upon the ridge where Dragons Roost would normally be were the ruins of a castle occupying the ridge line. Stars twinkled high above it in the night sky providing a magical backdrop for such mystical remains.

She looked back to the spot from where she had been expelled. There was no sign of anything indicating a portal opening—only the pumpkin patch in the moonlight. Standing here was getting her nowhere. At least she still had on both of the costume shoes, better to protect her feet in this unknown landscape. *It was more than chilly—a coat would have been nice.*

She began climbing up the ridge to the ruins working her way through the vines. Since the castle sat on the ridge line maybe it overlooked a town—at least long ago, giving rise to some sort of civilization in the present. For the moment this was the only logical direction to take.

The closer she climbed to the ruins she could see one section and tower were intact. A soft glow of light stood out in a window high in the tower. A wooden door was visible at ground level. If there was no sign of life on the other side of the ridge she would knock at the door—seek help of some sort. She had no plan yet, if, as she now believed, she was in some other reality—what *would* she do? Try to find that horrid Dr. Frank and convince him to help her get back—go home? *No, that was not an option.* Just the thought of *home* put a lump in her throat. Yes, she was frightened, but she couldn't allow herself to be swallowed by fear, that would surely defeat her.

Finally, she reached the ridge summit and crossed to the other side. It was just wide enough for the ruins. She stepped forward to get a better view of the valley down the other side of the ridge when the large flat rock she had been standing on gave way tumbling her a ways down the hill side. The shock of it caused her to yell out. She stood up shaken, brushing dust and debris from herself hoping she wasn't injured and just didn't know it yet.

Somehow, she still had on her complete costume, even that silly hat that tied under the chin—*why take it off now—what could it possibly matter?* Why hadn't she taken it off back in the car?

She looked back up at the light in the tower window then turned once more to check out the valley below for signs of life as she had before the rockslide. The valley too, seemed to be covered in those gigantic trees as far as she could see—were they a continuous forest? It was impossible to tell in the dark even in the light of the full moon; the land appeared to be foothills—even mountainous in the distance.

The darkness of the valley below gave no insight on her predicament. As she considered what her immediate options might be, a sinister voice told her. "Slowly turn and put your hands in the air."

She did, realizing as she did so this man spoke French—*Am I in France?* She wondered how this could be. *Hopefully I'm still on earth—my earth—just in France.* She spoke French herself. Haltingly she began. *"Monsieur,* I'm lost. I was at a party and through a strange accident I arrived here through no fault of my own. Could I use a phone, call for help, transport—and then I'll just be on my way?"

He said nothing more only motioned for her to go ahead of him and the gun he brandished at her back up the ridge to the ruins. He ushered her to the wooden door on the other side of the building that she had observed earlier. She knew she was being picked up for trespassing. Surely someone would listen to her—just not this person.

The door needed its squeaky hinges oiled. With him behind her they entered a dimly lit interior almost in as much atrophy as the exterior. A high arched stone door way farther in led to an area sparsely furnished with antique trash as far as she could make out—seedy.

She heard footsteps coming down the spiral stairs of the tower. The treads looked dangerous as there was no railing and many of the steps had begun to crumble. And—yes—of course. *Dr. Frank*! What was there to say on her behalf—let him do the talking. The man stopped at the bottom of the stairs seemingly not noticing that Georgianna lived and breathed.

"Haran." Dr. Frank said to Georgianna's captor. "You will take us to the city." He completely ignored Georgianna.

Haran, the quiet but well dressed, nondescript drudge of Dr. Frank spoke for only the second time. "What do you want done with her?" He indicated Georgianna who now felt her fear was so great she simply glowed with its energy.

"Benoit will take care of her—he comes now." Heavy footsteps ambled down the stairs. A gargantuan man appearing slow witted came to stand beside Dr. Frank who said only, "you know what to do with her." He nodded to Georgianna.

The deadly eyes of Dr. Frank told it all. He still wore the monocle. He took his time lighting a cigarette. Momentarily more footsteps could be heard coming down the stairs, only lighter—softer—a woman, one of youth and elegance. She went to the wooden door and stopped as if waiting.

Georgianna could tell little else about her because of the scarf she had tied around her head and the sunglasses she wore regardless of the fact that it was the dark of night; even so, there was a strange knowing between the indifferent woman and Georgianna, she said nothing, she was disconnected from Georgianna's plight—it was of no concern to her.

Dr. Frank joined her. "Come Haran." He said. "We go."

The three turned taking their leave. The door's hinges screeched loudly as it was pulled to behind them leaving Georgianna alone with this frightening Benoit.

She saw the flash of silver as Benoit pulled a long double-bladed knife from behind himself. There was no doubt what he intended. He stood between Georgianna and the wooden door.

It would do no good to take the tower stairs and surely be trapped up there or jump from the window she had seen the light in to her death.

There was only the grungy room behind her. She turned and ran looking wildly about for another door or window with Benoit at her heels. He quickly cornered her against the wall. Fear pulsed through her like cold fire. Adrenaline bathed every cell in her body. She slipped, slowly sliding down the wall's rough texture till she sat on the floor.

He stood over her with his knife raised above her for the deathblow. Even weaponless she didn't intend to go down easy for this evil brute. She remembered the rock hard heels on her costume shoes that had almost caused her to take a fall more than once on the dance floor at the ball. They were her only weapon—a spear at best—even if only a short one. She lashed out kicking as hard as she could with the sharp heel to the front of Benoit's shinbone knowing from experience how painful a blow to that area of the leg could be.

The man roared in agony attempting to clutch his leg with his free hand, causing the top-heavy degenerate to fall forward unsuccessfully clawing at the wall as he slid to the floor. Both his legs had flown back out from under him on the fine refuse of debris littering the floor while he still held tight the gleaming blade.

Georgianna rolled away to the side just in time as he landed hard face down on the floor heaving great heavy breaths. His breathing quickly became only shallow gasps, then, abruptly stopped with one last great heave of release from his lungs—then no more. He finally lay still and silent.

Using the wall as support she cautiously stood expecting him to rise any moment to come after her. He did not. She backed slowly away. Even in the low light of the shabby atmosphere she could see a fast moving pool of blood spreading dark and thick from where he lay. He had surely fallen on and impaled himself on his own knife—the one he had meant for her. She stepped back toward him only close enough to reassure herself he was truly dead before she made a run for it. She could tell his hands in death were closed around the knife that must have entered his heart. She could see by his head turned to the side in his last gasp for life, that his vacant black eyes had the glazed open stare of death.

This was her chance—in a flash she was out of this frightful place and through the wooden door, the sound of its hinges screamed, following her into the night. *Which way, which way?* She turned in a flurry and ran back down the hill amidst the pumpkin patch to where she had come through the portal. If pumpkins had been planted here it was likely that whoever had planted them lived nearby. She would seek help from none of those for they might be no better, on she would go for now!

She surveyed the very spot where she concluded she came through. Still there was no sign of anything out of the ordinary. No frame of sorts as one might expect as in the Dragons Roost lab. *Maybe a structure to frame a portal transit is not a necessity—but then what do I know?* There was nothing obvious at the spot to her way of thinking that could tell her anything that might be of help in getting home.

She wondered just how the portal might be accessed from this side. She glanced back up the ridge to the ruins in fear that maybe her executioner really wasn't dead even though she knew this was not so—he was dead! She tried to calm her racing mind and uncontrollable shaking. There was no doubt in her mind that a technology to open a portal was necessary which of course Georgianna did not have. She looked back up to the ridge wondering if the tower might contain such left behind by Dr. Frank; considering this not an option for her as she was afraid of being captured by those people again; indecisiveness caused her to nervously pace the small piece of ground she had arrived on. She was brought full square to the moment by slipping on an object that scooted aside from under her foot. Curious, she bent to see what she had stepped on.

It was the cell phone Ombline had thrown into the engaged blue portal hoping to distract Madame Seurat. *The phone! The phone!* Many scenarios flashed through her mind. What the hell! She thought. She dialed Mark, Peter and then Zorloff's number—even Serpentine's and Esmeralda's. Of course there was no response. *Could this set up some sort of beacon Peter could track?*

She didn't know.

One thing she did know, she would bury it here in the ground in case someone *did* come looking for her. She was afraid to just bury it in the dirt. *What to wrap it in—what?* She looked up at a flower petal dangling from her hat. *There must have been a reason that this hat has been with me all this time.* She untied it wrapping the cell phone in it and burying the bundle as deep as she could scoop out Earth. She patted the soil smoothly over her breadcrumb and strewed pebbles and debris over it to conceal it further—only the signal to be discovered was all she was concerned about. It gave her hope that she was doing something on her own behalf.

She stood, knowing she couldn't just wait here in a pumpkin patch forever to be rescued. She decided to strike out northwest after descending the hillside to an area that leveled out into a valley in hopes of finding an active road, a road to where and what she didn't know.

Chapter   Sixteen

Dragons Roost had become in a short time, a technological fort. Marc, Ombline and Serpentine joined Peter and Zorloff for dinner. Serpentine had brought a full gourmet dinner prepared by her cook along with several bottles of wine, some for dinner others for stock.

Ombline was beginning to feel better when she saw all that was being done to rescue Georgianna. The wine relaxed her as she sat in one of the chairs by the fireplace while Serpentine heated dinner for them. This gave comfort to both she and her father.

Marc had tried to reassure her that Georgianna would be fine, that Peter knew what they were about—what their next step would be—that they had been involved in such things before.

Ombline was shocked that her father was saying this—just what *kind* of things? She had never known such things of science were known to Peter or anyone. What lay behind all their veiled secrecy? She had a million questions that no one seemed to want to answer to her satisfaction.

All through dinner at the big round table and chairs brought in from one of the other rooms both scientists questioned her again as to even the smallest detail she could remember concerning any of the events she and Georgianna had experienced, even with the purple lightning the first day. No matter how inconsequential a detail might seem they jumped on it.

Zorloff said to no one in particular. "As simple as it sounds even radio waves can cause a disturbance traceable between dimensions."

"But you have the cell phone signal," Ombline almost shouted in excitement. "I threw my phone through the portal. I threw it through after Seurat discovered us in the closet just to distract her even though she didn't seem to notice. It went through maybe 30 seconds before Georgianna—it went where she went."

"Good to know." Peter said, reaching over hugging her with one arm.

Good to know? Ombline thought. Good to know—that's it? She had hoped for more exuberance from Peter. This cursed setting up shop that was taking forever was frustrating, and these strange little pieces of this and that, that Peter kept disclosing piecemeal at a time—why couldn't he just lay it all out once and for all?!

After dinner the two scientists moved back to the lab tables covered with a kind of technology completely unknown to

Ombline. So much of it seemed to be comprised of crystal arrangements unlike anything she had ever seen or heard of as new science. Just what *had* Peter been up to all those years in the cave lab on the Steffington estate?

Still, the blue frame stood in its original position in the center of the room—waiting to be used again she knew, for that would be the route used to bring Georgianna home. On their way back to Grey Hall Ombline wondered what Georgianna was doing this very moment, was she okay—what kind of world was she in?

At dinner Peter had explained as best he could in layman's terms how this inter-dimensional thing worked. "Most physicists now understand that all that we consider matter is only energy in an expressible form seeming to *us* solid. The smallest particles have been proven to be in more than one place at once." He was quiet for a moment. "Zorloff and I have been on a much different path of physics than science is today for many years and understand that these smallest particles of what we perceive as our reality exist at the same time in infinite locations—to make it simple, for example, the subatomic particles of everything that makes up what we perceive as an apple in our dimension are partial components of a tree in another and yet a river in another and so on. They exist as everything and anything all at the same time. All particles are not just as their makeup appears in our reality but comprise a multitude of other things in infinite realities. It's a matter of joining up with the correct algorithm of the energy of the destination via portal to that of the point of origin—a wormhole between two worlds in existence. Georgianna has been transferred to one of those realities and considering how quickly, I believe it was one Zorloff and I are very familiar with—one similar to this one here but called Irrieth." Peter paused, knowing this was a lot to take in.

Ombline was numb. She had nothing to say. This was like the science channel on steroids. How did these two men personally know of Irrieth? Could such a place really exist? Could Georgianna really be there? She was afraid she would not be able to sleep with so much plowing through her mind. And, most definitely had not been told the whole story which she was too tired to fight over now—did it really matter—if they just brought Georgianna home they could have their fantastic science secrets! Now that she thought about it she could never remember hearing anything of Peter's family history, and Zorloff, what of him? He could be Peter's twin. It was uncanny. Her mind was going off into the ethers with speculation, for now she wondered if the two of *them* were from Irrieth since they seemed to know of it, she was sure that that was just the way of it. There was no point in even questioning this for now. But why were they here in this world? She was so exhausted, physically and mentally. If both Peter and Zorloff suddenly sprouted little green antenna she didn't think for now she would even be shocked or bother to mention it. She knew her world and all of theirs was going down a road that none of them could ever return from—one so different she hoped all they were and had been would still matter.

Chapter Seventeen

Morning sunlight poured down through the tree branches above. Georgianna ambled along the shallow ruts of what had been a road through the forest. Sometime in the past the road had been paved but left to neglect for only small chunks of asphalt remained. Wild grasses had taken over, the farther she walked the more it had reverted to the lands natural state. Maybe she was going in the wrong direction—direction to where? But for some reason she didn't think so, so on she trudged.

Life of every sort seemed in abundance here. She had witnessed exquisitely robust forest animals—squirrels, foxes, birds and many she didn't recognize to be exactly like the animals she was familiar with—a knee-high rabbit that seemed to be a cross between a kangaroo and a rabbit in the way it hopped up right even without that kangaroo tail to balance it. None seemed afraid. Birds chittered as they ate the fruit at the top of the trees.

The strangest thing of all though was the fruit the trees bore (she was sure, now that she could see this in the daylight) was the same fruit they had stored for safekeeping in Serpentine's pantry fridge. This had to be where Seurat had intended to come since the fruit must have come through from here. Why—why—why was she so afraid of it—she certainly appeared human—but who is to say an alien wouldn't? It apparently was of no consequence to Dr. Frank. As creepy a pair as those two were, there was obviously something genetically different about the woman and her *extreme allergies*. No, Georgianna didn't believe for a moment after seeing the woman's frightened aversion to the fruit that Seurat had anything in common with the humans *she* was familiar with. And, after having been introduced to both Seurat and Frank, it would be hard to pick and choose which one was weirder or even an alien. Georgianna considered Madame Seurat's actions, an unanswerable mystery for the time being.

Earlier, she had been reckless considering how hungry she had been and picked two of the firm fleshed aromatic fruit laying on the ground and devoured them for breakfast. It could have been dangerous not being a native of this world, but she felt fine, in fact *very* fine, *even,* energetic, considering all she had been through with so little sleep.

When daylight had come about it had sunk in that she was not in the France that she knew. She had not walked far in the dark night (far enough though to be a good distance from the ruins) and had stopped and slept only till the sun came up eager to be on her way, to where she didn't know, but, she knew she should be on the move if she sought civilization. It would do no good to hang around the pumpkin patch where she came through. She thought that futile for now for she surely knew of no one here capable scientifically of offering her any rescue, she was on her own.

If she didn't soon come to civilization she needed to find water, already she felt the beginnings of thirst for the real thing. The juice of the fruit had helped. But still she needed water.

She walked until after mid day finding no sign of human life, thankfully though she did come upon a clear small stream from which she drank disregarding whether the water was clean and safe or not. Too, she needed to be higher to get her bearings instead of endlessly wandering in the forest valley.

She made it a point to be on the lookout for a higher promontory up on the spine of the ridge. *Where was the road Dr. Frank's party had left by?* She had seen none except for the disappearing ruts she had followed all morning. And—what was the city he spoke of?

Finally, a more prominent characteristic of the Ridge jutted out and above. She began to climb up it—hopefully this could give her direction—a goal, something to end this pointless wandering. Faster and faster she climbed up the dusty rocky hillside hoping to find purpose in her wanderings.

The very thought that she might be in a world where there were no humans gave her such a feeling of loneliness and despair she had no words for such emotion. But, then, the castle ruins on the ridge certainly were of human origin, and so was the building now just ahead of her.

She slowed as the hillside leveled out to its summit. She came to a halt, for just ahead was a square grey building squat to the ground. There were no windows on any of the four sides she found by walking around its perimeter, but what looked to be a lock of some sort seemed not to be engaged on the only door.

Pushing down a metallic bar of a handle, she ventured inside since no one was around outside. She could be considered a trespasser as she had not knocked or announced herself. So far Georgianna had not come upon anything that she could equate with her own world, the inside of this building was no exception.

A globe of differing metallic hues swirled in constantly changing colour atop a sizable block of white marble infused with gold. It gave off a low vibration barely felt as a rumble through the building. She ventured closer to the strange sphere only to be stopped in her tracks by what seemed to be an invisible wall. It enclosed the swirling globe centering the room. Nothing else occupied the space. Once again she was alone.

She was beginning to succumb to exhaustion, and, she knew, the overwhelming stress of her situation. The fruit could do only so much if one had not had enough sleep—which was becoming a weighty burden in itself. The afternoon was getting on. She was dusty from the climb and had lost one of the sharp heels of her shoes. Now she must somehow remove the other one. The only tool available would have to be a rock. She went back outside to find one with a sharp enough edge to use as a wedge.

She was down on all fours scrounging amongst the stones. A shadow silently moved over her blocking the sun. Fear washed over her provoking a flight or fight cat-like response, whirling her around to spring up in one motion to face whatever had come upon her.

She stood her ground, her ebony blue hair falling across her feline topaz eyes peering at the figure before her expecting to once again have to fight for her life. She felt strangely feral considering all she had been forced to do to exist since her arrival here—a predator of sorts on her own behalf.

A man taller than herself stood a short distance from her giving no indication her circumstances had changed. His sun-warmed good looks were not in keeping with his cold stare of accusatory recrimination most likely from her emergence from the building.

"*What*," he demanded, "are you doing here? Who are you?"

"*And*, who are you?" Georgianna shot back trying to control the quaking that now seemed to be racking her body.

"How did you get here?" He pursued his line of questioning, ignoring Georgianna's questioning of *him*.

She edged back slowly still holding a rock. "You first." She shot back again.

He moved slowly toward her repeating his question as if he had the authority to do so.

"I'm Georgianna Patrone, and I certainly never wanted to come here. I—I was," she hated to say the words, "shoved into a blue wormhole and shot out into a pumpkin patch!" There, she'd said it, the most absurd thing she knew she could have said to anyone. She felt herself shaking uncontrollably now, but refused to let herself cry. She was still looking at him through her hair.

He stepped closer as she backed up even more.

"You need to stop!" He cautioned too late.

She stumbled backward falling hard amongst the loose gravel ending up the center piece of a cloud of dust rising around her.

"I was going to say," he said shaking his head, "you're going to slide and fall in that gravel." He moved to where she lay. She sat up pained and dazed—exhausted beyond anything she had ever experienced before.

He reached down to her, helping her stand. "Are you all right?"

She didn't answer because she just didn't know anymore if she was what could be called all right or not and avoided eye contact as he helped her up. She was too tired and stressed to even defend herself if he had decided to execute her on the spot!

"Here," he said taking the cap off a bottle he pulled from a back attachment to his belt, "take a drink of the juice, it will restore you, then, we'll talk." He seemed both sympathetic and suspicious.

She did drink, for she was afraid her shaking was becoming more obvious. That fall was the final straw. She held the container and continued to drink deeply letting what she recognized as juice from the blue fruit, restore her.

Georgianna repeated her story. "I know how absurd this sounds, but, that is just what happened."

He did not smile as if weighing what she said. He took the container back when she was finished and re-capped it. "Were you at a costume party first before you were dispatched here?"

He looked at her filthy clothes, wondering if she believed her state confirmed her story.

He made her feel like some sort of lawbreaker—just what kind she wasn't sure—but she knew it had something to do with being in the squat building. She felt like he thought he had caught her and was mocking her story.

Again, just to watch her reaction he repeated his question. "And—you were at a costume party before being dispatched here?"

Regardless, she was going to tell it like it was. "Why yes I was, as a matter of fact," she stated with agitation. "I surely was. This is not my usual choice of attire for hiking the out-of-doors, or unsolicited form of adventure. By the way, since I'm divulging my circumstances, who are you—and most importantly—where am I?" He still did not give her any sort of a feeling of comfort for she just wanted to curl up somewhere for now and sleep for a few days even though the shaking was better thanks to the juice.

"Jack Stewart—my name is Jack Stewart." He studied her almost as if undecided on just how much to reveal. "You're in the region of Alsace-Lorraine in a major fruit forest."

Georgianna looked around her almost unbelieving. "I am at your mercy as I seem to be lost as much as I hate to say this, in an alternate existence somewhere—possibly even in time—you see I don't have any scientific answers for what has happened to me, or what, for the moment to do about it. I need any help you could possibly render me." The positive effect of the fruit was beginning to take hold—giving her more stamina and self control.

He didn't answer, but reached out taking her hand and turned to pull her on up the hill behind him stopping only to re-engage the stuccoed building's lock. A light on the door flashed three times indicating its security was in effect Georgianna believed.

"Let's go, transport isn't far." He said, indicating she follow him.

They climbed to the top of the next rise. On the other side a yellow and silver conveyance sat with no road in sight. He opened the passenger door indicating she be seated.

This confirmed her assumption that she was truly *elsewhere*.

After Jack seated himself, safety harnesses automatically crossed both passengers. Jack spoke to the vehicle and it soundlessly rose from the ground. They headed north and east quickly gaining altitude above the forest. She was astounded as the vehicle rose into the air and could not decide if she had been rescued or captured as she felt her head fall forward in a welcome dreamless sleep no longer avoidable.

Chapter Eighteen

Georgianna roused from the deep state of sleep she had fallen into wondering how long she had been out. They still travelled by air. Whether it had been a short nap of necessity or not she felt somehow revived and marveled at the view from the vehicle she flew in as a passenger well above the forest of trees bearing the blue fruit. It was as she had suspected, an orchard of sorts—one of vast proportions. Walking, would have taken far too long to find civilization.

They left the forest behind and flew over occasional small towns and other constructs appearing to be very methodized farming concerns—even futuristic.

She glanced at the man beside her, Jack, as he had introduced himself, the pilot of their transportation; still he said little seeming uneasy with her. What law had she broken—what jeopardy had she put herself in by entering the little building—casting what sort of suspicion upon herself—even spying? Some crime punishable by imprisonment—was she even now being escorted to that end?

They didn't fly at a great speed, no faster than a car on the open highway. She had seen maybe five other vehicles like the one she was in, different colours, but all the same design—and all at a constant airspeed that led her to believe when one was aloft the vehicles were under some other control than just that of the pilot. The ratio between air car and ground surface, seemed to always stay the same whether they were over the forest or countryside, the vehicle's altitude was consistent with the surface below it.

The sun was lowering in what she perceived to be the West. Their flight had been silent—at least while she was passed out. The experience and scenery below had made up for that she knew by giving her a boost of adrenalin and bringing her back fully awake.

Only now did Jack speak. "Feel better? You have been asleep or should I say unconscious for a space. When we arrive at the lodge you need to drink a goodly amount of the juice to restore yourself for the evening—it will be necessary I'm sorry to say, seeing your state of exhaustion."

Eventually, the vehicle slowed and began a spiral descent to a pine forest on the side of a hill; there were no visible roads below, even there. They were descending to the eastern side of a mountain range in shadow now that the sun was setting.

The air car settled in amongst a pine forest. Not far away stood a building clad in shingles curiously shaped like rows of feathers or fish scales—row upon row of protection—one above the other in mottled shades of light grey and beige so as to blend in with the natural tones of the mountainside—it was beautiful. Windows indistinguishable in shape as to whether they imitated clouds or ocean waves were located at odd intervals adding a mystical quality to the building.

The safety harnesses retracted and the sides of the vehicle raised to allow passengers to alight. Jack jumped out coming around to Georgianna's side. For all she knew she was a prisoner, but, her jailer was at least courteous taking her arm as she exited the vehicle although again silent.

She hobbled toward the building in the dusk still having only one shoe with a heel on it.

They climbed a few steps to a circular deck seeming to surround the structure. Jack halted at an arched wooden door saying only, Jack open, causing the door to swing inward.

The air outside smelled of forest pine—a subtlety inside also. A spacious living area was centered by a natural stone surround containing a fireplace. Roomy overstuffed chairs upholstered in a natural-coloured heavy linen were grouped around the fireplace—the kitchen a little beyond. A grey metal spiral stair wound upward.

An arched door stood ajar off the living area exposing an office-library hinting of a technology unfamiliar to

Georgianna—its walls as those of the living area were lined with books. The colours of the multitude of volumes infused the interior with warmth and a sense of civility.

Jack said. "Please be seated, shortly there will be those who wish to speak with you."

There it was. "Who are these persons I'm supposed to be questioned by?" Georgianna asked in this way, knowing she might as well lay it out that she knew she had committed some sort of illegality and was to be questioned by authority—or who?—Here in what appeared to be a private home? This concerned her. What did they intend to do with her in this out-of-the-way place where there was obviously no official authority—not the official kind that she was familiar with?

He ignored her question. "Would you like to bathe—shower? There is everything including clean clothing and shoes at your disposal up the stairs to your right, and privacy." He emphasized. "But first you need to drink the juice to restore yourself." He went into the kitchen bringing back a large glass of the orange-yellow coloured juice of the blue fruit.

"Here, drink down as much as you can—no sipping!"

She did just that and shortly regained most of her former momentum wondering just how long its effect would last for she had no doubt that eventually she would be out of it to the point that this super fruit could not even help her.

To be clean again would help to clear her head too, give her an added measure of renewed strength and initiative for her own behalf. She went up the spiral stair without further conversation.

Jack yelled to her on the way up. "Later we'll have dinner outside on the back of the surround, I'm sure you're starved; we can all talk and sort this out then."

Georgianna wondered who the others were that he had mentioned as *all*. She stayed in the shower luxuriating in the warm water longer than she intended. It seemed to wash away some of the stress and fear she had knowingly suppressed to make concentrating on survival easier.

Jack yelled up to her that the clean items of clothing he had mentioned were in the chest of drawers in the bath, and an assortment of shoes in the bottom of the linen closet.

She put on a natural fiber white shirt, matching drawstring pants and slipped on shoes in a neutral colour made of an unknown material but soft and comfortable; the clothing looked more like a man's pajamas than anything else—that was just fine she thought. They were clean and felt wonderful and her own outlook was improving—and yes, she could hardly wait for dinner.

Georgianna came downstairs renewed by the simple things one takes for granted to find Jack in the library talking to someone on something she considered a phone. She assumed that was what he held in his hand as he spoke.

He saw she was in the living area and discontinued his conversation. He walked into the kitchen setting out four wine glasses on the marble countertop and proceeded to pour red wine into two of them. He offered one to Georgianna as she sat in front of the fireplace where he had been busy building a fire while she had showered.

She only sipped on the wine afraid after being so relaxed she might fall asleep; she could feel her lack of sleep beginning to make it's fogginess felt even with all the strengthening juice she'd had and set the wine aside. She knew she would have to sleep soon for she couldn't keep this up much longer. She wondered if Jack intended sleep deprivation to produce some suspected admission of guilt from her. He seemed hard to know.

Georgianna's wine glass was still barely touched when the door announced two people entering.

A young man very similar in appearance and stature to Jack yelled. "Jack Stewart, your brother is here!" Another voice added. "And Storm too!"

The man was tall and lanky like Jack, dark haired and had the same grey eyes as Jack, but obviously of a more jovial and out-going nature. He was accompanied by a lithe-figured, pretty blue-eyed Oriental woman on his arm. Both seemed in extremely good spirits. Jack embraced them both.

He turned to Georgianna. "This, is our visitor, Ms. Georgianna Patrone from far away but not so long ago—my brother Ean Stewart and his wife Storm."

The young woman seemed both curious and pleased to meet Georgianna. "We have much to discuss this night. We brought a feast to have outback under the stars." She said this while scrutinizing Georgianna's reaction.

Georgianna wondered what this night would bring, but whatever it was she felt good amongst these people—why, she didn't know—but no longer did she feel quite so fearful.

Now Jack—that was another matter, she had never been a fan of those romance stories with dark brooding so-called heroes—arrogance was not an attribute she could abide in a man. He seemed to fit that bill.

She had questions of her own, this wasn't just about her— what were *their* stories and especially their intentions toward her? These, she too had to know; it would be a long night if she could stay awake. Her own curiosity would help.

Chapter Nineteen

Peter and the mysterious Zorloff were immersed in their work, oblivious to all else around them. The only help Ombline had been effective in offering was to run errands for the two. Still, she knew little more than she had—they were secret keepers, but eventually they would have to be up front with this mysterious business; for now they had her cooperation so her sister could be recovered, but any more than that, they would have to come clean with what she herself and the others were now a part of. She no longer intended to be a runabout for something she knew nothing of, even though she did trust Peter. These errands she was sure were to keep her not only busy and out of the way but to make her feel useful as if she too were part of Georgianna's recovery.

That was okay, she was for that. One of her errands had been to drive to Boston to pick up a specialized piece of equipment from a university friend of Peters.

On her return late in the day, she witnessed a very strange occurrence. Serpentine was outside Dragons Roost in the dusk with a large pitcher full of what Ombline knew (because of the familiar aroma) was mushed up blue fruit and water, dribbling the concoction around the foundation of Dragons Roost; no different than those who do such things with salt—believing it is a protection from evil. She knew without asking why this was being done—to keep Seurat at a distance since she so feared the fruit, not unlike garlic to vampires only much more alarming it had seemed. Serpentine said nothing and continued with what she was doing.

Ombline went inside with the big cardboard box she carried and set it on the floor.

"There is coffee just brewed." Zorloff pointed to the coffee maker. "Thanks for such a long drive, I'm sure you're tired."

"Not so much." Ombline said, taking in all the additional technology now a part of the ornate blue frame, and one monster of a cable up through the roof to what she believed must be connected to the lightning rods atop the building. But most mystifying was the thick round of blue Lapis, a dais, the frame now stood on completely surrounded by white quartz balls the size of grapefruit around the edge of the base all connected by two rows of heavy gold wire. Two three-inch diameter posts of gold disappearing down into the floor were connected to the gold wires of quartz balls on each side of the mirror. She thought the posts must descend into the earth as there was no basement under the building. She remembered seeing that it had been built directly on a short stone foundation. They had been busy.

Ombline poured coffee for herself and sat at the table quietly watching the two men with the new piece of equipment she had brought back wishing she had the ability to be a part of their work to speed things up.

Peter stopped what he was doing and sat down at the table with her bringing his mug along. "You've been a great help Ombline," he smiled, "all your goffering has saved us much time. There is one more drive we need you to make for us if you would. We need the insight of someone in an adjunct scientific field—someone we know we can count on and trust. You see, a close friend of Zorloff's passed away this past summer. The elderly man's nephew is just that person. He is a bit reclusive but *brilliant*. We've spoken to him and he has agreed to help, we need you to once again, drive to Boston and transport him here along with some of his equipment. Serpentine will be putting him up at Grey Hall so he will be close by."

"Of course, of course!" Ombline readily agreed. "It looks as if you're making progress Peter. One thing has concerned me though. Will this be safe?" She nodded toward the empty blue frame standing ready and attendant in the middle of the room. "I'm sure you've taken into consideration every possible negative. But my thoughts are concerned with such things as complete annihilation of this transference through the portal, or wormhole! Could that happen?"

"Anything is possible Ombline, but that is the very reason we are taking the utmost care in our preparations. We are involved in a science not available to the world today. It is (he paused, and looked directly into her eyes as if pressing a knowing into her brain that he knew by now she must suspect) beyond anything this world can imagine—a tangent science—one not invested in as yet. I say invested because more than one brilliant mind over the years has come upon its discovery but were frightened into abandoning it. Zorloff and I are not of that ilk." He paused, wondering if he yet should say more when Serpentine came back in with the pitcher placing it in the fridge.

"Okay guys," she smiled slyly, "Dragons Roost is *salted*, you're safe—at least as far Seurat coming in to get you. "She laughed, continuing. "I could spray the roof too if you think she might try to come down the chimney attempting to reclaim the little black box she left behind."

Zorloff gave a sanctimonious little huff of derision. "She knows by now we've *sucked the guts* out of her technology so she won't be after that. Anyway, if she had one, I'm sure she has others—never make just one of anything important. For the time we're *confined* here to the lab, we have the opportunity to do a little up-grading of sorts, hence, our need for Ledger Griffieth. He will fine tune a project we've already developed—just a tweak or two."

A mental picture of this Ledger, invaded Ombline's psyche, a messy-haired geek with thick glasses—probably a germ-a-phobe who would avoid all communication on the trip back. That would be just fine if it brought Georgianna home any sooner.

Serpentine again warmed up one of her cook's frozen gourmet meals for dinner for the four of them as Marc and Esmeralda were having a quiet dinner at Grey Hall, Esmeralda, not having been told the details of Georgianna's absence as yet. None of them had yet devised a story for Georgianna's disappearance or what should be in the telling of it. Hopefully she would be back before they needed a cover story.

Peter wrestled with the fact that he could not prevent all the details of his past coming to light eventually—even soon, not only to Ombline, but to Chloe and David as well—his beloved granddaughter and her fiancé that had been instrumental in her recovery and that of her archaeologist parents Francesca and John Steffington, from the clutches of this Seurat and Frank in Broyles, France at the end of summer, and ultimately himself from the hands of the very people they were now fully engaged in a final battle with, one of such importance to humanity that as painful as it could be, any of their lives could or would be forfeited if necessary. This had never been an undertaking for the faint of heart.

This moment, Peter and Zorloff had prepared for beginning in their youth, knowing their own science would one day be this world's only hope. Now that time had arrived.

Chapter Twenty

A brisk autumn morning found Ombline on the interstate to Boston to pick up Ledger.

She drove Peter's SUV knowing that Griffieth would be bringing equipment of his own. Peter reminded her, the vehicle had a trailer hitch if they needed to rent one for more space. This wasn't necessary. Ledger was very organized and compact considering the several heavy-duty plastic corrugated containers he had waiting in the lobby at the science building of the University where he worked. A student helped carry the containers and stack them in the back of the SUV. Everything miraculously fit and they were off.

Ombline was pleasantly surprised that Ledger did not fit the geek profile she had anticipated—but taller than herself and fine featured, a thick mop of dark hair and eyes enhanced a warm outgoing personality—that made the trip back an enjoyable ride, much faster than the ride up to collect him.

They talked of their childhoods and the avenues in life that had led them to their respective professions. Ombline's love of reading—its armchair adventure, history and hope for a future full of possibilities, Ledger's love of math, the challenge of materially overcoming adversarial scientific mysteries. He called himself the original erector set kid, he said he still found them useful to daydream a solution to a problem as simplistic as that would sound. By their conversation Ombline could tell that Ledger had a careful conservative bent—not an unnecessary risk taker without proven need to be so; so she was surprised when he admitted to being an expert skier since childhood. Many trips skiing the Alps with his parents, Zorloff and his late uncle Rutger had provided many pleasant memories for him.

Ombline told of skiing the Alps with their father Marc, Georgianna and their cousin Chloe on several winter holidays. At Georgianna's name she became momentarily quiet.

Ledger put his hand on her shoulder as she drove. "Try to keep a positive attitude Ombline, we will get her back."

"I assume," she said, "they told you the details and why they need you, they seem to think very highly of you."

"I'll do my best," he smiled, "I'm more familiar with Peter and Zorloff's work than you might think. The death this past summer of my uncle Rutger put me back in touch with Zorloff who I had not had contact with since my doctorial days at school.

As strange as it sounds because of my uncle's death a whole new branch of scientific discovery was open between Zorloff, Peter and myself making me useful to the problem we now front."

They arrived at Dragons Roost at dusk after stopping at Grey Hall to deposit Ledgers personal things in his suite.

Marc joined the group for dinner at Dragons Roost. Introductions to Ledger pleased Marc that one more, fine mind would be on the case to retrieve his daughter. Stress showed in Marc's face. Everyone sat to dinner around the table to another of Delia's meals.

Positive attitudes lifted the spirits of Marc and Ombline who had been quiet all through dinner for she had come upon a plan to satisfy a curiosity she had had brewing since the confiscation of the blue fruit. She intended to retrieve some of the fruit from Serpentine's pantry to have Thad with his professional expertise analyze it for nutritional and medicinal possibilities. This was something she felt they had overlooked.

Chapter   Twenty   One

The following morning, Ombline called Thad at Contraband sure he would be on duty by eleven for the lunch crowd. She jumped in the rental car and was at the bar just after it opened. She approached him saying only that a friend had brought back some unusual fruit from a Pacific island, and wanted to know something about it. The friend, she explained, was in the nutritional supplement business and suspected the fruit had great antioxidant value.

Thad agreed to use two of the fruit to learn what he could to assist in the possible discovery of a beneficial new food source.

Ombline was heartened that he agreed to investigate the fruits potential and promised to deliver it to him later in the day.

Afterward, back at Grey Hall just as Ombline pulled into the drive she spotted Ledger at the garages returning from a bike ride in a navy sweater and tan corduroy jeans. They talked while he put the bike back in the garage. "Ledger, are you a bicycling enthusiast too?"

"Actually," he smiled, "I bike every day to my work, errands and just for fun. I find it calming—I'm not a racer—I have always liked the feeling of flying low over the ground."

"I do too." Ombline said." Georgianna and I rode every day we were here before she—*disappeared,* we rode to town and up the Old Coast Road where you could see the waves crashing on the rocks below. Under better circumstances I would offer to take you on some of our day trips Ledger, but I'm sure you're much too busy," she smiled looking down to the ground and then back up to him knowing he would understand her meaning, "and, I *want* you to be. You must be under pressure with what you're here to do—we're all anxious to get on with it—get Georgianna back. It's very stressful as you can imagine."

"I *do* understand, I really do," he said most seriously putting his hand on Ombline's shoulder. "Since my part is done at night until late day I'm of no use to them. Is there a local eatery where we might have lunch? My treat!" He offered.

"Yes there is—I was just on my way to Smugglers Cove to Contraband on an errand, but first I have to stop at Serpentine's. Contraband is the best place to eat in town—or so I'm told," She laughed at herself, "and since I haven't eaten anywhere else yet I guess I'm prejudiced—but yes, it is good." She took Ledger's hand pulling him toward her rental. "I'll be our chauffeur for now so you can absorb the local beauty." She said this, hopping back into the driver's seat and Ledger into the passenger side. She drove slowly down the country road barraged with the grandeur of autumn toward Smugglers Cove.

Ombline and Ledger found themselves severely drawn to one another—each knowing that under different circumstances their meeting would be a life altering event—but then why *not* now—life never holds back in the unveiling of its own agendas, and fate, always decides its own schedule.

They made a quick trip to Serpentines for the fruit and then back to town.

Ombline ran in ahead and delivered the fruit to Thad in a simple cold pack container with his promise to get right on an investigation into the fruit's possibilities. She and Ledger then had a late lunch in one of Contraband's alcoves, afterward, taking an afternoon drive up the Old Coast Road stopping twice to admire the ocean view below the cliff side.

At the last stop they stood quietly shoulder to shoulder looking out over the crashing waves on the rocks below. Ledger turned, drawing Ombline to him, kissing her forehead.

"Well!" Ombline hissed in jest. "If that's all I get, a peck on the forehead, I'll just remedy that right now!" She caught him by his shirt collar pulling him down roughly to her and kissed him hard on the mouth.

He grabbed her to him, a kiss lasting so long she thought they might be permanently melded together and she liked it—a lot! This was the last thing she would have expected to have happened in her life just now, but here it was! They were quiet in each other's arms for some time before they noticed the sun advancing to late afternoon.

"We need to get back. When darkness falls," Ledger said, in a mock Count Dracula voice, "I vrill be *needed*."

"Okay Count Ledger, let us be on our *vraay*," she laughed, reciprocating his Dracula-speak.

They drove slowly down the winding coastal road not wanting the day to end so soon, but unexpectedly, Ombline's keen eye picked up on an isolated and out of the way, but, fortuitous occurrence.

She grabbed Ledger's arm. "Pullover to the side of the road! No, not the cliff side—our side!" She directed. As soon as they stopped she jumped out of the car running across the road to the ocean side of the highway with Ledger on her heels.

"What's wrong—what is it?" He looked down over the cliff where Ombline peered. Two vehicles had turned off the highway and were driving down a narrow dirt road that ran precariously close to the outside of the cliff wall.

Ledger watched, saying under his breath. "How very strange, two most unlikely vehicles on such a road, and together, a Bentley and a black delivery truck—and to where are they going taking such a chance?"

They looked questioningly at one another. "Ledger, I believe that's the Bentley we saw Madame Seurat being chauffeured in—did they tell you about that? You don't see many Bentleys around Smugglers Cove—if any."

"Yes," he said, still captivated by the absurdity of the dangerous stunt of the drivers below. "That vehicle following the Bentley looks like a souped-up delivery van, high, square-topped, a very heavy set of racks on top—almost looks like it would be top-heavy, maybe outfitted to carry some sort of satellite equipment—at least that's what comes to mind." He looked to Ombline.

"I agree, this is very strange."

Ombline recounted all that she and Georgianna had witnessed *before* her sister's dispatch. "It has to be Seurat. I think there's some sort of hideout or lab or something like that down there. What better place to continue what they've been up to than a cliff-side cave, almost undetectable. I wonder how they found such a place? And another thing—why did she need to use abandoned technology at Dragons Roost? How did she even know of it?" Ombline looked to Ledger as if *he* would have an answer. "Seurat seems to know an awful lot."

"Come on Ombline." Ledger said, steering her away from their observation spot while the two vehicles still meandered on down the road below. "We need to let the guys know about this right away; it could be important." They ran back across the highway to the car and drove down the coast road to town. On the Way, Ledger called Peter to let him know what they had seen.

Strangely, he did not seem surprised but said they would discuss it further at dinner. Ombline thought he seemed awfully calm and accepting of this news.

They stopped at Grey Hall to shower and change after the day's outing before returning to Dragons Roost for dinner. The sun had set dropping the temperature of the autumn evening considerably. Ledger had put on a black wool bomber jacket while Ombline wore a wrap jacket of indigo cashmere accentuating her shoulder length pale blond hair and lavender-blue eyes. Her Nordic beauty was inherited from that of her and Georgianna's maternal Swedish grandmother, a woman whose heart had been in that of the theatre like her granddaughter Georgianna, even though the two looked nothing alike.

The family had all agreed that Ombline had inherited their grandmother's ice queen beauty while Georgianna, a beauty in her own right, had inherited their grandmother's love of the theatre; each sister seeming to know from birth what they were to be about in the world.

Marc wasn't at Grey Hall when they arrived back. Ombline brought two glasses of champagne into the common room before they left for Dragons Roost. Both she and Ledger sat quietly before the unlit fireplace. "What will your work be like tonight Ledger?"

"I set everything up last night for tonight's preliminaries," he said, seemingly in his own thoughts. "We'll see how it goes."

"Why does this have to be done at night?" She asked, wondering about the timing of his work.

"It's necessary for the greatest potential benefit when the earth is turned away from the sun—less interference from solar flares." He explained.

"I see," Ombline said, not really understanding the why of it but was curious for she was not all that familiar with the intricacies of Astro-Biology or how Ledger's expertise would pertain to Peter and Zorloff's work. She had always enjoyed her science courses enough to pass with good grades but had never delved into those particular subjects more deeply.

The autumn night now ruled with a zenith of stars overhead in contrast with the barely perceptible silhouette of mountains on the far distant Western horizon. The Milky Way Galaxy, our own solar system flung far out on the outer rim of said galaxy, was not yet evident, needing complete darkness to be viewed in all its splendour.

The night air was chilly as Ombline backed the rental car out of the garage. They buckled up in silence and set out for Dragons Roost. No sooner had they left Grey Hall's drive than Ombline slammed on the brakes and pulled off to the side of the road cutting the engine. They had not even been on the road long enough to turn on the car lights. "It's them!" She exclaimed. "That black van parked off the road up there Ledger—it's that Seurat bunch at it again! What are they up to now?"

Ledger stared out into the dark at the vehicle. "It does look like the delivery van we saw this afternoon, although, I can't imagine why they would be here now. It doesn't look like anyone is around does it?" He looked to Ombline.

"It doesn't—they must've parked a ways away and then walked on down the road and climbed up the ridge."

Ledger tried calling Peter on his cell. "No one's answering," he said after trying both Peter and Zorloff's numbers.

"Okay." Ombline said. "Let's leave the car here and get up there." This time as they started out on foot she remembered her mistake with her phone before and put it on vibrate urging Ledger to do the same.

No sooner had they started down the dark road than Ombline felt the phone in her jacket pocket. It was Peter.

"No," he said when she quickly related the details of their discovery. "No one's around, we have an assortment of alarms— outside and up the drive too—be very careful—get back in the car and get up here! I'll open the gate for you from here, don't waste time!"

Peter disconnected abruptly. Should they wait to see who came back to the parked vehicle or do as Peter said. The question was settled for them. Sounds of movement in the brush coming down the hillside decided what their position would be. Garbled voices could be heard in the darkness up above as two figures stumbled their way down from the top of the ridge through the brush.

"Come on!" Ledger commanded. "Now Ombline! Back to the car!"

She didn't seem to be listening. "We need to see who these people are, where they're going." She said under her breath.

Ledger grabbed her arm pulling her toward the car.

Just before they reached the rental Ombline pulled away from his grip, turned and streaked back up ahead to the van climbing up the back of its ladder in a flash to the top and lying down perfectly flat between two of its bulky racks.

Ledger was stunned. He felt he had been thwarted by the stealth of a human badger in the blink of an eye. *What the hell is she trying to do by climbing up there?—It makes no sense.* He felt like a complete ineffectual boob to have been so taken in by her reckless and dangerous actions—and now it was too late, he crouched beside the car fearful of Ombline's discovery, for there was nothing he could do about it but watch while the two figures emerged from the brush and entered the vehicle not realizing they had an extra passenger on top. In a burst of gravel they pulled onto the black topped road towards Smugglers Cove. *She hasn't flown off—yet. Hold tight Ombline—hold tight!* Ledger silently pleaded as he hung behind pursuing the vehicle down the dark road, not knowing what else he could do to protect her.

Chapter   Twenty   Two

Ledger had jumped into Ombline's rental car giving chase as best he could. He was furious at what she had done but relieved to have found she had left the keys in the ignition. He dared not turn on the lights for fear those in the van would know they were being followed. They had a good head start and he hoped their destination would be down the cliff side road where they had seen the two odd vehicles earlier in the afternoon for at least that wasn't so far away.

He hadn't seen another car on the road yet. It had always seemed deserted out here in the short time he had been here; he hated driving in the dark like this with no lights knowing it was dangerous, but he had no choice. He called Peter dreading to tell him what Ombline had done and that he was following as best he could at a distance to where he believed the vehicle was headed. He followed the car lights on the road up ahead hoping to see Ombline on top, still, hopefully, unbeknownst to its inner occupants. At least she had the racks to hold onto, but what about when they stopped. He'd think about that when it happened. *Just hang on Ombline, please, just hang on.* He pleaded silently once more, as if this would make it so.

He knew now why she had done what she did. She had, in the moment thought they couldn't follow in her car right behind the van without being discovered. If she had taken the time to think it through, together they could have done what he was doing now without endangering herself.

He pulled closer. He could just barely see Ombline's silver hair blowing in the wind revealing her position between the racks. He dropped back satisfied she was still on top. Just before they reached Smugglers Cove he dropped back even further just long enough to turn on the headlights but not lose sight of their direction. Once in town he pulled to the side of the street and parked turning off the headlights as if that had been his intention and waited as long as he felt it was prudent.

He stalled two long minutes while the van wound its way up the street out of town and into the dark of Old Coast Road hoping its occupants would believe him to be just another motorist stopping in town; then, when he could wait no longer resumed pursuit. Not long after both vehicles were out of town and travelling up the coast road, Ledger saw the lights in the distance turn off the highway and down onto the cliff side. He was relieved that was their destination. What to do now, he didn't have a clue, he could only follow the truck down below the cliffs on foot and respond as events played out hoping for a safe escape for Ombline.

He felt she would still be able to hang on going down the cliff road, but was direly afraid of her being discovered when they stopped. He had to be there when that happened. He felt sure once the van was below the highway his vehicle would no longer be visible above them. He stopped, pulling well off onto the other side of the road and extinguished the car's lights. He had no flashlight and wouldn't risk using one if he had. There was enough of the waning moon to illuminate his way down the cliff. He followed as stealthily as he could under the circumstances, sliding on gravel.

Far below and just above the water line a small cove was channeled in by treacherous rocks pounded by insurgent ocean currents. Wan moonlight glistened off the Atlantic farther out where the current had not yet encountered the rocks. The car's headlights revealed the vehicle pausing and then turning left into the dark of the rock wall down below. Ledger moved as fast as he could slinking against the cliff wall along the rough roadbed, halting just before the cavernous opening of a large cave. There was no light to indicate where they had gone, only darkness into the cliff opening.

He moved further back from the cave opening and crouched just outside listening for any sort of sound. Voices inside were barely audible as a flash of light far back inside the space came on dispelling complete darkness inside. He jumped back and moved farther still away from the mouth of the cave wall outside hoping he hadn't been seen. He could tell in the very brief time that the lights had come on that the interior was camouflaged by a sharp turn to the right after entering.

Ledger straightened, intending to risk creeping closer again, fearing Ombline had been detected, yet wondering what he would be able to do against several who most likely had guns. He stuck his hands into his jacket pockets in fearful frustration trying to decide the best course of action on Ombline's behalf when a soft warm hand reached from behind him covering his mouth. Shock coursed through his body until a familiar pair of lavender blue eyes framed by wisps of flaxen hair peeked around from behind him. Full rose lips brushed his cheek. Ombline grabbed his arm shushing him with her finger across her lips pulling him backward with her up the road. They silently broke into a run up the dirt road to the highway, jumped in the car, locked the doors and headed back to town.

"How did you get off the roof without detection?" Ledger asked in awe of Ombline's escape.

"As you drive down the cliff road, a high dirt bank closely parallels the road bed, I noticed that earlier when we first saw them driving down there, so I just rolled off onto the soft earth as we passed by. I was still close enough to see where they entered the cave in the cliffs. That was all we needed to know for now—their entry, as I don't think anyone is around there in the daytime if, as you say some of the best work of this nature is done at night. I didn't mean to frighten you back there when I jumped on top of the van, but I knew I had to do it then or we wouldn't know their exact destination, if this is truly Seurat's hidey-hole! I was pretty sure I could do it and not be found out."

Ombline looked at Ledger sheepishly. "I do apologize, I'm not normally this irrational, acting in such haste—frightening the people I'm with. I just knew I had to do it and didn't have time to sort it out with you. And—thanks for being my wing man." She smiled, reaching over squeezing his hand.

"Ombline, you took an awfully dangerous chance, why didn't you stop me before I got to the cave?"

"I tried to, but you flew by so fast I couldn't grab you *speed racer,* so I had no choice but to catch up to you at the entrance."

Ombline was quiet for a moment. "There's an aspect of this that puzzles me. Serpentine introduced Dr. Frank, Seurat's sidekick, associate or whatever, to Georgianna and I at the ball saying that Seurat was going to be a new resident of the community—real estate needed or already has?" Ombline raised her brows in question to Ledger. "Serpentine must know Seurat, being at the ball and all—in business maybe? She must know where she's staying—how to get in touch with her. I know she doesn't live in that damp cave—that's only her place of business so to speak, Dragons Roost didn't work out so how *did* this cave thing come about? It makes no sense! Even in those campy old 1930 movie serials the bad guys had a more comfortable hide-out, not a toad hole! She doesn't impress me as one who would willingly give up the comforts of the sophisticate she appears to be. There has to be a scientific reason they're in such a place. Everything has happened so fantastically, I forgot to ask Serpentine how she knew Seurat and Frank to even invite them to the ball."

Ombline continued just letting her thoughts unravel on to Ledger. "If you haven't noticed, those three main pieces at Dragons Roost are surely immersed in a web of esoteric secrecy so deep I can't imagine why they're even allowing us to participate except for the fact that they need us—especially you, and have no others they can trust to turn to. There's a little obvious touchy-feely going on with Serpentine and Zorloff that's kind of hard to ignore if you haven't noticed. I'm sure they've *more than known each other* before this. Peter and the two of them, even my father, are keeping to themselves something a lot more sinister than they are willing to reveal and for all I know maybe they are right to do so—secrets, secrets and secrets."

"What makes you think that?" Ledger asked keeping to himself the secret of the letter he had passed on to Peter from so long ago, glad now, knowing what he did, that he had been able to do so—also glad he had tested the authenticity of the document himself, not allowing it into the hands of others. He also knew as Ombline did, there were so many missing puzzle pieces here—some of which, as Ombline had said, just didn't make sense—and that they were being purposefully kept in the dark as to the whole story. *Was it for their own good—their safety as Ombline suspected?* He had always felt Zorloff an honourable person, so did the others seem to be.

"I'm not completely sure," Ombline replied, "I suppose the zealous overnight arrival of Peter with such an extensive complement of equipment as I never dreamed existed, a—a—sort of crystal technology which you obviously are privy to in your work with them. I was surprised when he brought Zorloff in tow, it makes one think he's out to not only recover Georgianna but save the planet—change the world, it appears to me his and Zorloff's science has very little to do with this worlds!"

"It does make one wonder—that, it does."

Ombline's instincts told her Ledger too, was included as part of an inner circle that she was not. Maybe then she shouldn't have said as much as she did, but she didn't believe she had said any more than Ledger already knew. He seemed to add little to her observations—only a sort of quiet agreement adding nothing new.

Back at Dragons Roost they were greeted with relief *and* reprimand for Ombline taking such a chance—endangering herself and Ledger. She explained her actions, reiterating what they had gained from what she had done.

Peter reluctantly intervened on her behalf. "It's behind us and you're safe Ombline, that's what matters, at least we know of a new tangent concerning this Madame Seurat—an unexpected discovery, a point for our side, but tonight we have more urgent concerns, a bunch of people in a cave cannot presently do us harm. Now let's have dinner."

Ombline was no longer surprised at Peter's nonchalant attitude seemingly so unconcerned with danger they all could be in. How could he be so—oh well—la-de-da? It was just, well let's have dinner now. Serpentine had held dinner for some time. Even so, they wanted to hear the details of Ombline and Ledger's short-lived adventure.

Ombline was perplexed that her father didn't question how this new bit of information might affect their attempt to recover Georgianna, he seemed almost tranquil in his relief that nothing had happened to her and kept hugging her all evening even though he did voice strong recriminations for such a dangerous stunt; he didn't mention the part about *stupidity* that she had expected. She did appreciate that. At least for now they knew where Seurat was carrying out her attempts at inter-dimensional travel *in the neighborhood,* but not the purpose, for none of the older generation offered any more enlightenment to those outside their small circle contained by controlled calm.

There was an unspoken understanding amongst the older generation that the climax they had long awaited and secretly prepared for was now to be fully engaged. They would face off with mankind's enslavers whatever the outcome for there was no turning back.

Chapter Twenty Three

Jack Stewart, his brother Ean and his wife Storm sat around a clay fire pit on the back surround of a mountain lodge with Georgianna, who was fast giving into a great need to sleep despite all she had learned during dinner. They were alerted, she was told, as soon as she had come through the portal and was allowed to continue on until they had been sure of her intentions, that she was an innocent not involved with this Dr. Frank.

She related the events leading to her present predicament, starting with all she and Ombline had witnessed starting with day one at Dragons Roost up to her unexpected transit through the portal activated by Madame Seurat—the terrifying Benoit's attempt to murder her under the direct orders of Dr. Frank, and Benoit's accidental death by his own hand resulting from her attempt to save her life. Fighting her compulsion to sleep, she listened to *their* tale as best she could.

Storm cautiously related that *certain things* were at a critical point—just what that meant Georgianna certainly didn't know and Storm didn't offer to elaborate. Jack further explained that their world was defended by a grid technology, each location independent of the others; any singular station could be incorporated into the grid pattern as a whole if need be or respond individually using the planet as the source of its power. If for some unforeseen reason one station was lost it would not affect the rest which would together take up the slack of lost stations. This prevented inter-dimensional or other incursions. This system warned the Guardians of any such attempt to enter their world from other existences. This arrangement could only be interrupted if the Guardians so chose. This protection was of general knowledge and approved by Irrieth's citizens. (Irrieth being the name of this parallel world—similar to her Earth but not a copy).

Georgianna was sure the squat building with the metallic globe inside was one of those grid stations, thus Jack's suspicion of her having been in it. *Well, why had he left it unlocked—to entrap me?*

The system had been developed and put in place seventy-five years earlier when a need for such existed to once and for all protect their world from a species of human who called themselves the Vraang—they had always existed on the planet secretly as far back in history as could be later discerned after *The Great Cleansing*, as the liberating of their world had become referred to. The accidental discovery by two scientists of cloaked collectors in high orbit around Irrieth was the initial catalyst for the discoveries to follow.

The purpose of the collectors was for the harvesting of an incidental component of human adrenaline more precious than any riches known to the Vraang, it promoted extremely long life spans with almost perfect health; only the physiology of the Vraang benefitted from the substance—no other branch of human. All through history they had kept this world and others in constant turmoil, its populations in war or on the verge of war and destruction, political upheaval—a planetary garden if you will, producing an atmosphere satiated with fertile adrenaline for the cloaked collectors above.

Georgianna's dinner companions continued with details of Irrieth's final break for freedom from the Vraang.

Secrets were easily kept with all the Vraang's wealth. Ancient puppet masters they had been—some believed the Vraang had even seeded this world with humankind just for the harvesting of the treasured component of adrenalin, that, they hadn't just come upon this planet in this dimension by accident.

Eventually it had been learned that behind the scenes the Vraang incessantly created chaos never moving aside for mankind to evolve to its better heights—it's golden possibilities. The Vraang's snares and plots were behind every human failure to finally *get it right*—they would not allow it. Their need controlled their souls irrevocably—it was now part of their DNA—mutated to be the species of human they had become. There would be no going back. They had become forever the monsters they had willingly allowed themselves to genetically evolve into—a scourge to life.

They lusted after Sesca as they called this component of human adrenalin—the ultimate Vraang elixir, culled from human sorrow and the coerced failures of mankind. There had been no boundaries for their immorality in attaining it. After the great cleansing it had been discovered in vast stores at certain points around the globe, most of which after collection would have went to the Vraang home world. It had all been destroyed except for a small amount so as to scientifically study it. *The tears of man*, Sesca had been called, because that had been its origin—mankind's great sorrows and disappointments.

At first the presence of the collectors had been kept secret from the publics of the world until a solution could be found for humanity to liberate itself from such beings, ones that had forever owned them. At the time there had been no way to differentiate just who was Vraang and who was not. With the discovery of the enslavement of humanity by the Vraang, a secret war between a small select group of humans desperate to free their kind from this evil species of human was clandestinely carried on behind the scenes to no avail, for, at that time, the Vraang technology was far ahead of Irrieth's—there was no solution. Fate stepped in. Almost at the same time that this was all taking place, another serendipitous happenstance took place. A little-known scientist secretly working out of the way on his own made a fortuitous discovery—the ability to travel between parallel worlds. He told no one—kept his *travels* to himself, bringing back to Irrieth a blue fruit he had found so enticing on another parallel world—so invigourating, that he planted the seeds of the fruit in his garden and gardens of friends around the world. The fruit restored health and vigour to all who consumed it. The trees propagation was uncontainable—unstoppable once they had gained even a small foothold and spread like wildfire around the planet as these fast-growing seeds grew into mammoth-sized trees in short weeks feeding the world's hungry populations, solving world hunger almost overnight. The fruit served all health and nutritional needs, but of course the human palate does require variety even though one could live on *the fruit* (as it became called) indefinitely in perfect health.

A defining event followed as dependence and enjoyment of the fruit progressed, certain groups and individuals dissolved into a gaseous vapour dispersing into thin air when within close proximity to the blue fruit, completely evaporating into nothingness; not that many actually, only an incidental percentage of Irrieth's population. It was as if they had never existed, their molecular structure disengaging. The miraculous fruit destroyed Vraang it was discovered, only Vraang—Irrieth was free at last—saved by nature!

So—what Sesca had done for the Vraang and all its unconscionable cruelty, the fruit did for humanity in bounty and goodness.

With these strange deaths the truth could finally be told. Sadly though, a final great revenge by the last few surviving holdouts of the insidious Vraang sequestering themselves away from civilization in a mountain laboratory unleashed upon the people of Irrieth, a virus so deadly, that the survivors believed it was the end of everything they had hoped their world could have become without the Vraang. In the aftermath of the Vraang's assault, many of those who had survived had done so, thanks in part, to the miraculous fruit. The last vestige of Vraang had been discovered ensconced in their secret mountain bastion in the Alps. They were bombarded with the fruit's juice as simple as that would seem to those not familiar with the circumstances. The Vraang were not found when finally their last refuge was stormed and overrun by humanity's victors. It was assumed it was the fruit that had done its job but others were not so sure, for considering a technology left behind in their mountain citadel some of Irrieth's scientific minds believed the evil Vraang had been able through their unknown technology to escape to another parallel world. No one knew for sure, but Irrieth's people knew they were on a new bright path and didn't ponder this dilemma for long. They knew whatever the truth they were finally free! Only now, after so long ago, had Irrieth's population begun to recover from its loss in numbers.

Finally, decade by decade, a golden age of enlightenment had come upon the citizens of Irrieth free at last of the Vraang, life on it's own terms, that which it had always starved for, and knew within its collective heart was supposed to be. Without the undermining cruelty of the Vraang, the world's people were to reclaim their rightful place in existence and live in a world unhindered by subversive cruelty serving no master at last, but the best of their own devising to live in harmony.

Science of every discipline had made monumental strides turning the planet back to the verdant garden for which it had been originally intended. The inter-dimensional defense system had been put in place to guard Irrieth from invasions from interlopers from other existences, even, the occasional poking and prodding of the Vraang to once more enslave their population knowing as they did so that their attempts were futile. Never again would Irreith's people submit to being cabbages in someone's Cabbage Patch as they had been, for now, they knew what life could be—what it had originally been designed to be for all.

The collectors in orbit were finally destroyed after scientists from several disciplines learned all they could from them.

Jack, Ean and Storm were part of generational scientific teams of Guardians that constantly monitored the safety of Irrieth—thus their knowledge of Georgianna's arrival and just before her that of Dr. Frank. Unknown to him, he and those he partnered with were under surveillance. His intentions *would* be known. They were aware at this very moment of Dr. Frank's whereabouts along with his two companions. They were giving him and those connected with him uninterrupted ease of movement—waiting to see what revealed itself.

The evening had produced answers to their questions—what had led to Georgianna being here. Puzzle pieces had been found; now it was the responsibility of the Guardians to assemble such to ensure Irrieth's safety. The Vraang were not the only subject of suspicious activity needing investigation and protection from those hoping to profit from such a progressive civilization.

Georgianna startled herself awake not realizing she had fallen asleep. She could no longer contain her exhaustion even if the world exploded. Again her head fell forward to her chest without rousing this time as she gave in.

Storm's sympathy intervened. "Jack! She has to have sleep! Can't you see she's practically unconscious?"

He relented and stood, picking Georgianna up in his arms as she tried to open her heavy lids, no longer able to do so. Sleep was so necessary, it was her drug. She was out!

Jack carried her up the spiral stairs to the guest bedroom laying her on the bed and covering her with a blanket of white softness. He shut the door and went down stairs to Ean and Storm.

"I believe her," Storm said. "Remember how we got here—certainly none of our doing—not in our plans. Twenty years ago we were on a boat crossing the Channel in a fantastic thunderstorm on our way back to our respective schools, the two of you to Scotland and myself to school in London as my grandfather had provided for me when an extraordinary event occurred. A portal opened engulfing our boat in the magnificence of the storm, depositing us in the channel of this parallel world." She added. "Georgianna and the details of her story are as innocent as ours. We must help her home Jack."

He said nothing as he stood staring off into the night.

Chapter Twenty Four

Georgianna awoke from a very deep dreamless sleep slowly realizing where she was. Sunlight streamed in at an angle through an eastern window indicating she had slept very late. The forest house was quiet. She needed coffee—did they have such here? But first she would shower and see if there was a change of fresh clothes, something *not* like pajamas.

The shower restored much of her vitality. There was even a sort of hairdryer. She finally felt renewed. *Amazing*, she thought how just brushing your teeth changes your viewpoint. She went through the drawers of clothing and found something similar to jeans that fit. In the closet there were clothes belonging to a woman, one of very elegant and expensive taste. She chose a beige plaid silk blouse and dusty lavender jacket not knowing what the day would bring. Dark grey short heeled ankle boots gave her back her self confidence—she had always loved a bit of heel—it just felt right to her dancer's sensibility.

There were a few cosmetics in a separate medicine cabinet. A compact of rouge served as a colouring agent. Georgianna had always had long thick dark lashes so she didn't always apply mascara, but she did use the rouge for lips and cheeks.

She went downstairs to the quiet kitchen intending to find something to drink. One of the cabinets had a note attached where anyone would see it. It was from Jack saying much to her delight they did have coffee on this world. There was no cord to what she discerned was the coffeemaker. Jack's only instructions said to just tap the top it was ready to go. She did so once and immediately a brew began.

In the meantime she found a yellow pungent bread that smelled of cheese. She broke off a chunk finding it at once delicious and satisfying. A pitcher of deep orange coloured juice she now recognized as having come from the fruit sat in the fridge—this she drank first even before coffee. Other foods recognizable lay on its shelves, others, she was unfamiliar with.

She took her tray outside to the back surround where they had feasted on the food provided by Ean and Storm last night. It seemed to be close to midday and felt like the unusually warm vibrant autumn she had left at home. Just to think of home started a fear and aloneness building inside her that she knew in her own best interest she would have to suppress to be able to concentrate on how to *get home*. She was sure if she could get here there had to be a way back.

It had sounded last night like the people of Irrieth were so advanced surely they could help her as she believed they understood she was no threat to anyone, just unexpectedly scooped up in strange circumstances she and Ombline had had no understanding of, as she had explained.

Peter, she knew, would find her if anyone could, obviously she couldn't hang around indefinitely where she had been deposited from the portal. She had no way of knowing, but just on a chance, hoped the cell phone she had buried at her spot of entry would help her rescuers.

Briefly she thought of Peter and Zorloff, she knew the word that now struck her describing the two men—why had this only now come to her—they were sentinels! Yes, that was just what they were, sentinels! Last night's conversation, her own adventures here and everything she had unconsciously absorbed concerning Peter Steffington down through the years had verified this. Even as a child she had realized as kindly as Peter was, there was something different and closely guarded about him and his private lab on the Steffington estate. There had always been that little twinge of suspicion that she had never before been able to put word to.

She needed to discuss this with Jack now that she was *back* so to speak. She needed hope, for she could not face never seeing her loved ones again. These people had to help her go home. A shadow interrupted her sunshine—and her thoughts.

"I'm glad you found everything to your liking," Jack said as he sat down on the other side of the table. "Are you feeling more rested today? You were dead out of it last night. I'm sorry we had to keep you up with all the discussion but it had to be. You know," he paused studying her, "you are a uniquely beautiful woman—very unusual colouring—I'm sorry," he apologized embarrassed that he had said such. "I just wanted to say that."

"Don't apologize." Georgianna said. "At least such a compliment helps to make me not feel so—so illegal," she struggled for a word to express her feelings of not belonging—alone with her fear of, or maybe, never seeing her loved ones again, of the need to control such forlorn hopelessness—stranded in a world she had no part of.

Jack laughed. "You're certainly not illegal, just caught up in things you shouldn't have to give thought to. You have my word on it, we will try to help you. Try not to be fearful. Our science, from what I can understand from our talks last night is much more advanced than the world you came from, you see, I believe your world is one that is under control of the Vraang like ours once was."

His statement did not give her comfort, it caused her to shiver knowing what she now knew of the Vraang she could well believe this was most likely the case. A passing cloud cast a shadow over them. She had always suspected as she believed the humanity of her own world had in their deepest being intuitively known that something wasn't right—no one had ever voiced or considered such a thing as the Vraang—how could it be? If true—what could be done?

Jack could see she was fragile under a brave exterior, this he could understand, for he himself had felt the same hopeless fear when he and his twin brother Ean had been deposited in this world as adolescents—at least they had each other, and Storm; Georgianna was all alone, but with the new science that also protected their world they would return her to hers. This they could do with a certain amount of cooperation—for initially those long years ago it had been done by one scientist's secret experiments—he wanted to *wander* as he later put it; his *wandering* had helped lead Irrieth to the dawning of a golden age by bringing the fruit home with him.

Jack put his hand on Georgianna's shoulder. "Don't be afraid, you will go home—and soon; but before you go, you should see what a world can be like without being enslaved by Vraang."

She smiled at him trying to hold back tears that would no longer stay in her eyes, but spilled down her cheeks.

Jack took her napkin and gently blotted them away. He stood, pulling her to her feet. "Come on," he said, "let's go for a ride. I want to show you a beautiful world of great possibilities. I hope you'll always keep it in your heart when you return home." His confident attitude helped stop the silent tears running down her face.

As they left the mountain lodge he said. *"Secure house."* A chime tinkled as he shut the door after them.

Once again they entered the silver and yellow air car and lifted to become part of the sky, this time in a westerly direction.

Chapter   Twenty   Five

"Where are we going?" Georgianna asked once they were aloft. Few clouds were visible as far west as she could see, the air was clear and pure without any trace of air pollution. The land below appeared a healthy verdant landscape. They did not pass over the blue fruit forest they had flown over yesterday.

"To Paris." Jack smiled. "And yes, there is a Paris here too. Preserved of its history and glorified also in its newness."

So different he seemed today. "How is that—glorified in its newness?" She asked. "What does that mean?"

"It means, we treasure and protect all that is and has always been good about us, the arts, beauty, the finest of creativity, but also embrace the new of those fields—enlightenment—if you will. You, Georgianna, being a successful actress in the theater of your own world (she had explained her profession at dinner the night before saying how all her life she had so loved the theatre and all it's tangent arts) will feel at home in the Paris of this one. The city is respected and loved as our world center for all that is creative. Before the great cleansing there was little room for distinction of diversity—a narrow view of what was artistically acceptable, a few great masters at the top excluded all others not approved. That is no longer the way of it. If you feel it is art and brings joy without harm—then, it is art!"

"There's so much I would like to know of Irrieth." Georgianna said. "It sounds inconceivable—progressive in all the right directions. I'm sorry about the tears earlier. I just felt so alone and I had such fear of never seeing my family again—I didn't know what to expect. At first I wasn't even sure this place was populated by people. I tried to keep my cool and survive, especially after that Benoit tried to kill me. As I ran out of the ruins and back down the pumpkin patch I was shaking so uncontrollably I became freezing cold. I thought I was having a seizure, the walking helped; yet, I saw no evidence of civilization and feared I was going in the wrong direction of maybe a dead world even though the forest and its animals looked so vibrant.

I understand your feelings—anyone would feel as you did, you see, Ean, Storm and I are not natives of this world either. We've been here since we were twelve and Storm, ten." He continued. "The three of us were on a boat just leaving the French coast to cross the English Channel at the end of the summer of 1920 when somehow a freakish thunderstorm transferred our boat through a portal to this world and this time. We were cared for and brought up with great kindness and well educated by the now elderly Duchess of Granby and her son Leopold in the English countryside. We were never close to our own father, our only other relative was our cousin David Stewart. The three of us were like brothers and spent summers together on his mother's estate in France. We have always missed him. I'll just bet though he turned out to be a great scientist, it was always his bent. I've often wondered what his life would have become—maybe someday…" Jack didn't finish.

Georgianna didn't pursue this not wanting to intrude on something she knew nothing about.

Jack seemed at ease relating how his life came to be in this world as he continued with the story of Storm. "Storm's grandfather had been brutally bludgeoned to death in the Paris of the previous spring to the channel crossing. The nuns her grandfather had entrusted her care and education to were sending her on to a private school in London when we three being on the same boat found ourselves in such altered circumstances as you find yourself. When we arrived here there was no hope of going back—at least that we were privy to at the time—but for you it is possible. A friend of ours has been doing just such work in a field of science as brought you here—he's—(Jack smiled mischievously at Georgianna) he's very proficient at such work—you see—he's the great grandson of the original discoverer of the fruit—the renowned self-described scientist, *The Wanderer*, but in his own right—Benjamin Fouchard, too, is a *Wanderer*."

"If you're up to it I'd like you to meet him tonight at a fancy dress ball at the new Paris Opera House—Musée du Printemps—a magnificent architectural work of art, hailed as one of the great structures of the new age after the cleansing. You will hear that term—*After The Cleansing* as a reference point in our society, so much is measured by it. And, if you haven't noticed by now, the term *the fruit,* is understood by everyone."

"I can see why, its life altering." More relaxed now, especially since Jack had brought up her way home—that it could surely be a reality—that she could really *go home*! Georgianna tried to control her elation at what Jack had just said and concentrate on enjoying the travel through the clear sky. She knew full well there were those who would envy the position she was in, to experience a parallel world; she tried to concentrate on her circumstances objectively. They had not flown over many towns. The populated areas seemed sparse as compared to her world. She understood that the release of the deadly plague by the Vraang had killed off a large part of the population but had understood that humanity had at least partially replenished itself through the years, still, the landscape appeared not as populated as her Earth. This she voiced to Jack.

"I'm sorry to say this is true." Jack's face became somber. "I've only briefly mentioned this, it was the revenge by the Vraang. It happened long ago before our arrival, right after the fruit gained an irreversible foothold on Irrieth. The Vraang tried to force the destruction of the trees of the fruit. Humanity refused to destroy them (which it is almost impossible to do anyway as the roots of the trees run so deep into the earth that they almost become part of the planet as a self protection, propagating from roots as well as their seed) and remain slaves of the few remaining Vraang, so, as their final act before escaping Irrieth they tried to destroy humanity. It came about as a last-ditch effort by them using a biological weapon on Irrieth's people murdering three fifths of the world's population. It's been a long slow recovery as many people of that time were so despondent by the loss of their loved ones that they feared this happening again even knowing the evil species had been permanently done away with, they found it too painful a prospect to start new families—there was such deep sorrow—many suicidal. The final physical dissolution of the Vraang and the destruction once and for all of the collectors in orbit helped to dispel humanity's despair and bring people out of their great darkness and start anew."

Jack continued with the story of Irrieth's people. "The destruction of the collectors was done on every side of Irrieth specifically at night to appear as heavenly fireworks of great magnitude representing humanity's final great independence from enslavement. It was inspiring to the populations of the planet. You can still watch the recorded glorious celebrations of that time. Millions of tears, only this time in joy. The celebrations went on for weeks all over the world, mankind, finally masters of their own destiny!"

Georgianna was impressed but thoughtful. "You make it sound like Nirvana, Jack."

"No. It is not that." He said. "I hope I haven't given that impression. But without the constant undermining and encouraging humanity to stray into the wrong direction, steering us into the worst we can be, to use us as we used to use farm animals, everything evolves to the light and eventually will leave the dark by the wayside as it is unprofitable and disillusioning for all in the end."

"As you know Georgianna, we have the Guardian force—not an army—or even military, but a group of scientists who are the protectors of Irrieth from any form of outside disruption detrimental to life here, and yes, we do have local law enforcement as each locale might need. Irrieth's decisions are decided by planet wide referendum, and, if ever necessary, we do have the means to defend ourselves."

Something she had wondered about just came out of her mouth. "Jack, whose clothes am I wearing?"

"A friend of mine who occasionally visits."

Georgianna smiled knowingly. "She has excellent taste, I hope she doesn't mind my choices from her wardrobe."

Jack smiled, realizing this might be awkward. "I doubt it. Her name is Canquetyne, she will be in attendance at the Musée du Printemps. You will meet tonight, she acquires art for the Musée; but more importantly you must meet Benjamin, he will be your avenue home."

She had so many questions, like *when, where and how* would this take place, but felt somehow they should wait for now. It was comforting to be in this lofty blue sanctuary of calm, and now there was hope that yes, she was going home.

Jack took her hand squeezing it softly with that same look of studiousness he had had earlier. "Now, I hope that I've put your mind at ease a bit, we're going to a late lunch in Paris—afterward you need to find something to wear tonight, and, something for while you're here."

They flew on in silence for now nothing more need be said. Georgianna had much to think on.

Chapter Twenty Six

On the outskirts of Paris automated control of the air car took over. Jack stated their destination and relaxed as the car was guided to the nearest parking within walking distance of the heart of the city. Georgianna and Jack lingered over lunch at a small café.

Jack said. "Ean and I have apartments here in the city. You can shower and dress at mine tonight. For now it is up to you to find something suitable for a formal evening. Being a stranger here I suggest you use this to make your purchases."

He extended to her a small black disk that would fit snugly in the palm of the hand. She believed it was similar to a credit card. "Jack, I'm at your mercy here, I'm not familiar with your ways." Making her point she held up the black disk. "In my world we use little rectangular pieces of plastic called credit cards. How do I use this—give it to the salesperson?"

"Yes." He said. "You will not be questioned, I've already taken care of that." He gave her the address to the apartment with instructions to enter also using the disk. He would pick her up at nine o'clock so she had the afternoon at her disposal.

Georgianna spent only two hours shopping for what she needed. It was a wonderful experience, the citizens of this Paris did not believe in wearing anything that was not a work of art. The fashion of her own world seemed a little drab compared to here, everything from the abstract to artful elegance could be seen on the street. She purchased the casual clothing she would need for what she hoped to be a short stay leaving the best for last—something smashing for tonight. She pulled herself up for thinking this—why would she even care so much how she looked for this event, she just wanted to go home! And—why had she asked Jack about the woman whose clothes she wore?

Jack, Ean and Storm, all three, appeared to be successful and self assured in their positions, they had treated her well and believed her, but she knew they had the technology to verify all she had said. What would've happened to her if they had not? These things she had no answer for so concentrated on finding what she hoped would make the evening a distraction from her concerns.

A small shop of nouveau couture fulfilled the artistic expression of Georgianna's sense of fashion in a fitted simple design of dusty rose silk woven sparsely with metallic threads and scant petite crystal beads. The fabric of the gown flowed to shoe top level following the lines of her lithe body taunt from years of dance. A narrow strap of the fabric flowed over each shoulder crisscrossing the low back. A short matching evening capelet longer to a point in back than front completed the design. It was an haute find. Metallic pewter fabric evening sandals completed her outfit. It needed no jewelry other than the simple silver locket her aunt Lily had given her that she always wore. She purchased a crystal encrusted evening bag along with cosmetic colours she felt were her most becoming, deep lavender eye shadow, rose lip and cheek colour, then of course intense black mascara to accentuate the feline element of her eyes!

Georgianna had always loved fashion, it was one of her personal joys of expression. This was a world where one could easily become indulgent in such. She had shopped the fashion capitals of her world, but now she shopped a parallel world's Paris! She chided herself for not being more appreciative of such an experience, after all she *was* going home!

She easily found her way to the apartment. It was spacious, bound by two-bedroom suites, a kitchen, library and a tastefully decorated lounge containing high ceilings and walls hung with art—some she was familiar with and some unknown to her. The decor was sophisticated yet inviting, eclectic.

She drew a bath luxuriating in its relaxing warmth and dressed in her purchases. She was studying one particular painting in the lounge when Jack walked through the door.

He smiled in admiration. "You did well." He had apparently dressed elsewhere for he wore a traditional black tux and was ready for the evening. "We need to go now." He said taking her arm.

She gathered the gown's matching capelet around her shoulders and carried the crystal bag. They left the apartment and out into the Paris night filled with partygoers pursuing their own entertainments.

Again the air car took them on their way when called. They rose above the city heading to the southeast, shortly settling in line with other vehicles whose passengers disembarked from them in order of arrival. There were no parking valets as in Georgianna's world. A voice command sent the empty conveyances to a place of storage until they were instructed to return for their passengers.

She had begun to think more positively of her predicament and to find some joy in the uniqueness of her situation. An atmosphere of Carnival lit the grounds surrounding the Musée du Printemps. The grounds were magnificent adding to the beauty of the night. The structure was aglow from within created from large plates of softly coloured swirls of glass sustained by massive sandstone columns of thread-screw design.

A gently graded ramp infused with pastel swirls of colour as in the glass instead of stairs lead up to the entrance which contained no obvious doors—it was simply framed by the twisted columns. Georgianna knew this was an evening she would never forget. If only there was some way to let her family know that she was safe; she hoped her father had not told her mother Octavia back in London what had happened to her until there was a resolution to her circumstances.

Her parents had divorced when the twins were small and had led very different lives through the years. Even so, their daughters were the light in each of their parent's lives. Georgianna and Ombline had grown up living for the most part with their mother Octavia and her husband Sir Gregory Pritchard in Octavia's London town home and Sir Gregory's country estate. Several summers and holidays had been spent with their father on the Steffington estate in Michigan.

So now, no matter what reassurances Jack gave, if necessary, she *would* find her way home with or without his help. And for Georgianna Patrone, that, was just how it was! To comprehend such a thing as parallel worlds existed was one thing, but to be able to safely traverse them back to your own original home world was another she felt, wondering how it would be possible to discern the right one. She hoped this "Wanderer" person knew what he was doing.

She smiled in remembrance of something Peter had said to her in his lab as a child, comically explaining a scientific precept. "Always remember Georgianna, if you can *think it*—you can do it. You just have to find out how, that's all!" She laughed to herself at his silly English. Tears could not fill her eyes again for her strength had returned. No giving into hopelessness tonight. She had never forgotten those words, a simple little moment in time that helped her even now.

The magnificence of the architecture was impressive, such an edifice of pastel swirling glass had no equal on her own Earth. They made their way up the ramp to the entrance. On the way, Jack paid respects to the occasional acquaintance. They meandered into the central affair containing new acquisitions of art in many forms that would later be installed for public viewing. Tonight was a private showing for contributors, wealthy supporters of the Musée. An adjoining ballroom offered dance music, cocktails and an epic buffet of many foods Georgianna was unfamiliar with.

The grand edifice also contained a theatre for the opera and other theatrical arts of high acclaim. As an actress Georgianna was in the glory of her profession. Her subtle unease had given way to the experience of the moment, one she knew she most likely would never be part of again.

She and Jack danced to music unknown to her, but being a quick study as a formally trained dancer was soon inventing her own moves to the sounds. She had had two glasses of champagne, her limit, when a slow dance found them still on the dance floor. Jack grabbed her to him, cupping her whole hand in his. She was surprised seeing as how he had seemed to stay purposefully distant since their arrival, at other moments, as in the air car, a warm caring person, see-sawing between that and "let's get this business sorted out and done with—just the particulars ma'am!" She found it hard to determine which he might be or when.

She knew he was purposely keeping his distance as she certainly was and had avoided any opinion of him personally. Until this moment with his arms around her she had avoided wrestling with this dilemma. And yes—she was a big girl—one that certainly understood biology and chemistry and did not appreciate being the victim of either. Resentment at her own turn-coat biology plagued her.

Their cheeks brushed in an electrifying fire that unexpectedly ignited their very beings. Georgianna was both surprised and crestfallen that she should feel this way toward someone she did not feel entirely comfortable with. In a way she hated that this had happened. She had her own life—one that was fulfilling—a life she loved—and all those she loved in it—all she wanted was to go back to it—an encumbrance from this alternate reality was inconceivable and unacceptable. She would not allow it! The music changed to another rhythm. Still they danced as one, afraid to part and lose this moment of existing as one being of fire.

"Biological betrayal of self!" She hissed silently to herself as they moved together in sync across the dance floor.

Circumstances changed abruptly. For one of frost moved in, bringing this paradoxical experience to an end—actually, an escape for Georgianna from a predicament she couldn't seem to extricate herself from on her own.

"Might I have this dance Jack?" An arresting woman, fine of feature sporting short dark hair in a straight, chin length cut, and dressed in elegant simplicity—most recherché, stood behind Jack. An arrogant condescending smile played across her deep red lips as her dark, almost black eyes evaluated his dance partner. The woman displayed a not so subtle amusement at Jack's choice. Right away Georgianna wanted to back away from the presence of this woman, a feeling she could not explain assaulted her, a feeling of revulsion, so overwhelming she could feel her heart beating, it seemed to strike in waves.

Jack turned around disengaging and dropped Georgianna's hand.

"Canquetyne, I didn't see you earlier," Jack said. "I'm glad you're here now, we must talk." He seemed to forget Georgianna and then excused himself for his rudeness. "Canquetyne, please meet a distant cousin's daughter from out of town. Georgianna, my friend, Canquetyne, Acquisitions Director of the Musée."

Georgianna hesitated, preventing herself from backing away from the woman's outstretched hand, for she was positive this Canquetyne was the silent woman with Dr. Frank when he had so callously ordered Benoit to execute her in the ruins.

Chapter Twenty Seven

Next day Ombline and Ledger made lunch plans for Contraband, needing to be out and away from the heavy atmosphere that had begun to feel confining, to enjoy the fast fading New England autumn. They were warned repeatedly—begged by Marc to be watchful for what was going on around them. Before they left, Peter asked them to stop at Serpentine's to collect a few of the blue fruit (which still showed no signs of decomposition) and have them over-nighted to Mona Steffington, who had advanced degrees in botany and had had for many years a thriving business in herbal healthcare. On the way they stopped at Serpentines and picked up a specially prepared cold pack container to be sent to the Steffington estate, then dropped it off to the overnight shipper.

This done, they had no sooner been seated at Contraband than a very excited Thad rushed over to their table. "I've got to talk to you Ombline," he said trying to contain his excitement wondering how much he should say in front of her lunch date.

"It's okay Thad, Dr. Thaddeus Hawthorne meet Dr. Ledger Griffieth. Yes—both doctors," she smiled, "but very different fields. Thad and his fiancée Prudence Farthington—a doctor too, are to be part of an exploratory expedition after the holidays to discover new plant pharmaceuticals in the South American rain forest—so, considering his expertise I asked him to investigate our own biological specimens." She explained this in a subdued voice looking knowingly to Ledger, not wanting to be overheard.

Thad said. "Good to meet you Ledger."

"And you, Thad." Ledger agreed. They shook hands.

"So what did you find?" Ombline asked in a hushed voice knowing he had found something unusual or he wouldn't have come around during lunch time considering he was the only bartender on duty then.

"Something—something," he looked around not wanting to be overheard himself, "something—fantastic!" He stretched out the word fantastic. "You need to see this for yourself. As you asked, I've kept all of this to myself. Can you come by my father's house on Chestnut Street after 2:30 this afternoon?"

"Yes, yes and yes!" Ombline said, excited at Thad's excitement.

Thad gave them the address and quickly went back to his bartending.

A wave of knowing passed over Ombline, something she couldn't express with words, a connectedness she sensed and out of habit put her hand up to touch the silver locket she always wore—a matching one to Georgianna and Chloe's given to them years ago by her aunt Lily. The lockets were cherished antique pieces the three young women kept a connection through, a sort of talisman of heart. "Oh, my gosh—my locket! Ledger, we have to go back to Serpentine's, I left it on the powder room counter. My hair had somehow tangled to it in the back and when I removed it and combed my hair I forgot to put it back on." Aggravated with herself she told Ledger. "I don't believe I did this, I never take it off! How could I be so careless?"

They finished lunch, paid the bill and drove out of town and back up the coast road to Serpentine's estate. They pulled up the drive and around back of the building so they could expedite this little unplanned side trip and be pointed back toward the highway when they were ready to leave. Ombline ran up the steps and rang the bell while Ledger waited in the car.

The butler escorted Ombline to the solarium where Serpentine directed several men in overalls, padding and boxing up the magnificent male fertility statue that dominated the center of the solarium. Serpentine looked askance at Ombline. "Yes"—she smiled hurriedly, "we found your locket." She went over to a little side table opening the drawer and removed the locket. She held it out to Ombline.

"Thanks so very much," Ombline said in relief, "this has always meant so much to me, I'm never without it."

"I'm so glad we found it dear."

Serpentine seemed rushed and uncomfortable. Ombline knew she was in the way of something, she could sense it—it hung in the room like thick swirls of fog. *Why, was this beautiful piece of statuary being crated up and removed, and to where?* She felt it would be an intrusion to ask. Visible through the back of the solarium a very large transfer truck was guarded by two armed guards dressed in black with earpieces. They stood at the back and front of the truck. Ombline was puzzled by such extreme precautions.

Could it really be this priceless—had Serpentine sold it? No—somehow she didn't feel that was what was happening She pretended to ignore what was taking place, thanked Serpentine and left. She said nothing of this to Ledger for what was there to say? One had a right to do with their art what they would.

They drove back to town as it was now after 2:30. The Chestnut Street address Thad had given them was easy enough to find. The well kept yellow two-story Victorian had a wraparound porch, white trim and grey shutters which evidenced pride of ownership by several generations. A waist high picket fence surrounded the property. A tire swing still hung from one of the lawn's trees.

Thad answered the door promptly seemingly relieved that they had arrived. He led them through the spotless parlour and down a hall of polished wood floors flanked by a dining room on one side and a library-office on the other where Prudence, his fiancée, worked on Contraband's books.

She yelled out to them as they passed by. "Hi guys!—Wait for me—you won't believe this!" She joined the group of three as Thad led them on through the kitchen to a lofty spacious greenhouse beyond, full of plantings. The far end of the greenhouse's glass enclosure was joined by another building. Thad led them through such intensely packed greenery Ombline felt as if she were in a jungle.

"We'll come back in here shortly." Thad said, "but first, we'll go into the nursery *prime*." The four people entered another section of greenhouse not as large as the area they had just passed through. Its high humidity and warm temperature provided the perfect environment for the germination of seedlings—sprouts. They were everywhere. But they all paled in comparison to the back wall of the humid enclosure. Everyone just stopped in the middle of the aisle. Veritable trees nearly touching the ceiling grew out of the enormous containers—all had already produced the blue fruit! Other containers were in various stages of growth—some only sprouts, others plant pot-size on up to the trees bearing fruit.

"Every seed I've planted has survived," Thad said, "and with implausibly aggressive growth and fertility." He walked over to a potting table and pulled from underneath a plastic container. It was full of navy blue seeds from the fruit. "I have fresher ones in the fridge in the greenhouse. Prudence and I have discussed the possibility that such a plant is uncontainable—uncontrollable."

Prudence cautiously interjected. "You might say—a plant takeover of the world!"

Thad, more than suspicious of such a plants source, asked. "And—where did you say your friend found this specimen?"

Ombline didn't answer his question directly. "I'm not sure Thad, but I can find out, oh, and what about the nutritional value?"

"That," Thad nodded to his fiancée, "is Prudence's area of expertise."

"I'm astonished with what I've discovered in such a short time." Prudence said seemingly awed at her own findings. "Such nutritional value I've never found to be in one food source—just incredible, you could live on it in perfect health. It has components I can't yet identify; I need more time, I'm overwhelmed with its possibilities."

Thad said. "We're both considering not going on the South American expedition and devoting our time to this." He indicated the trees with a wave of his hand.

"What can we do to help?" Ombline asked.

Thad said with what he felt was great justification considering the trees were outgrowing his greenhouse space almost overnight. "We need to move these *suckers* to a place where there is more room to grow. I believe with winter coming on they're large enough and hardy enough, or certainly soon will be, to be transferred to the out-of-doors, it needs to be done right away. We will find out if they do well in the cold, somehow I believe they will—otherwise they are going to burst through the green-house roof."

Ombline had an idea, but first she must call Peter.

Chapter   Twenty   Eight

The actress in Georgianna disguised her jolting physic affront at meeting the very woman in compliance with Dr. Frank's orders to murder her as if she were of no consequence. She played her part well, even complimenting Canquetyne on her acquisitions for the museum. She had no doubt that the woman recognized her, she could see it in her very being, seeming to secretly savour this confrontation unbeknownst to anyone but the two of them—a powerful chess game, an opportunity to exercise control over those Canquetyne felt had no relevance.

Georgianna could feel a perverted aura of omnipotence surrounding Canquetyne, flaunting what only the two of them knew, that she could get away with being an accomplice to murder in front of the very one who was to be done away with. Canquetyne's disdain for her was as evident as if Georgianna had been an insect under glass—raising the dome and flicking away the little winged one.

In this very instance of meeting, two warriors of opposite morality played their parts for now, but both knew there would be a reckoning.

Georgianna had no fear, in fact, she looked forward to doing whatever battle would come between the two of them as strange as that would seem even to her. She was over her original feeling of revulsion now understanding it for what it had been—an intuitive perception of Canquetyne's very essence, a being of such darkness anyone of the light would find nothing worth salvaging.

If all the Vraang had not been done away with long ago the woman would be what Georgianna would expect a Vraang to be—supremely arrogant, a vile despicable creature unbounded by any sort of virtue—a true predator, human in form only. This knowing had assaulted her very senses as if she were a sieve straining out this knowledge as the waves passed through her.

Canquetyne's underlying darkness did not refute the fact that she was a woman of great allure and manifested her magnetism in elegant simplicity, a one-shoulder gown of dragongreen silk accessorized only by a chunky crystal bracelet on one wrist. When she walked she glided as silently as a phantom of the night, a creature that could be expected to spring upon one in the dark. The flowing lines of her gown closely followed the lines of her body as she moved.

Georgianna found Canquetyne's presence as yet a mystery... what was her game?—and the peculiar repulsive aura accompanying her physical presence—possibly a chemical effect since she had noted this sensation only when in close proximity to her, for as she had initially upon introduction to Canquetyne felt compelled to step back from her as if a wave of sorts emanated from the woman. Suddenly it struck her—it was the same odd feeling that had come over her and Ombline at meeting Seurat at the ball! The very same! Georgianna knew this was important, but she didn't know how. She felt more than uneasy with her disturbing impressions.

She needed to talk to Jack who had left the dance floor with Canquetyne and could see he was now engaged in close discussion with her on the other end of the ballroom. Georgianna had no indication that Jack intended to return anytime soon so she ventured by the colourful and vastly varied buffet offering many foods unfamiliar to her of an agrarian nature selecting slices of nut pate and what she knew to be *the fruit*. She had, since her initial arrival developed almost a craving for the stuff when on that first morning she had, out of hunger, relented and eaten two. Once tasted, it seemed to call to one's vigour.

She finished the plate of hors d'oeuvres and seeing no Jack, wondered when she would be introduced to this Benjamin he had spoken of tonight. She'd had no indication that any of the acquaintances he had addressed on the way in was this person—not knowing how things worked here she wondered if this was to be a secret meeting—how would it take place (returning her home that is) when a tap on her shoulder caused her to turn around. A pleasant face covered in freckles and slicked-back red hair smiled broadly and introduced himself as Benjamin Fouchard. He gave a slight bow from the waist barely causing movement in his long lanky body—almost robotic—indicating a formal nature, *severely* aristocratic—yet, somehow likable. He was dressed in tails, a bit overdone for this affair, lending an air of eccentricity to the man.

"So-o-o-you're Ms. Georgianna, so charmed to meet you." He bent from the waist once more and lightly kissed her hand. "I must leave soon but Jack insisted that I meet you for myself—so glad I am—I will say no more now, but I believe I can be of great assistance to you in your *travels*." He spoke quickly never losing his broad smile. An unquestioning knowing was communicated, as if a secret between them was understood. "And now, I will take my leave." Once more he gave a slight bow, quickly turned and walked away before Georgianna could respond.

Wow! That was fast! Well, so much for formal introductions. At least she had met this Benjamin who obviously was aware of her situation and seemed to be interested in helping her. She had immediately liked this man who had seemed in such a hurry. It had happened so fast she hadn't even had time to speak. She wondered about this; was there some reason he should not be seen talking to her?

Irrieth, from what she could tell was certainly a civilization to be proud of, and, she was enjoying herself. She had never been one who needed a date to have a good time. Jack and Canquetyne had disappeared together some time ago so Georgianna cruised the perimeter of the ballroom and wandered back to the exhibition when without warning she tripped in her pewter evening sandal. The delicate little buckle at the back had come undone. To re-buckle it was no easy task as it had to be done sitting down with one's foot up to get at its back.

She hated doing so, but, removed it and limped over to a gentleman who seemed to be an official of the event and inquired as to where she might take care of her mishap.

He saw what had happened and personally offered his arm to an out-of-the-way ladies room not heavily trafficked now as were those of the ballroom. It was small, only three stalls, but beautifully executed in pale green silk covered walls and floors that appeared to be white opaque quartz with streaks of pink and gold running through it. A lone mauve silk settee sat against the wall opposite the stalls. An ornate gold-framed oval mirror hung over the sink also of the streaked quartz.

It wouldn't work to try to buckle her sandal sitting on the settee. She needed to put her foot against the wall. She entered the center stall, pulled up the skirt of her gown and sat sideways on the toilet seat putting both feet up on the wall beside her finding it easier that way. She didn't bother to shut and lock the stall door as it would only take a minute—the stalls were roomy.

No sooner than she had done this than someone entered the room, quickly turning and locking the door. Georgianna could see who it was through the crack in the stall door. It was Canquetyne. Georgianna remained quiet and as she was. Was she in danger?—in a locked room alone with a murderers accomplice? She wasn't going to find out if it was preventable just by being quiet. She could see through the crack that Canquetyne thought she was alone.

The woman stood unmoving and silent in front of the sink's mirror. She threw her head back and breathed deeply. Abruptly, her head came forward as she grappled in her black evening bag bringing out a syringe. She removed its cap and quickly injected a solution in her forearm so green it matched in colour her gown. She then replaced the cap on the needle end of the syringe and put it back in her bag. She leaned forward over the sink holding each side of it as she took deep even breaths obviously waiting for the injection to take effect. Slowly she seemed to recover from what ever it was that had afflicted her.

Once again Canquetyne opened the evening bag this time removing a small zip top plastic bag of what appeared to be bloody raw meat—possibly liver, or so it appeared to Georgianna who sat frozen to the toilet seat as she watched this macabre scene.

Canquetyne opened the plastic bag bringing it to her nose, again breathing deeply for what seemed to Georgianna an eternity. Finally the woman sealed the bag and reinserted it in her evening bag. She wet a paper towel and proceeded to clean a spot of blood from her nose, threw the towel in the garbage can, quickly unlocked the door and left.

Georgianna, still frozen to the toilet seat was incredulous. She sat unmoving for a good five minutes not wanting to run into the woman again tonight. She was more than disturbed by what she had seen. She was frightened.

What the hell was that, sucking in the stench from bloody raw meat? What is Canquetyne? What kind of drug addict breathes the fumes of raw meat…just what is she? That repugnant act would fit in a with what I would expect a Vraang to do in private!

What form of disgusting darkness had Georgianna been witness to? Shaken, she finished buckling her sandal, stood and left the ladies room.

Again, the dark and strange haunted Georgianna. She was anxious, since Canquetyne seemed to be connected to Jack who was her only hope of getting home.

She had to talk to him now! She had told Jack, Ean and Storm everything she could remember about Dr. Frank and the woman with him, every detail she could remember, had that been a mistake?—And now, she had to identify Canquetyne as that woman—and the disturbing events in the ladies room were just plain creepy. That meat bag thing could have been in a horror movie.

She rushed back to the ballroom with Jack nowhere to be found. The music still played to a full dance floor. She didn't want to return to the apartment without him, so she danced with a young man who enjoyed dancing as much as she would have under different circumstances. Two dances later they were starting a third when Jack tapped her partner on the shoulder. "Can I have this dance with my date?" He had switched back to the lighter side of his personality.

Georgianna's dance partner walked away as Jack grabbed her to him. They danced with the same fire between them as before. Jack said. "I'm sorry to have left you alone so long but there was something I had to take care of right away, I do apologize." He held her close savouring their warmth. She could feel his breath on her neck, the strength of his body and his vitality of spirit—and yes, she liked it even though she would rather not admit this to herself—it was there. This was just biological—his personality was too inconsistent for her taste!

"Jack"—she ventured, knowing what she had witnessed was important but should she bring it up here or when? "There's something strange happening, we need to talk about very soon. I—I—don't know how to say this but there's something you need to know. It could be *very* important."

He stopped dancing stepping back a little from Georgianna. "Let's go—I think we put in enough of an appearance here tonight."

Once again in a veritable instant he had flipped to his one-eighty self. He had seemed so different on the dance floor and now returned to his reserved indifferent side as if he had taken off a coat. *Why would she even care—she didn't—she only wanted to go home, let the Irrieth people deal with their own world as barbaric as he led her to believe hers was compared to this place, she would take Earth any day—it was home—all she loved was there.*

The air car came around for them taking them back to the apartment over a brilliantly lit Paris. No sooner had they arrived back than Jack answered his cell in the library, five minutes later he emerged in a state of urgency. "Get your things together as quickly as you can Georgianna, we need to get back to the lodge tonight—there's an emergency." He disappeared back into the library shutting the door behind him.

Chapter   Twenty   Nine

The sun was just setting in the mountains far to the west of Dragons Roost. The figures in silhouette on the ridge scurried to finish planting trees around the building before it was too dark to do so. Thad had moved, by closed transfer truck, the larger of the blue fruit trees from his experimental greenhouse on Chestnut Street to the seclusion of Dragons Roost to find out if they could survive being transplanted to the colder temperature outdoors preferring to keep their existence a secret for now—anyway, he knew they would for sure break through the nursery roof in a matter of days.

It had been Ombline's idea knowing they could also provide further protection for the work being done there, no more sprinkling mushed up fruit around the house as Serpentine had done. "This ought to keep Madame Seurat at bay," she said. Zorloff had agreed. She wondered at first, why they hadn't seemed shocked at her suggestion, but rather pleased with Thad's progress.

Peter made an unexpected request of Thad and Prudence inviting them to dinner that night. Again, Serpentine provided the group with excellent fare.

Thad was curious as to the strange laboratory equipment he was completely unfamiliar with arrayed in Dragons Roost. Zorloff explained that their work was something he and Peter had worked together on for years and were close to a resolution, he gave no further explanation.

"We know you understand the great importance of *the fruit*," as they had all come to call it. Peter spoke to Thad and Prudence in particular knowing they must become familiar with the enormity of their involvement without yet knowing all. "I can't yet disclose to you the origin of the fruit but let me say it's one of the most important things that will ever befall Earth and all its life forms."

Thad was more than eager to know what lay behind all the secrecy. "And surely, *you*, must understand our inquisitiveness—the fruits origin Peter—it's what we do—of *course* we're raging with curiosity. We can't begin to know everything we can in the short time we've had the specimens—these are only our immediate observations, not yet scientifically proven by only our initial testing. We need more time, but Prudence and I believe this fruit is not genetically altered—purely an unaltered biological line. We worked as fast as was possible considering how quickly the seeds sprout and start to mature overnight, we've never even known of any rain forest legends portending such as this. One thing we're very concerned about—the trees taking over the world so to speak." He smiled as he said this knowing how sci-fi it sounded.

The two older men looked to one another weighing just how much to disclose. Peter said. "Not to worry Thad, we've had more than a little experience with these trees and their effect on other botanicals—actually promote the vigour of other agricultural species, magnificently positive—if you're concerned about a takeover rest your mind, the trees are self-regulating—blend in but don't overwhelm biodiversity—live well in any climate never losing their glossy leaves and produce year round for the long life of the tree." Peter paused, choosing his words carefully, still not answering Thad's question as to the fruits origin. "We have a proposition we'd like to propose to the two of you if you are willing—all of you," he corrected looking to each of the young people.

Thad looked to Ombline and Ledger completely bewildered by Peter's statement too.

Ombline said. "We're just as mystified as you guys are. Tell us more Peter, we're all ears."

Thad and Prudence stayed to dinner. Everyone sat around the table discussing what would have to be done to *change the world* as Peter defined their mission of the fruit and its protectors while enjoying a dinner of crispy artichoke, spinach and tomato pizza along with white wine and later, coffee and cherry pudding soufflé with chocolate sauce for dessert. The gourmet pizzas of Delia's had become a quick and easy favorite—no one was complaining of nutritional redundancy—Ombline continued along with Ledger, her bicycling, to neutralize the effects of all the pizza eating at night.

After dinner Zorloff sipped a second cup of the rich black coffee in front of the fireplace explaining what would be necessary for their success. "We've planned for a planet-wide random distribution of the seeds in out-of-the-way places to give rise to the fruits unimpeded propagation before certain factions realize it's too late to stop it."

Ledger said. "Zorloff, are you saying there are people on this planet who would destroy a solution to world hunger?"

"There certainly are." Peter quickly interjected. "That's why this has to be covert—the distribution of the seeds—and keeping it secret for now. Just dropping them from the air randomly all over the world will do the job. It's—*been done elsewhere*—worked extremely well. Our other preparations are almost ready. It has to be done as soon as possible though. There are factions now doing all they can to prevent this from happening—we can't even consider interference an option. Some of their minor players you have tangled with."

Ombline said. "You mean, of course, Seurat and that bunch."

"Correct."

The four young people knew they had become part of something more important and clandestine than they could possibly have imagined only a short time ago—and the fruit was only the beginning—they realized they had not yet been told the whole story, but were filled with plenty of suspicions that certainly seemed to indicate other existences of some sort—a knowing that enticed each of them.

When Peter mentioned that this had been done *elsewhere,* Thad and Prudence looked to one another understanding that there had been a click in the turn of reality—an altering of humanity's path beginning with the seed sowing, but more revelation they knew would soon follow for all was surely not told in this endeavor. They would discuss this later amongst themselves. Peter had avoided revealing for the time being where the fruit came from, or where this *other place* was that it had been successfully used. Even so, they were fully invested in what they were a part of, and, the integrity of Peter and Zorloff. As naïve and gullible as they would earlier have thought themselves to be that no longer mattered.

So, for now none of the young people pursued *the rest of it* for when those questions came up Peter finally said. "For your safety, all in good time. Oh—by the way, have any of you tried the fruit yet—it's really quite delicious—and—very invigourating." He just smiled as if extending an invitation to do so.

Of course this only whetted their curiosity, being a part of something so cryptic, to advance possibly the greatest humanitarian effort in human history. For now though, they were satisfied doing whatever was needed to help make the world a new place, but soon, Peter knew they would demand to know the rest and rightly so, for their help would be needed with what lay beyond the dispersal of the seed.

Chapter   Thirty

A gentle but chilly autumn wind skittered the few leaves left from summer across the lawn and under the mighty Oak trees of the Steffington estate. The sun warmed the early afternoon air compensating for the frost earlier in the day.

Timeless beauty and elegance graced the tall slender woman just past midlife standing on the front lawn of the estate. A lifetime of Sun enhanced freckles added to her classic bone structure. Full lips and sparkling green eyes denoted a woman still full of life's vigour and goodwill to all creatures—her vitality seemed to know no bounds as could be attested to by all who knew her. Mona Steffington anxiously awaited the transfer truck from Serpentine's estate on the New England coast.

She, Peter, Zorloff and Serpentine had longed for this day when all would be in place to free their world of humanity's enslavers—the despicable Vraang. Once more she checked the prepared ground under the central Oak tree of the maze garden where the placement would adhere to the right connection with the Earth. This was crucial—it had long ago been plotted perfectly.

They were so close. They had allowed Dragons Roost to seem abandoned for years. Now it had been reclaimed—reanimated if you will, to perpetrate a simple laboratory of collusion between two scientists. A cavernous laboratory had been created under the ridge in the beginning long ago with Dragons Roost built above to disguise all it concealed below in a laboratory light years ahead of anything on the planet. Because of this, their coming and going between that location, Peter's lab—the Cave, as it was called on the Steffington estate, and Zorloff's laboratory in the mountain forests of Sweden, their secret advancements and preparations had been cloaked well over the years. Still with all their secrecy one Vraang had somehow determined *something* was happening at Dragons Roost and had shown up attempting to use the old original portal frame from years ago—one that had been created as a diversion—a decoy for just such an eventuality, it had worked well as a moth to the flame—for now, it was just that! The unexpected involvement of Georgianna and Ombline had put everything on the fast track with unanticipated results. Now they must follow through.

They had secretly worked in the three locations over the years. Only the four knew of the extent of the laboratories. Marc

Patrone had been a tangent fifth to their group having been early on apprised of the life-altering intrigue surrounding the four, playing parts of his own through the years to assist where he could. Travel between their labs had been undetected thanks to the development of portal travel early on.

For some time Serpentine had guarded a planet altering weapon disguised as a mythical fertility figure of art in her estate solarium as had Mona in the twelve faerie statues in the central maze garden of the Steffington estate. Now they were ready at long last to be linked together—the thirteen pieces would become a formidable weapon (their function neutralized after the one use they had been designed for) that would, along with the fruit finally free Earth's people to define their own destiny without the evil interference it had always unknowingly been subject to—coerced barbaric self-destruction repeatedly throughout history.

Mona was relieved her granddaughter Chloe and her fiancé, David Stewart, were away on business in France and Scotland. She wanted to be able to carry out what their small group and its background affiliations had put into place so long ago without any kind of interference or worry. This effort would only have one chance at success.

She had packed up their beloved dog Thistle and their seven cats to stay at a secret location with old and very trusted friends not wanting any of their loved ones endangered by what they would attempt. All the servants except for Sedgewyck had been given time off. The estate would become a fortress for a space of time. As soon as all was in place and then executed she knew the change in humanity's fortunes would be on a fast track with no going back.

It had been unfortunate Georgianna had been caught up in the portal transference to Peter's home world Irrieth, thanks to that meddling Vraang, Seurat, but, with Peter's technology they would be able to safely bring Georgianna home. She did not fear for her knowing she would be discovered by Irrieth's Guardians right away.

Irrieth's civilization was so advanced in comparison to Earth simply because of Irrieth's having been able to rid themselves of the Vraang many decades ago. Most importantly, always first, was the acquisition of the fruit. Irrieth had had to deal differently with the Vraang than it now appeared Earth would if everything went as planned. Hopefully, Earth would be free without the horrendous tragedy that had befallen Irrieth in yanking off the yoke of *its* Vraang enslavers. Even with all their scientific advancements through the years an unsettling fear of what-ifs haunted Mona, and especially now that the time had finally come. What vengeance would the Vraang attempt in an effort to maintain their hold on humanity here on Earth—an unspeakable retribution in what form? The Vraang had tried to store up as much Sesca as they could by destroying most of the human race on Irrieth with a deadly biological weapon once the fruit had taken hold. They had almost succeeded, but many of

Irrieth's citizens were saved *because* of the fruit. What horrors would the Vraang attempt to unleash on the humanity of Earth in a last ditch effort to save themselves? This fear gave Mona no quarter—always she had lived with it, but now it was oppressive.

The descendants of those who had for centuries known of the Vraang but been powerless to rise against them remained secretly in the background of this project waiting for the day when victory could be claimed for humanity. They had supplied much along the way that was needed as had Marc who had early on been enlightened as to humanity's enslavement by the Vraang, yet not knowledgeable of the details for ridding the planet of this scourge—and didn't want to be—hoping to be a help in the process with what he could contribute with his great wealth and ability to move internationally as he had always feared his involvement too closely could endanger his daughters. So he had contributed at a distance.

A think-tank on what the most likely scenarios of vengeance the Vraang would take had been considered with no definitive answers—or what steps could be taken to prevent such from befalling Earth as it had Irrieth. This, they would have to deal with as things played out for this was their one great fear.

Everything had to be done in secret. Even allowing this Seurat woman and Dr. Frank to assume they had discovered a secret advancement in Earth science leading them to Dragons Roost, in the process, exposing themselves to some of the original Four's *watchers*. Ombline and Georgianna's discovery of

Seurat's meddling—her attempt to use old outdated technology in Dragons Roost, had stepped up the Four's time table forcing them to enlarge their circle at the last moment.

Marc Patrone had been fully initiated as a fifth into the group of four after the unavoidable death of his wife Ursula. He had been heartbroken at Georgianna's loss initially until Peter hating to see such sorrow overwhelm his old friend enlightened him even further, allaying his fears, saying that Georgianna's fate was in good hands and why his fears for her were not to be. Now Marc knew what the four knew, he was one of them and resigned to what had to be done. He too was in the thick of it now.

A call from the front gate alerted Sedgewyck, the Steffington's long time butler and manager of all concerning their day to day family life that the truck had arrived. From events long ago Sedgewyck had been guardian and keeper of secrets for this small group of revolutionaries—knowing from painful loss at the hands of the Vraang early on, where his lifetime loyalties would lie—he had always been the Steffington's personal sentinel.

A relieved Mona and Sedgewyck watched from the circular drive in front of the grey stone mansion as the truck entered through the falcon-topped pillars hedging the gates of the estate. It slowly drove up the long blacktop lane through mature Northern Oaks to stop at the northwest entrance to the faerie maze fronting the Steffington estate home.

Two armed guards in black jumped down from the truck, one in the cab, the other from the back. The driver presented a clipboard to be signed for the delivery. Two more men dressed in dark suits emerged from the entrance of the Steffington home joining the others with the delivery. The crate was lowered out of the truck to the ground by the trucks hydraulic lift.

The huge object d'art was un-crated after being lowered to the ground. Mona indicated the shortest route to the center of the maze to where the fertility spirit was to be placed on the specific plot of earth covered by a sizable dais of pure white quartz streaked with gold veining. Only a few of autumns leaves clung to the massive oak tree centering the maze where the statue would be placed underneath its sprawling branches, giving it the appearance of the lord high phantom of autumn and his coven of twelve.

The silent guards did not realize they had just taken part in humanity's deliverance—only the transfer of a valuable piece of esoteric art.

The over-nighted cold pack container had arrived as an early morning delivery to Mona giving her the opportunity to right away remove seeds from the fruit potting many of the deep blue seeds in the greenhouse farther back on the estate. This greenhouse she used for the botanical studies she incorporated into the herbal products of her self care line. Botany and all that involved had always been her great fascination and life study. Now the greatest mystery of the plant kingdom had finally arrived at her doorstep for her own investigation—just a few for her to work with for the satisfaction of her own curiosity since before now such delving into the study of the fruit could have gotten away from them and inadvertently revealed all their efforts before all was in place—such a shame that would have been, even though so much good could have been done for so many starting long ago, but it had had to be until all was in place. Mona had been elated all morning at finally getting to work with the fruit. She had so long anticipated this day when it could be revealed to the world, besides being anxious to get on with all the positive change it would bring to Earth life.

Long ago she had discussed with Peter how imperative it would be to acquire an abundance of seeds to assure a successful foothold—the intense proliferation of the fruit would come later when there would be no stopping its spread across the world. Hours ago she had planted seeds in the ground among the cherry orchards abutting the back of the estate grounds too. Surviving the Michigan winter, they would be hidden in the orchards until their height towered over the cherry trees, but by then the fruit trees would be a sensation all over the planet.

* * *

At Dragons Roost Thad expressed his fear that there would be a shortage of seed even though they had recovered much in a very short time thanks to the fecundity of the trees. Peter was forced to release a little more of his promised disclosure telling them that they had years before, amassed stores of the seed from their sources and secreted it away for this time. "All your long hours to recover seed have not gone to waste Thad, shortly it will be in great demand. Without all of your and Prudence help this would have been a lot more difficult. There are not enough words to convey all the thanks you young people deserve for your unquestioning trust and loyalty in this great project to deliver Earth's population from hunger and the beginning of a whole new world of hope."

Dragons Roost's small group discussed all the optimum out-of-the-way places on the planet to disperse seed so as to gain footholds in secret—specifically wild areas that were thinly populated—a sort of Johnny Appleseed approach. Peter wanted to include everyone of their small group in this decision for many destinations overlooked originally might be of great consequence. The original group of four had always known the greatest challenge before destroying the collectors of Sesca was the seeding—it would be a massive undertaking requiring exact timing, stealth and coordination with the assistance of those in shadow who had for so long remained quietly in the background waiting with whatever would be needed, doing their part in this day of deliverance.

Zorloff and Peter, with their years of covert preparations had had help in engaging hundreds of small planes to disseminate the seed over the planet when the time came. Marc's many international connections had been an insurance policy against anything that might go awry at the last minute. None of the pilots were aware of the others. All the pilots had their own flight plans and destinations—some a cross-check on others so nothing of import was neglected. Everything had to be succinctly orchestrated. There would be no allowance for failure, for if that happened there would not be a second chance.

All was in place.

The sowing would be done all at the same time as the earth turned away from the sun into the darkness of night—the planes would fly into and stay within the encroaching darkness until all the Earth was sown. Irrieth's contribution of seed had been safely stored in secret locations around the globe in years past so there would not be the problem of transportation to points of departure. *Those in shadow* had provided for this. Regrettably, lives had been lost to preserve this fearsome secret—one humanity could not conceive of, one that if known could only defeat them further realizing that all they aspired to had always been undermined, that there was no liberation available to them—dashing all hope. Those in shadow had always until now lived with the sorrow of such knowledge. The knowing had been almost unbearable at times realizing humanity was steered away from all it's possibilities—led to purposeful failure.

The deed, once done, would be irreversible for the trees once entrenched, could never be done away with once they took root for they became so abundant dispersing their seed into the earth it was as if they were protected by the very planet itself to become one with it—there would always be the trees—any destroyed always replaced themselves, the very ground protected and concealed the seed from destruction. Earth's people and all its creatures would be on the way to endless unobstructed possibilities—but Peter, like his dear Mona, was haunted by a sense of unease. He hoped this was only because so much depended upon what they did.

The mass sowing began on the side of Earth just turning away from the sun as planned, sowing eventually, the whole planet with swarms of blue seed spiraling down to the waiting dark soil's nurturing protection. It welcomed them. They settled softly to their long awaited destination to work their fated magic, burrowing deeply and safely to spring to life on yet another world needing their deliverance. The group at Dragons Roost waited anxiously for the completion of the first phase of their mighty struggle. With the pop of a champagne cork Peter announced that the last of the small planes had taken off with their precious cargo. Now they waited as the fleet finalized its mission flying at last into the sunrise of Earth finishing at their point of origin with the spread of the cargo of light. Mona would wait on the estate until what she guarded would be needed. Ombline wished Georgianna could be with them. She and Ledger held hands waiting for it to be over—be done with. For a celebratory group everyone was quiet—within their own thoughts—their private hopes and wishes—and yes—fearful something would go wrong. It did not. By the next day they knew all of the earth had been successfully turned over to the fruit. Even now the little blue containers of hope worked their way deep into the earth in unsuspected out of the way places and too, the more obvious as well, to ensure the survival of the fruit. It would soon make itself known everywhere. There would be no hope for the Vraang for at long last their time was over on *this* world.

Chapter Thirty One

Jack had been silent and grim as they left the apartment in Paris. Georgianna wondered what had so disturbed him into such urgency; she was sure it was most likely to do with his work as one of the Guardians. He had carried her newly purchased bag stuffed hurriedly with her few belongings. She had changed into casual clothing while Jack had sequestered himself in the library.

He had thrown her bag in the back of the air car. It rose with them into the Paris night leaving all the revelers of the city far behind. They soundlessly passed over countryside below and a star filled night sky above. The car had quickly attained its ritual zenith and flew effortlessly on through the night.

Georgianna could wait no longer. She had to talk with Jack now no matter what his troubles were. "Jack, I have to—I just have to relate to you something that happened tonight that I find so very unsettling, I'm hoping you can give me a reassuring answer for it but, then maybe you can't."

He could tell that she was deeply disturbed. He remained quiet suspecting that somehow she had discovered things she was better off unaware of—at least for now.

She turned, looking at him surrounded by the beauty of the heavens above, wishing that it wasn't necessary to ruin it with reality. She just blurted out what she had dreaded having to say that she herself had found so disturbing. "Canquetyne is the woman who was with Dr. Frank in the ruins when he ordered Benoit to kill me."

Jack's response was even and seemingly unaffected. "How can you be sure Georgianna, you said this woman had on sunglasses and a scarf?"

"Trust me Jack, it was her. I knew right away it was Canquetyne—and she knew I knew. She recognized me, I'm sure of it!" Georgianna continued, ill at ease with what she had to say. "I don't know how things work in this Irrieth of yours, but the worst is yet to come."

She proceeded to explain the circumstances which had brought her to the out of the way lounge and made her unobservable. "I was alone when Canquetyne flew in and locked the door behind her thinking she was alone. She seemed under some sort of weakness or duress. She removed from her bag a syringe containing a vile green solution and injected her forearm. She held to the sink waiting for the injection to bring her around.

I could understand if maybe it was a medical condition that required such, but that's not the worst of it." Georgianna took a deep breath. "When she recovered she brought out of her bag what I would term on my world a zip lock bag of bloody raw meat and breathed deeply into it for what seemed like a long time to me, at least a minute or two. She had blood from it on her nose and cleaned it off with a wet paper towel, replaced the zip lock bag back in her purse, unlocked the door and left." Afraid his answer might be one of derision she asked. "Jack is that how things are here—people carry around bags of bloody flesh to inhale?"

Disgusted with her description of events he reached over grabbing her hand looking into her eyes. "No—No! Georgianna—No! This world is so unlike anything you can imagine it's as close as human kind can come to Paradise—a civilized existence—so unlike your present Earth. You see, we three, myself, Ean and Storm remember well what a horror life on Earth was for so many.

He continued. "The people of Irrieth no longer even eat animal products—certainly not the flesh of any living being. You should have noticed that by now. We still produce a laboratory version, not from any living creature, strictly for some of the very elderly who couldn't give it up due to the conditioning of their youth. Man's desire for flesh food was quenched once and for all when a greater percentage of the world's population died at the Vraang's last ditch effort to harvest Sesca immediately after the fruit had taken hold. The biological weapon that the Vraang released killed over three-fifths of Irrieth's population—there was no alternative but to cremate the dead in the out of doors. It could not be done in a respectful civilized manner there were so many. The stench of burning flesh permeated the planets very atmosphere for months. A nauseating reminder to the survivors of the loss of loved ones; the stench of death so pervasive in the memory never to be forgotten—the horror stopped for ever the desire to eat flesh again. All animal food sources became abominable to the survivors and went by the wayside permanently. Then, along with the fruit came a new industry of agriculture—that of developing new plants, ones with unimaginable nutritional value, tantalizing taste and aesthetic value. The health of the world's population after decades became almost free of disease—old age halted in its tracks, our life spans have doubled and seem to be increasing as time goes on simply due to the incredible effect of the fruit and having less stressful lives."

Georgianna was quiet remembering the robust health of the people of Paris now that she thought about it—no one that she could recall appeared very elderly or ill of health confirming all Jack had related, then she suddenly remembered the man who was to be her ticket home. "I meant to mention that I met Fouchard tonight—very impressive, lanky, red hair, very formal. He surprised me by introducing himself and then just as quickly disappeared."

"Oh, did you now? He's an eccentric *original*, but brilliant. I didn't see him myself. Georgianna, I too, am concerned at what you saw tonight, but I have to be forthcoming with you, in all truthfulness, we know who and what Canquetyne is—that's we of the Guardians—she is Vraang—always they are pushing and prodding trying to retake our world even though they know it's useless, their greed and immorality—their cruelty knows no bounds. Before they were finally ejected from Irrieth they conducted horrible experimentation on some of our people attempting to undo what the fruit could do for us, their efforts failed of course—you can't defeat the fruit. Many have searched for it's origin in other parallel worlds—is it a freak of nature? Has some science far beyond ours created such? If so, what else did they give birth to that might be a boon to us all? This is a very necessary quest—to one day find it's origin."

"That's very thought provoking, but Jack, hasn't anyone ever tried to do the reverse with the Vraang?—alter their need for Sesca the same way that substitutes are used for people who have drug problems—drug intervention?"

"It's not that simple. Many protocols have been tried, none indicating a hint of success. I don't think at this point in their existence they would want a substitute even if it worked, as their very DNA is, after eons, dependent upon the Sesca. Some scientists believe that their species would die out without it—and to be honest, I don't think anyone really cares, the rest of humanity just needs to be protected from them. And that is what we do. Canquetyne injected a drug devised to counter the effects of the fruit. We know what she used. What you described is an indication she is suffering the inevitable effects of that drug, the drug itself can be as dangerous as the fruit. Most of her species can't tolerate the drug at all, it's an immediate death sentence for most, killing even the strongest Vraang. We don't yet know the reason she took such a chance coming here—we believe it has something to do with your world, considering her connection to this Dr. Frank. Canquetyne has been here two months, a vial a month. She has to leave soon or she dies a very ugly death. What you saw no doubt was the third and last injection, for three are all that can be tolerated. We knew when and where her point of entry was. She's been under surveillance from the moment she arrived. In no time she inveigled her way into acquisitions for the Musée, a position that would open doors to her—we even assisted. As to this Dr. Frank she's connected with, he too, is a mystery. We don't yet know his intent or other involvements, but we will—he is not Vraang—possibly only mercenary, looking to profit from his association with them in some way. You see, we have more than the fruit as a test for that."

Georgianna said nothing for the moment, her mind filled with more questions than she had answers for, then suddenly she remembered sensing the wrongness—or now she could call it like it was—the Vraangness of Canquetyne, knowing as woo-woo as this sounded she had to relate her bizarre experience.

"Jack, I know this may sound peculiar, but I could sense Canquetyne's otherness—I don't know how else to describe what I felt at our introduction at the Musée—it seemed to be only in close proximity to her. I was shocked at first by what I would term an invisible blow upon my person—almost a psychic assault, but, again I use the word *felt*, that it was some sort of chemical reaction, why I say this I don't know—it just seemed so, for when I stepped back from her, as was my first instinct, the overwhelming feeling of revulsion disappeared—step back to her immediate vicinity and again I was buffeted by it—I purposely did this just to determine if what I was experiencing was valid, and there was no doubt—as unseen as the wind, but it's effect just as real."

"I'm not surprised, some people do sense them, I understand their presence brings on a feeling of dread, anxiety or in milder cases, a feeling of disturbance, unease, even exhaustion."

"That's exactly the way of it, my sister Ombline and I had the same unsettling experience in the company of this Seurat woman I told you about—so I guess she's one too, especially since you say my world is infested with them!"

"That would be my interpretation." He said no more for a long moment seeming not to want to talk more of the peculiarities of the Vraang tonight, at ease with the peaceful beauty of the night sky they glided through thanks to the transparency of the vehicle's roof. The heavens stretched from horizon to horizon, only an occasional shooting star disturbed the calm.

"This is beautiful is it not Georgianna?" He smiled at her obviously enjoying their time together high above Irrieth flying through the silence of the star field together. Jack considered just how much more to reveal to this beautiful young woman knowing that her fear of never seeing her loved ones again encumbered any enjoyment she could experience in this world. He had hoped to see this evening's festivities bring relief from her latent distress that he could feel just below the surface. He spoke anyway. "There are people of your Earth who have been planning to rid your world of the Vraang for a long time. We are assisting, we have sent more fruit and seed so there is no shortage of seeds to disperse; there is no going back Georgianna—your world *will* be free of its darkness."

"I believe that. I think I've known for some time people I'm close to were about something spectacular, I just never knew what, I guess I didn't want to know—considering how unbelievable all this is, I wouldn't have believed it if I had been told—it's so fantastic! My uncle Peter Steffington and his friend Zorloff came overnight when my father called him to tell him of Ombline's and my encounter with Madame Seurat at Dragons Roost. We knew something very serious was up but didn't have a clue and they sure weren't talking."

"Well, there's no point in keeping it a secret now Georgianna. Peter and Zorloff are brothers—originally citizens of Irrieth and when they were young hot-blooded risk-takers they worked together on a scientific experiment that accidentally dispersed them both to your parallel world. It took time and research for them to locate one another having initially been dispatched to different times and locations on your world which was far behind, and, on a different path scientifically from that of Irrieth's. Working in secret together, they were finally able to traverse at will between Earth and Irrieth. They've returned here several times in the last few decades for help and advice on how to go about freeing your world—believe me, it *will* happen. They are attempting even now to put all in place to proceed with the same process that happened here, but without the Vraang's vengeance raining down upon Earth's people as it did Irrieth—that will be the trick of it. They are close, and, they have help—even more than they are aware of. Their greatest concern is revenge by the Vraang on Earth's people as the fruit takes hold. Like here, the Vraang will do anything to retain their grip on power, storing up Sesca, saving the collectors in orbit at least until they find a way to survive. The Vraang science is not as advanced as you would think considering how ancient their species of human is—more one of a predatory sort of psychology and subversion than technology. Once Sesca became their life, the means of obtaining and collecting it, further knowledge seemed not to matter so much to them any more. In a way they became lazy. That at least is in your favour. It has taken centuries for your world to reach the technological apex that it has arrived at—one of those points the Vraang like—for you, so much more to lose after attaining so much—they would call it, a good harvest. You see, destroying your civilization would net them much Sesca. I don't like voicing such a fearful thing to you, but I believe you yourself would come to such a conclusion knowing them for the merciless creatures they are."

"I'm so afraid I do." She was quiet for a moment needing to have an answer to a question she had feared asking. "One thing you haven't covered Jack, is why the Vraang haven't, or, is it *possible* for them to mate with us—I mean can they or do they? Are we interbred with them?"

"Not possible, a completely different species of human—copulate, yes—reproduce?—no! No different than Dogs and Giraffes or fish and parrots—*not gonna go*! Vraang consider their species superior because of their predatory prowess anyway and wouldn't consider tainting their gene pool with a trait they consider a weakness—a conscience, even if it were possible."

Neither said anything more about the grand darkness that Earth would soon have to deal with. For now, there had been enough said, for the magnificence of the heavens intruded upon reality—an experience Georgianna would not soon forget.

She had been curious since Dragons Roost, "what was that burst of the fruit through the portal Seurat tried to step through when she was spit out—bombarded with the fruit? That's how Ombline and I got it."

Jack laughed. "It's just a little joke on the Vraang when we don't allow them in. We are always alerted to a portal attempt—if we want to allow them in to keep tabs on what they're up to—no fruit—if not, it's just fun to launch the stuff at them!"

Georgianna too, thought this was cunning. "I see—good plan!" She laughed. "One thing I don't understand though, with Peter and Zorloff able to travel between our two parallel worlds why didn't they themselves bring the fruit back with them before this?"

"It wasn't time yet. The Sesca collectors in orbit always have to be destroyed right after or at the same time the fruit takes hold on the population, the Vraang will be desperate—their destruction inevitable. They're a vicious species who relish revenge if challenged or defeated. They will attempt to bring down as much death and destruction as possible on your population, at the same time, collecting as much Sesca as they can before they die or escape for wherever, or, try to hold up on your world. It was necessary to make sure the weapons to destroy the collectors worked perfectly and were not detected by the Vraang or negative forces of your world who would put them to use as weapons against each other since Earth is not yet in a position to live in peace. There was no point in giving you weapons more terrible than any you've ever known. The weapons had to be tweaked to perfection so once the collectors are destroyed there will be no debris raining down on Earth. After that the weapon will be destroyed so there will be no trace of the existence of such an omnipotent force of nature. You see a fog of Sesca raining down on humanity could be deadly to humankind—such a concentration of this particular component of adrenalin can cause mass suicide—it would be like drugging the whole planet into a depression so dark they couldn't climb out of it.

Jack hoped he was giving Georgianna some reassurance that her world could be free of the Vraang—not adding to her fears.

"I understand that Peter and Zorloff are in the process now of preparing to disperse the seeds in every out of the way place where they will survive unimpeded or unnoticed at first. This will be quite an undertaking, more important than the weapon at the moment—fruit first." Jack hoped as dark as the truth sounded it also gave hope for a much better future for Earth—and she was going home to be part of it! He thought it best to lighten up all this talk. "I suppose you had some of the fruit in one of its many forms at the Musée tonight."

Georgianna, suspicious at his abrupt change of subject just nodded not sure of his motive—maybe bored by her constant pity party.

"Good," he said. *"It vill make you not so tasty to a Vraang Earth lady!"* He laughed, only this time at his own cuteness, adding as a positive afterthought, "I hope you enjoyed the Musée, but it is nothing compared to what is going on back on your Earth at the moment—the planet's future is on a very fast track."

"Well," she said," I guess I'm missing the big party back home!"

"I'm very sure you are," he said, squeezing her hand.

A trail of several bright meteors streaked across the heavens putting on a stellar show just under the band of the Milky Way.

For the first time since her arrival, she felt more at peace knowing for sure that she definitely would be going home and that she too, could be part of humanity reclaiming itself.

Chapter Thirty Two

Georgianna had so many questions that would do no good to do to death for now. She felt better, it was hard not to in this beautiful place that made one feel a part of the heavens themselves, so much more prominent because of the clear rarefied air of Irrieth—a world that had been able to *purify* itself she felt sure because of it's liberation from Vraang control. No sound disturbed their comfortable silence as Jack had tried to answer much that he knew she had questioned. Although, *other* answers she needed pushed their way back into her present. Was Jack involved with this Vraang woman whose clothes she had worn? If so what was he doing holding hands with "her"? It wasn't just to relieve her anxiety, she wasn't a fearful child needing consolation for her plight. This was man-woman stuff and to deny it was to ignore their attraction even though she still clung to her own assessment of their draw upon one another as only biology—not to make it more than it was. Somehow a knowing had crossed her mind like an encroaching dark shadow when she had seen Canquetyne with Jack at the Musée.

"Jack, are you involved with Canquetyne?" She wanted a forthright answer if that was possible.

He seemed not surprised at her question—almost casual about it. "No—not really."

Ha! Georgianna silently mocked his answer. *No, and not really, are for sure a weasel's words—really! You wuss! You know that means yes!* Acting had taught her great self control and it took all she could muster up just now to keep from pitching him overboard!

Jack knew in that instant that without considering the vagueness of his answer he had verbally hung himself with those three little words *no—not really,* but it was the truth. He had not expected anyone knowing the truth of who Canquetyne was could possibly believe he would be involved with a Vraang. He realized too late he had responded without thinking. He was afraid anything else he might say would only shorten the noose already around his neck but he did anyway. "She's been at the Lodge once or twice for a weekend getaway, just to have a breather from the city." He knew the more he said the worse it sounded. *Why didn't he just shut up!*

To Georgianna, this was a condescending insult to her intelligence. She disengaged her hand. "So, I suppose," she cooed, "this was just undercover work on your part—feel out the

Vraang—get her to spill all her secrets to one of the Guardians I suppose?" Even in the starlit night Georgianna could see Jack was uncomfortable with her assessment of his relativity to a Vraang. "You spent the weekend with a woman who wants to suck the life out of Irrieth again if given the opportunity and most assuredly you? You've slept with the enemy so to speak?— gave your all for the cause?" In a way Georgianna felt disgusted—disappointed that Jack would think such involvement with the dreaded Vraang was necessary or acceptable considering his vile opinion of them.

In a society of such high technology why would boots on the ground (or the bedroom) tactics even be necessary? Maybe he just liked the drama of the chase of an alien species—being a participant in high games.

"Such unpleasant torturous work, spying, I'm sure!" She added sarcastically.

"It wasn't like that Georgianna, we hiked, talked and spent time with Ean and Storm. You never know what little bits of things you might learn just in casual conversation. You know the adage about keeping your enemies close?" He was trying to clean up her perception of his honour but every word out of his mouth tightened the noose—he seemed to be in a free fall of self destruction. What was wrong with him—he had never been so dislocated with the opposite sex *before?* He had not realized until now how very important this woman's opinion of him had become.

Before Georgianna could respond, a bright flash of light beamed upward from the countryside below cupping the bottom of their transport with a sizzling burst of energy mimicking the crawling flash of an electrical charge. They were rocked violently. The air car started a spiral descent to the forest below.

"Brace yourself!" Jack yelled out trying to manually regain control. "We'll be okay," he shouted to Georgianna, "the car's designed to land on a cushion of air in an emergency."

A low whining noise and the increasing speed of descent did nothing to dispel Georgianna's increasing panic. "Just when do you expect that to engage?" She screamed. "Now would be good!" She had no problem with heights, but to fall out of the sky like this was doing nothing for the fast approaching hysteria she felt sure she would soon be dealing with.

Their descent came under control after the initial jolt resulted in a brief nose dive then slowly settled down into the darkness of a forest meadow ringed by thick growths of underbrush, a pronounced pinging sound and then all was quiet finalizing their landing.

Georgianna felt frozen to the seat, immobilized by adrenalin even though they were solidly on the ground.

"Get out!" Jack yelled, jumping out of the car and around to Georgianna's side pulling her out so fast she thought her shoulder might be dislocated. He dragged her into the dark underbrush crashing through the thick forest beyond. After they were a ways from the crash site he turned back stooping low pulling her down with him peering at what was taking place back in the direction from which they had escaped.

They could barely discern three people in the dark converging on the downed vehicle, outraged at finding it empty of passengers—they could see one of them slammed the vehicle with their fist. The figures scanned the darkened forest in all directions and finally gave up, moving into the underbrush in the opposite direction away from where the two passengers hunkered down. Georgianna started to rise as the figures disappeared off into the forest thinking they were in the clear but Jack pulled her back down, his finger vertical over his silent lips. "Wait for a bit they might be watching to see if we return." He whispered.

"What happened?" Georgianna whispered back. "Who are those people Jack? Were we shot down or *what*?"

"The car has been illegally disengaged, but a distress call locator was sent out as we settled to the ground—they're not able to block that, so they won't hang around long." He didn't explain further or who *they* were. "We had better get moving as it seems we are what they're looking for."

With stealth, they crept away from their place of concealment and proceeded through the valley forest bracketed between a mountain ridge above them on the eastern side and a lesser ridge leveling out on the other. They continued the north easterly direction they had been travelling originally keeping well into the cover of the thicker parts of the forest. Moving at as fast a pace as they could in the dark they stumbled on slick moss-covered rocks and clawed their way through thorny undergrowth which made a speedy escape difficult. An hour later they seemed to have put the worst of the entanglements behind them.

Jack said. "We're actually close enough to the Lodge to make it on foot. It's not an easy hike for we need to go through a bit of a marshy area—cattails, reeds and such—the worst of the route has a lengthy footbridge. We'll be okay, I've done this before, hardly any snakes this time of year," he added, smiling in the dark at his little thorn thrown in.

Georgianna wasn't amused. Was he being cute or was this meant to be reassuring? She wasn't sure.

They tramped on in silence. Light from the star-strewn night sky was visible through the canopy of tree branches overhead. Shortly, they emerged within the border of the swamp verified by Georgianna sinking over her ankles in black mud. "Good g-r-rief, I'm in quicksand!" She hissed, clutching at Jack as she sank even deeper.

He grabbed both her arms pulling her up and away from the unstable ground she had fallen victim to. There was a sucking sound as she pulled each foot out of the fast grip of the mud. At least the slimy black stuff hadn't sucked her shoes off when she disengaged! A miracle in itself! How was she always able to keep on hats and shoes in even the most egregious situations?

"We're almost to the bridge." He said, pointing to a long elevated footbridge ahead. "Come on. This will bring us over the worst of it." He led them to a set of steps leading up to the surface of a narrow bridge of wooden slats. It had no safety railing, just a quick means of traversing the swamp. It was so narrow they had to walk single file.

Jack stopped suddenly, listening to *what*, Georgianna could not say, she feared they had been discovered. She scanned the abundant cattails and forest on both sides of the bridge seeing nothing. "What is it Jack, what is it?" She whispered, hearing nothing but owls hooting in the distance while other night prowlers seemed to answer with their own warnings.

He seemed to hesitate in answering. "I—think we're all right now. Once we get to the top of the ridge," he pointed up the mountainside above them, "then it's all downhill to the Lodge—easy enough for you barbaric Earth girl types," he teased, again smiling to himself in the dark, attempting to make light of their situation.

Not taking into consideration how very narrow the bridge really was, Georgianna shot back at him, "barbaric huh-huh?" giving him a hefty shove to the shoulder—too late to consider just how hefty. It was enough to put him off balance and over the bridge, at the last moment twisting and pulling Georgianna with him into the brackish mess of cattails below.

Recovering from the shock of their predicament they clawed their way through the mess alternately slipping and regaining ground as they held onto one another trying to get back upon the bridge.

In vain they grasped each other for support when Georgianna finally slipped on down under the bridge pulling Jack with her into the decomposing muck underneath. They struggled to regain at least the positions they had had and ended up facing one another on bended knee. A savage attack of ferocious kissing overtook them. Locked together in passions grip they fell over back into the muck again. Georgianna wrapped one leg around both Jack's incorporating a stand of cattails against the back of his legs in the process. No one was letting go of anyone.

Suddenly, a small creature with thick wet bristly fur slithered across their entwined legs spooking them into disengaging from such reptile-like ardour.

"Oh—oh—oh!" Georgianna squealed in revulsion. "Something is going to eat us if we don't get out of here!" She shoved Jack back away from her seeing his bewildered face faintly in the dark.

They wasted no more time scrounging around in the slimy muck. Georgianna threw one leg up on the bridge surface with little effort this time managing to pull herself up with instant success thanks to the rush of adrenaline brought on from the slick haired little animal whose home had been rudely invaded by the sudden thrashing around of the two trysting people. Jack was right behind her. Neither said another word as they made their way on across the bridge lickety-split looking for all the world like a Sasquatch couple so covered in black ooze and dead leaves they were. Only dazed and befuddled could describe their state of mind as they tramped on into the night, each, wondering just what raw wanton insanity had befallen themselves as they hiked up the mountain and on down the other side to the Lodge.

Georgianna showered for some time trying to *cleanse* herself from the swamp—such things as flesh-eating bacteria floated through her mind (such fear of deadly germs seemed to run in her family) reflecting on the possibilities of what they could have come in contact with in the slime they had rolled around in. She showered and scrubbed till she was red and at last felt reclaimed.

Jack, in his filthy state had, as soon as they had walked through the door of the Lodge secreted himself in the Lodge's library attending to the emergency he had left Paris to take care of in such urgency.

Georgianna was mystified at herself, unsure just what savage wantonness she had been a victim of—*completely* out of control, she just wanted to dismiss the incredulous attraction she and Jack had had for one another after falling off the footbridge as momentary insanity—after all, out of control was not part of a great actress's repertoire. She was still in shock at being so out of control—disgusted with herself for whatever it was that had overtaken her—what was she thinking? She wasn't sure she even liked Jack—his clandestine relationship with Canquetyne, a Vraang…the most vile and despicable of beings ever in existence as far as she knew. This was just biology, she told herself, nothing could stand in her way of going home—certainly not that—not biology! Rats—rats and rats! Georgianna wanted her mind cleaned out of these Jack thoughts!

She came downstairs dressed in more of Canquetyne's clothing. *What the hell!* Her own had in their escape into the forest, been left behind in the downed air car. She really didn't care anymore, for now, these pajama things were clean and dry.

Disquiet still hovered over Jack as he rushed past her on his way up the stairs, saying only, "I'll be down as soon as I shower—find something to eat, and we'll talk as soon as Ean arrives."

She set out what she found appetizing from the fridge onto the table in front of the fireplace and nibbled while Jack showered. Once again she found herself drawn to the fruit—she wondered if one could become a fruit junky. It was more than good and so-o-o satisfying, and—it made her feel terrific! She could hear the water running upstairs when a loud banging commenced on the front door, not a door alarm, but a loud banging. Why, she wondered, would Ean do this when he could enter at will?

Jack's voice rang out from upstairs. "It's Ean, I forgot to give him the new code—let him in if you would Georgianna!"

She put down the fruit she had been munching on and wiped her hands then cautiously opened the door expecting to see Ean.

Before she could protect herself, the figure in front of her puffed a spray of something into her face. An acrid odor filled her nostrils. She felt herself melting down to the floor as a black hood was being pulled down over her head. She struggled to remain conscious, attempting to call out—yet feeling no sound come out of her mouth. She could do nothing on her own behalf. She heard the door being quietly closed as she was dragged outside and then was picked up and carried by the man she remembered Dr. Frank addressing as Haran, back in the ruins.

Her last conscious thought was that of being placed in a vehicle—an air car, ascending and gaining altitude as she lapsed into darkness losing the fight.

C h a p t e r   T h i r t y   T h r e e

It was late. Dinner had long been over with at Dragons Roost. Thad and Prudence had left for town. Only Ombline, Ledger and Serpentine remained along with Peter and Zorloff. A discussion ensued. The topic of conversation was the cave entrance off the Old Coast Road and just what that could mean to them. It was necessary to know and there was only one way to find out. With Ledgers help they had almost completed a method for controlling all portal traffic on the planet by DNA identification, origin and the ability to block or transfer such traffic from or to, either the Steffington estate, Dragons Roost or Zorloff's lab in Sweden—a necessity for what would most likely follow if all went as planned. Peter had developed a time block to be used if necessary since the dangerous adventure involving his granddaughter and her fiancé David Stewart the previous summer. The portal transference technology and time travel were one and the same science—you control one—you control both. This included not only the Vraang's doings but any other. To interfere with linear time was something not even the Vraang cared to engage in as it could with the smallest change in the past alter negatively what they would do in the present. Time intervention could be deadly for anyone foolish enough to interfere with it as had been experienced by Ursula, Marc's deceased wife. For the moment though, they could only depend on a hands-on approach until this newer system was a go. They had to know what they dealt with at the cave site though. Could there be an unanticipated hindrance to their work? If so, it would be dealt with!

Ombline and Ledger were both adamant that they were the ones to carry out this clandestine surveillance. Marc was determined that Ombline was going nowhere near that place as Ledger felt the same, saying since he was young, agile and also a scientist it should be he who *"cased the joint"* as he had said in jest of the situation.

Serpentine had a better idea. "The caves location is not that far from my property. My ancestors were not town fathers—they were irascible pirates described in the brochures at Grey Hall. There was a secret underground way from the cliff's caves to the estate ending underneath my home, it's still accessible down through the cellars. I'm sure I have an old map of its ways, where it starts on each end etc., I can find it easily and be back in an hour." She didn't wait for discussions on the matter grabbing her coat and slipping into the night before anyone could protest this.

More coffee was drunk while they waited for Serpentine's return. Ombline and Ledger took a walk around Dragons Roost amazed at the growth of the trees they had just planted. They seemed to have doubled in size, loaded already with the fruit. They both pulled one from a tree and munched freely in the dark knowing now it was safe to do so.

"This is so delicious." Ombline said. "To think something that tastes so good can also change your life for the better. What do you think our world will be like if all this works Ledger?"

"I don't know, it would be difficult to anticipate what or how long it will all take to play out. It's so unimaginable—is this only a dream, I hope not, think not."

"I feel the same," Ombline said throwing the seed filled core back over the ridge behind Dragons Roost as headlights pulled up to the gate down on the road.

Serpentine's black Mercedes continued on up the drive parking with the other vehicles around back. The gate down below had closed quietly with the new self locking mechanism that had been installed and changed to one of Peter's design. She jumped out of her car carrying a thick folder and entered the building with the two young people in tow. Serpentine spread out the folder's contents on the table, some of the fragile documents were age yellowed and tattered. Peter and Ledger were examining several of the old yellowed pages when an exultant Serpentine exclaimed. "This is it! A map of the tunnel, I'm sure this is what we're looking for!" She spread it out for all to see.

It was brown and water marked with discoloration but obvious broken red lines indicated an underground route from land to water side and cliffs.

"Holy Moley!" Ombline exclaimed. "A real secret tunnel that leads right into Seurat's lair!"

Chapter Thirty Four

Ombline convinced a still reluctant and fearful Marc she would be an asset in reporting what they would find being a writer and observant of detail. He was distrustful of the whole thing being safe or sane, questioning the very idea that it was necessary. Finally he just threw up his hands in acquiescence. They were at least all in agreement that it would be best to do this in the wee hours before dawn thinking this was the most unlikely time anyone would be about in such a place.

The three adventurers, Ledger, Ombline and Serpentine set out for the Pendergast estate with the map after only a few hours sleep. They had dressed warmly and in dark clothes. Serpentine advised that the route down to the cave would be cold and damp; the way would be comprised of many steps carved and roughly cut in hard coastal stone nearly two centuries ago—in an unknown condition leading down toward the direction of the coast; it could be precarious. They would need to be watchful. If it became too dangerous they should return—another way of reconnaissance would have to be found.

The three adventurers all carried flashlights and cameras just in case any one of them lost theirs.

Peter had been adamant about the danger they could be in, that they should take no chances, just observe, photograph everything—do nothing—touch nothing, then get out!

At the Pendergast estate they walked through a heavy wooden door in back of the pantry off the kitchen, it had creaked with age, its wood swollen with damp when unlocked. It was weighty with iron fittings. They pulled the door shut behind them making their way down into the dark crumbling tunnel and cautiously proceeded in single file down into the unknown. Already the temperature had dropped and felt chill and dank.

The farther they went the more profound the smell of salt water became—ocean life—that of the sea. The route alternated between long stretches of flat areas and the steep rough steps downward, all the while curving south and then eastward. This, Ledger took specific note of, having brought a high-tech compass-pedometer to record the time and distance the trip was taking—the depth underground all along the route. One of the most important observations was to be sure they were arriving within the same location he and Ombline had discovered the night of her ride atop the delivery van.

Sooner than they had expected, they could hear the crashing sounds of the Atlantic on the rocks somewhere ahead. Almost immediately, their route opened into a small cave to their left, then at the end, narrowing and expanding into a much larger cavern that defused the sounds of the wind and waves—almost soundproof, strangely quiet. Darkness and the unknown prevailed.

In this moment unease overrode their sense of adventure, wondering if they were walking into some sort of trap.

Ledger shined his flashlight around the darkened cavern revealing an array of unfamiliar technical equipment. From what they could tell nothing was in use at the present, but the most significant site fronting them was astonishing in its unexpected beauty, a monstrous oval over fifteen feet in height comprised of crystals sparkling from the light shone on them from the flashlights of the three people. The crystals seemed to individually have a life of their own. This crystal frame too, like the blue one in Dragons Roost stood on a massive frame for support. This appeared to be some sort of metal the colour of pewter.

It vexed Ombline why they would need a portal so large if only people were transported through it—what else would it be used for? There was no time to discuss this, only take quick pictures of everything—this they did once again in triplet in case anyone lost theirs. Simple cameras were used not knowing if signal strength would even be evident underground.

Ledger's camera was different from the others, specific in its technology to measure heat, radiation and most importantly time-space differentials. Before they had left, he, Peter and Zorloff had discussed the specific requirements for what they would need to finalize the portal blockages and transferences. Anything brought to light would help.

Ledger worked quickly then froze, for a sound he had dreaded to hear caused him to whirl around to the way they had come. Footsteps echoed off the hard surfaces back in the smaller cave. He quickly stuffed the specialized camera down into his boot where it could still record three-dimensionally their surroundings and events through the very fiber of his boot, then quickly pulled out an ordinary small camera like the ones used by Ombline and Serpentine preparing before they had left for just such a scenario.

A voice of discovery came from the connecting entrance to the smaller cave they had just traversed. They had been discovered!

Three sinister figures, two men and a woman of self-possessed authority and intimidation confronted the three interlopers as lights flashed on throughout the cavern. Ledger had never seen Madame Seurat but from her description was sure this was she. Ombline of course was very familiar with her—the dispatcher of Georgianna. Darkness seemed to snake its way around Seurat's essence like a sort of malevolent smoke—a part of her hideous nature that always companied with her.

Her men had their guns trained on the three. Seurat carried with her a little black box that immediately came to life with an array of blinking lights, appearing to be the same one that Ombline was all too familiar with—the same as the one she had used to engage the portal in Dragons Roost.

The crystal frame came to brilliant life—a pearlescent spiral filled its frame. Ledger recognized the engaging of the control of time and space—felt its sharpness of crystallization in a controlled environment. He greatly feared what would come next—and rightly so.

Seurat triumphed, revealed by her affected smile. "The three of you will hand over your cameras to Washburn—*now!*" The quicksilver smile left her face being replaced by a mask of hatred.

The burly red-haired Washburn took their cameras stuffing them into his coat pocket and then silently retreated.

"Now." Madam Seurat smiled again that demonic smile that seemed to come and go with her in an instant. "I have a message for your people." She made adjustments quickly on the black box. A disruption within the crystal frame took place. Ledger could feel it intensify, the pearlescent glow deepened, swirling at what seemed to be a hurricane force within its frame—it seemed monstrous and threatening when engaged.

Again, Madam's face turned to one of vicious delight as she nodded to her henchmen.

"Take her!" She nodded to Serpentine.

Ledger came hard on at the two men intent on rescuing Serpentine. The beefy Washburn came at him knocking him to the ground as Madame Seurat pointed her gun in Ledger's direction all the while keeping a good distance between herself and the prisoners, giving Ledger the feeling later that she feared some sort of contamination from them. "Stay as you are she shouted at him directing the gun toward Ombline. "Or she will die."

Ledger slowly and reluctantly got to his feet as the evil woman indicated. She then waved her gun at Ombline, indicating for her to stand with Ledger away from the portal.

Serpentine struggled as the two men held her before the portal. Seurat's face had returned to its former mask. "If Zorloff ever wants to see Serpentine alive again, immediate cessation of his endeavours will be necessary."

At that she nodded to the two men. They cast Serpentine into the portal. She disappeared. Gone—their friend gone.

Satisfied, Madame Seurat turned to Ombline and Ledger. Vitriol contorted her face. "The two of you are free to go—go and deliver my message!"

The two men pointed back through the small cavern. Ledger and Ombline wasted no time on the route back up the underground tunnel to the estate and back to Dragons Roost with the dreadful news.

At least the specialized three-dimensional camera was still in Ledger's boot recording everything as it happened—they would need everything he had recorded if they were to recover another of their number.

A great sorrow played across the face of Zorloff at the news of the loss of Serpentine. He was consumed with anger at such a failure with what had seemed such a circumspect attempt at helping their cause. Even so—he was comforted by Peter's attitude that they must proceed with great haste regardless, assuring Zorloff that somewhere Serpentine was safe seeing as how Madame Seurat wanted to use her as blackmail against their efforts. In all their years of preparation for this one great moment they had known they might be confronted with such loss, even so, it was painful to bear for this man for he so loved Serpentine. What had for so long seemed a grand adventure was being replaced by reality.

The three scientists set to work at once with what Ledger had recorded—there would be no stopping them as the seed of the fruit was even now taking hold all over the world. This was *the* historical showdown mankind was to have! It *was* being done! And, Serpentine would be recovered! Peter assured them of these things laying his hand on Zorloff's shoulder understanding the depth of Zorloff's despair. He knew if this had been Mona he might not be able to be so rational as he was asking Zorloff to be.

For now, there was a comfort at least to Marc that it had not been Ombline that Seurat had taken. He did not like Ombline's seeming attitude that this was some great adventure that she could participate in free of deadly consequences. He was quiet and yes, fearful. What had they all allowed themselves to become part of—for the first time he was beginning to question this struggle, would it really be worth it—where would it end—and especially for his daughters and any others being barter for these evil people so easily.

Chapter   Thirty   Five

Georgianna slowly began to regain consciousness realizing that a head to toe covering of protective clothing was being pulled on her. The word HAZMAT came to mind. A separate hood was pulled down over head and pressed lightly around its edges to the body of the suit; the hood was fronted by a clear face screen. The two doing this, also wore the same suits they had pulled on her. She couldn't see their faces very well as they had struggled to put on Georgianna's suit. She was still woozy as she was lifted under her arms to stand by the two people then dragged to a black metallic oval ring about eight feet tall. In her foggy mind she thought this portal reeked of cheap—put up in a hurry—why was her mind zeroing in on such things?—was it the drugs they had given her or a for real observation?—she didn't know but she vowed to herself she would remember her impressions in case she got out of this; they could be important. She feared what would come next having been an unwilling participant in such technology before! A figure stepped in between her and the black frame, one immediately recognizable even through the view screen of Georgianna's suit—Canquetyne!

The Vraang woman said dismissively. "Take her through," and sped away saying only, "I'll be there myself shortly."

The black oval came to life with a dark purple glow. This was visually fear inducing for the portal at Dragons Roost had a sort of etheric beauty. This one appeared dark and draconian. The two men dragged her forward with them, all three entered. Georgianna felt sick with the swirling mass around her and her captors but tried not to throw up inside the suit, still, she was so sick! Was it just this portal or a result of the drugging? She feared where she was being taken. If they had wanted her dead she was sure she would have been—what did they intend doing with her? Where was she being taken to?

Shortly they emerged. Her two captors removed their headgear leaving hers intact. The light was painful to her eyes after being in the dark purple transference even with the view screen. The nausea was subsiding as she became more fully conscious and attempted to ascertain just where she was. Large oval windows looked out upon a city teeming with very dark buildings far into the distance. She seemed to be high above a city—a location of some prominence—for Vraang elite maybe?

For some reason she suspected that was where she was—on a Vraang world. Why, she felt that she could not say. It could result from Canquetyne's attitude of complete authority. She believed she had been brought into the midst of the Vraang stronghold—the home world. From the view through the oval view-ports of windows it was a place constructed of a most rigid and dark form of architecture.

The circular space they stood in was divided by the span of a five-foot wide chasm dropping down below through a multitude of floors, this she could see without any effort, a deadly drop without benefit of safety railing. What was the purpose of such a canyon down through the floors below? What was this place? It could freak her out if she allowed it to. After all she had gone through she was starting to learn how to control her fear better and concentrate on the moment and what had to be done.

The portal they had just exited continued to be in operation for it still contained the purple miasmic swirling energy that she believed had contributed to her nausea. Her captors didn't have to wait long for Canquetyne, for she came through in a rush ignoring Georgianna as if she didn't exist.

She spoke to the two men as she swept by. "Take her to the lab and chain her, my injection is becoming a hazardous burden. Keep a tight grip on her I can feel the fruit on her—she reeks of it. Go now and secure my newest lab rat."

With that she turned and smiled malevolently at Georgianna and then entered a door between two of the thick-walled oval windows.

Georgianna felt the evil of Canquetyne's words wash over her even in her new found attempt at controlling her fear. And— what was this negative effect being experienced by Canquetyne from her most recent injection? Was this a normal reaction for the third and last one, or, a bad reaction? Was she even now in search of antitoxin? This too could be helpful to know. She felt stronger addressing these things instead of giving in to her pumping adrenalin—be observant of every detail.

Georgianna was steered toward the chasm. Reluctance to go near such a drop filled her. Why would such a thing exist? One of her captors clicked a small hand-held unit at their approach resulting in a narrow link of flooring devoid of any sort of railing to shoot out bridging the space. They moved her slowly and carefully onto the bridge, one in front and one behind, to where, she knew, she was to be Canquetyne's lab rat. *This* she was *not* going to be—*not gonna do it!* She looked back at the portal gate, it was still operational. If she could manage to get to it, it would most likely be the route back to Irrieth.

Her chance had to be now, there would be no other. Her hands were free; with her captors in front and back of her she would have only this moment to save herself. She reached up to her head piece frenetically yanking on it finally able to rip it off from her head flinging it to the depths below. The man in front of her turned to see what was happening and in an instant she blew breath on the man's face causing him in his fear of her fruity breath to fall to the depths below, vaporizing on the way down. The horrified man in back of her shoved her on across the chasm, all too late, for once across she quickly turned and came at him too, blowing her fruity breath into his face before he could reattach his head covering; terror filling his eyes as he evaporated before her.

Georgianna stood safely on the other side of the chasm just as Canquetyne emerged wearing a lab coat from a door between two oval windows now on Georgianna's side of the chasm. Georgianna could see the fury upon Canquetyne's face realizing in the absence of Georgianna's head covering what must have happened. The Vraang's hand flew up to the wall at her side hitting a button withdrawing the drawbridge over the chasm.

In this most grave of moments Georgianna dared risk it all as she backed up against the wall and prepared to leap the empty space between herself and freedom. She knew she could do this. She had played the Black Swan in Swan Lake having attended an all girls' school. She was chosen for her ability to take great flying leaps that no one else was capable of. Her most adored ballet teacher Mme. Lietzke had taught her a trick for practicing her leaps through the air to rival that of the fabled Phoenix. She had practiced running as fast as she could toward a wall attempting to run up it and then at the last moment flipping around and using the wall as a springboard into the air as a bird in flight.

This had been her claim to fame. Such a leap Mme. Lietzke proclaimed she had never before witnessed.

Now this unusual talent of Georgianna's must save her life.

With the fear of death or worse facing her, Georgianna pulled up her right knee in a flash of time placing her foot flat behind her on the wall and with a great launch propelled herself faster, harder, even higher than she ever had for her ballet teacher soaring with the grace of a giant bird high into the air and out over the chasm with only inches to spare on the opposite side to freedom.Canquetyne howled in furious rage at losing her lab rat as Georgianna, airborne, flew over the chasm and escaped. She was in such momentum of force and intent she couldn't stop nor did she intend to, but continued on with one more great and final leap diving headfirst into the swirling abyss of the dark purple portal, wherever it led. Mme. Leitzke would have been proud of her!

Chapter Thirty Six

All the animals in the encroaching darkness of the autumn forest remained still and quiet—even the great owl who never feared its own voice. Their domain had been briefly invaded by an oval of foggy brightness spewing out the form of a dark clad woman. She did not fall to her knees or roll out as if pushed but stepped lightly into a new environment making a soft crunching sound on the recently dropped autumn leaves of the still forest. Fear did not hold her, but aggravation at her circumstances did.

She turned back toward the direction from which she came and angrily kicked up a storm of leaves. Serpentine Pendergast was infuriated that she, Ledger and Ombline had been caught and she as barter dispatched to this world—*wherever* it was. Mainly, she was angry that most likely she would not be present for the culmination of all they had planned for these many decades. Always she had been in the thick of it—the plotting and intrigue—living on the edge, such was her fuel of life. Whatever her lot, she would find her way home from this place. Peter and Zorloff would not allow her being taken to interfere with their plans. Long ago they had discussed such possibilities as this many times and each participant understood and accepted the dangers involved. They had saved samples of all their respective DNA and that of all those close to them for just such as this that she now found herself in. That would facilitate their tracking just which parallel world she had been shunted off to, in the meantime her survival would be her own doing.

Dusk was edging into the full indigo of night—a night with stars visible up through the tree branches overhead. Dried autumn leaves still clung tenaciously to the branches rustling in a gentle wind through the treetops. The night sky was clear and free of any cloud cover. The star patterns were not quite the ones she was familiar with anywhere on Earth—similar, but yet, not exactly the same. Only a soft glow remained along the distant horizon which she believed must be a westerly direction. She heard the soft twittering of small animals finally losing their fear enough to question what had just happened in their world, but, with the coming night all avian life would naturally be quiet anyway, this was their time to tuck their heads under their wings and sleep with the onset of darkness.

Serpentine wondered if this parallel world had any geologic similarity to her own. This was certainly not the seacoast she had left. It seemed in the increasing darkness that she was on a high point of a rolling mountainous region—no lights of civilization were visible in any direction. Conceivably, she was concerned that this was not a world technologically advanced enough to illuminate itself against the dark—medieval, or worse. She realized time would not necessarily be in sync with her own either. Although, it did appear to be autumn here too from what she could tell. She had left before dawn, the sun was just finished setting here. What did that mean? A world far down or up on a scale comparable to Earth time? She had no way of knowing. The glow of her watch in the dark told her nothing. It was in sync with what it would have been at home she determined.

She decided to keep moving as her energy was still high—better to be on the move in the cover of darkness so she could exercise a sort of reconnaissance without being discovered. It would be necessary to take on an identity of the locals until she could assist Zorloff in placing her location; then, they could set up a portal for her extraction home. She knew all this would be tricky—but such things they had planned for and were capable of carrying out, but for now she would be on the move as location would be no obstacle to her assisting in her own rescue. She was just so damned disappointed that she might have to miss it all.

In the distance the hooting of owls could be heard dispensing with their chosen camouflage of quiet to declare their hunting territory once again. Serpentine carefully tramped through the forests heavy underbrush maintaining a north easterly direction considering where the sun had set. She thought of all the forested regions of her own Earth that would fit the same geologic identification here—none in particular came to mind—there were many. On a parallel world similar to Earth, this could be any continent. She still had her flashlight inside her jacket but knew better than to expose herself with its light.

She continued, slowly making her way through the dark, sometimes being snagged by brambles and tripping over fallen tree branches. The night air was cold and this difficult trek in the dark forest would soon sap her energy. The terrain eventually began a gentle descent toward what in the dark looked to be a rolling plain, fewer trees, more of a meadow-like hillside. She stopped for a short break to consider her progress. Sticking her hands in the pockets of her jacket she was surprised to find an energy bar which she broke in half and chewed slowly saving the rest for later if the worst came about—that any sort of civilization was far away or nonexistent. Thirst was beginning to gnaw at her, but for now she forced herself to avoid thoughts of water. She knew water always ran down hill and expected to find a stream eventually.

The careful hiking in the dark (as the moon was just rising on the far distant horizon) was becoming exhausting, farther ahead thick forestry began again. Crossing several gullies on the hillside it was necessary to wade through washes of fallen leaves to enter once more the thicker growth of trees for she knew it to be to her advantage to still be in the cover of the forest when the sun came up. She had to soon release her body and mind to the peace of sleep. Eventually a grove of trees were the cover for a mound of boulders that would make a better temporary shelter than the bare ground. She crawled beneath an overhang of rock giving a sense of protection. What else might shelter here she dare not dwell on and curled up and slept until the breaking dawn brought her fully awake and somewhat refreshed, then continued on in the same direction after savouring the rest of the energy bar.

Daylight not being fully engaged yet and defeating to one so used to the caffeine from a good cup of coffee, she set out in the same direction she had chosen the night before, only to lurch forward on some slimy squishy things in her path downward to the plain below. As she jumped and leaped in an effort to stay upright she could see there was a slide of fallen fruit in a gulley wash down the hillside. She was finally able to stop with one last leap to the side jumping away from the slash in the ground. With the sun almost above the horizon now she could tell she had stumbled on a swath of the ripe blue fruit that had fallen from the trees above. That had not been discernible in the dark. She was surprised that she had not been cognizant of the presence of the trees as she had made her way through the forest during the night.

At least for now she believed this was no Vraang controlled world—*good for humans, bad for Vraang.* The fruit, she knew, could save her from dying of thirst until she found water and proceeded to sort out such pieces as were not damaged by their fall to the ground, devouring two right away then stuffed more inside her jacket for later. In doing this Serpentine discovered she had lost the flashlight—maybe back at the rock overhang or avoiding the slippery gully ruts, wherever—there was no use looking for it now. She felt completely reinvigourated by the fruit and wandered on till midmorning. The land had leveled out to a more rolling countryside with fewer groves of trees and soon came upon the sound of rushing water. She followed the sound to its source.

The water raged along its banks as if fed by a recent storm. She bent down to the swollen torrent drinking her fill. Satiated, she sat back on her heels admiring the prolific scenery around her. This was certainly a beautiful country—rolling hills doted with forestry. Eventually she lay back on the grassy bank above the stream soaking in the warm sun. Serpentine was in that most relaxed of states just between wakefulness and sleep when a deep male voice full of authority and accusation bellowed in her direction. "Woman, you're trespassing in the forbidden forest—full no doubt of the cursed blue fruit. You will be tested as one of the revolutionaries!"

Before she could get up, two black-uniformed men, some sort of armed guards, dragged her to her feet to stand before her accuser, a hefty official similarly clad but obviously the superior of the other two. His dark red beard and moustache bristled as he dictated what he had vowed his duty to be in such a case of trespassing—one of punishment. Once again Serpentine had been captured by someone, this time too, there was no doubt about it, this, did not look good. What was going on here? Were the Vraang trying to keep control where the fruit had just recently gained a foothold by violently enforcing the population to accept that the fruit was deadly? That had been tried elsewhere, but there was no being rid of the fruit once it established itself. Their attempts to do away with it were always futile in that regard. In no time people always fully realized its benefit and the Vraang were always the losers; sometimes that had been a deadly process in the sorting of it. In the meantime, she could be one of the casualties of the Vraang's attempts at damage control. She had to think fast, was it better to escape now or after they transported her to a place of holding (providing there was no immediate execution) she decided to chance it and wait, for if she had to be here in this world for a space she needed to be in a civilized part of it. She allowed herself to be towed back up from the stream to a road she had missed in her hurry to get to water. The conveyance they approached was startling in its incongruity for it appeared to be a highly stylized version of a coach of sorts—if you wanted one that encompassed a high-tech appearance. It had wheels of a metallic spoke design, the coach itself long and pointy at the front and back. Neutral coloured metals formed the body. But strangely enough there were no animals to pull it!

This place seemed to be ahead of, and in back of it's self. What had happened? A sort of twisting of reality—the timeline itself maybe. Serpentine was roughly shoved into the coach by her captors after having had some sort of small hand held tube-like sensor run over her from head to toe. Red beard nodded to one of his subordinates indicating she had passed whatever it was they scanned her for. Was it the fruit? If so, they certainly hadn't detected it inside her jacket! She did not know, but held her tongue not familiar with how things worked with these people thinking it best to remain silent for now—revealing nothing that could possibly worsen her situation. The fruit in her jacket could be an asset as long as it went undetected—or condemn her eventually since she was accused of being full of the stuff as if she were some sort of serious lawbreaker! Two of her captors climbed into the coach behind her, the third man climbed to the front top of the futuristic coach and engaged the vehicle. It moved slowly at first and then rose off the ground and into the air! The view from inside the coach was one of building speed up over forested countryside similar to that of Europe or the British Isles. Occasionally they passed over small towns below. She attempted to engage the two men in the coach with her in conversation to see what she could learn. This was futile and soon gave up. They stared straight ahead ignoring her as if robotic or conditioned. An hour later the coach slowed but kept a consistent speed as if approaching an inhabited locality where speed would not be acceptable. She began to see buildings similar in style to those of medieval Europe only more grandiose—newer—more recently established. Flags of colourful standards flew in the breeze from every turret along the way as they began to descend.

The coach slowed even more now as if in reality horses truly did pull it, not this unknown power source. They were entering the center of a magnificent walled city, one modeled after European castles clustered upon a central high hillock most likely the seat of a governing body.

The vehicle slowed, hovered and finally settled to the surface of a busy cobblestone boulevard in front of a tan stuccoed block style building, austere in its execution compared to the pageantry of the other structures surrounding it except for its colonnaded pillars fronting its several stories. *Was this a place of judgment—imprisonment—even execution?* Serpentine knew it most likely was.

One of her guards stepped down out of the vehicle indicating for her to do likewise. The other one followed. Immediately an armband of red metal was placed around her upper arm, its chained end was connected to the wrist of the red bearded man who towed her through hefty rust-brown metal doors into the buildings interior and on through another set of similar doors, then down a hallway supported by wooden arches reaching high above. Tall double doors lined the long hall on both sides reminiscent of offices of governmental affairs of state. Guards stood on either side of some.

Before one of the guarded doors they stopped. The guard leaned forward and opened it for them to enter. A court room scene dominated the far end of the space. Still nothing was said. Serpentine and her jailer moved toward but stood a goodly distance in front of a high ornate bench such as those in Earth's civilized countries where judges presided over those before them.

Shortly, a clean-shaven man of stark skull-like bone structure entered dressed in flowing purple robes and a square flat headpiece followed by a guard in black. The man in the purple robes seated himself in the chair of authority with his guard standing quietly in attendance.

Serpentine knew this was not looking good, she could only hope for a delayed execution, that they didn't just take you out and *off* you right away!

The official she was connected to edged only one step closer fronting the robed one as if forbidden to get too close. A metal railing in front of the raised dais prevented their standing in the immediate vicinity of the judiciary—justice was apparently done at some distance. Was the man in judgment of her Vraang, needing protection from any sort of contamination by the fruit? Interesting. Serpentine mused to herself.

"Honourable executioner." Her guard began.

There it was! Everything she had feared—no defense—just a proclamation of her guilt and voilà, get popped at this so-called exalted ones discretion.

The red bearded man said. "This woman was found in the forbidden Forest of Kirth. She is here for your dispensation of execution in the group for tomorrow." Serpentine's heart beat rapidly. Apparently this was the worst thing you could do on this world—be caught in the forest of Kirth! Worse even than murder—an indefensible crime demanding the ultimate punishment! So—the Vraang were somehow holding tight here!

"I condemn you woman!" The robed one on high bellowed. "On the morrow you will join the group of revolutionaries to meet your fate in the center square of Handeleine." He angrily continued. "The blue fruit trees of the forest encroach upon the city ever closer surrounding us and ever more you revolutionaries assist in their dispersal to destroy us, your betters!

Now you will pay for your crimes. How many of us have evaporated before the eyes of all because of the accursed blue fruit and yet you continue."

How, she wondered, had they not discovered the fruit inside her jacket if that was what that scanning procedure had been about?

His voice reverberated in hatred off the hard walls of cruel justice in this supposed courtroom. "Take her to the dungeons with the others." He commanded his attendant in black beside him, waving dismissal to the two before him.

All the while Serpentine had begun to wonder why no one had searched her for the fruit physically knowing how it was a death sentence to the exalted Vraang—was it just oversight— how even now could they be so oblivious to the presence of something so deadly in such close quarters—why had they placed such unassailable faith in that little scanner? Well, if executed she was going to be, it might as well be for something really egregious. There was slack in the red line to her captor. She edged a little closer to the railing before the executioner's bench. She knew she had to be fast, at least it was her right arm attached to the grizzled man beside and a little forward of her—lucky she was a southpaw and a dead on base ball pitcher of some renown in her youth—how all of a sudden handy! Slowly she raised her left hand as if to wipe her face, then, in a flash pulled out an overripe piece of the fruit flinging it hard into the executioner's face dead on before any could stop her. It smashed into a juicy blue and orange pulp covering his face and running down his neck into his robe.

The guard froze as terror gripped the face of the esteemed executioner. He gasped for breath as the molecular structure of his physical body disengaged. His countenance grew pale and quickly began to evaporate before them leaving only the purple robes of court and some under things on his chair of authority. Serpentine was quickly disconnected from her captor, dragged away out of the courtroom, brutally shoved to the end of the hall by the guard in black into the darkness of dungeons below. He was no Vraang as his molecular structure still held. She was thrown roughly into a single cell alone. The harsh metal sound of the locking mechanism brought home her hopeless state. She could see the faces of other prisoners in cells across from hers. Their silence was deafening in meaning. She came up to the bars holding one in each hand, her face between.

"Anyone have any ideas how to get out of here?" Her voice rang out hollowly against the walls. No one spoke.

"Just thought I'd ask." She yelled out sarcastically, angry at the fine mess she found herself in. She turned back and sat on the filthy pallet against the back wall drawing her knees up with her chin resting on her arms across them.

As time went on, she tried repeatedly to get her fellow prisoners to communicate with her. *Surely, if they all expect to be executed in the morning why keep quiet now?*

As the day came to an end there was no water or food given them for what she thought would be at least their last meal. Thirst was again racking her existence—it was hard to put aside. Still, no one spoke, so finally she lay on the filthy pallet and drifted off in an exhausted sleep covered with her jacket no longer containing fruit. They had made sure of that after she killed her Vraang executioner.

She wondered why the guards willingly served Vraang who they must know would use, and dispose of them as they chose— none of their population had anymore hope of a future than these people imprisoned around her. Most likely their loved ones were held hostage to get cooperation from them; it had sounded like the Vraang's days were numbered as the executioner had said the city was surrounded by the advancement of the trees—the revolutionaries had tried to infiltrate the city with seeds and/ or fruit, thus, the mass executions of anyone importing it. The Vraang surely had no plan other than hostages, so, how did they hope to escape? This could only go on for so long before the fruit won out.

Serpentine awoke later in the evening, thirst a hot knife in her throat. She could tell it was late, dark, for the two barred slits of windows at each end of the corridor of her damp dark prison were devoid of day light, still no food or water. She had come to realize there would be none. The adrenaline of suffering would provide any Vraang present at the executions with Sesca. There would surely be a portable collector at the event just from the fear of the prisoners and onlookers.

Darkness dominated, for there were no lights in the dungeon. She felt she understood why no one talked, they were intent on controlling their fear, hence, no adrenaline. It was an attempt as their last act to deny the Vraang their Sesca—strong people! She imagined that would be the same practice of tomorrow's crowd of onlookers; she did not feel she could do this herself. Another fear took hold of her. They would most likely be subjected to a most painful execution, one which would produce adrenaline from all those concerned regardless of how practiced they were at control.

Many forms of execution filled her with an admitted fear realizing escape was nigh to nothing from what she could tell for now. She considered her options, none of which seemed hopeful. There were no guards to bribe or foil, they were just locked away down in the dungeons to rot like winter vegetables in this cold filthy place till tomorrow.

Chapter Thirty Seven

Chloe Steffington, soon to be Steffington-Stewart jogged alongside the black-topped country road in between her and her fiancé David Stewart's home, the Château Rose, and the resort town of Broyles, France. Autumn held a tenacious grip on the land although few leaves still clung to the trees partially lining the road; many skittered across her path as she ran by.

The day had been beautiful, a clear blue sky dotted with a few clouds, and she knew, a deceitful warmth for this time of year. She and David had lunched out-of-doors at Le Cigne Noir (a local restaurant prominent in their past) and realizing since this would be their last visit here until just before Christmas she would enjoy one last jog through this place she so loved and left David after lunch to run the country roads of the area, for later in the afternoon, they would leave for Paris to return to the states.

Peter Steffington, Chloe's grandfather, had sent an urgent message for her and David to return to the states at once, saying only that an emergency of monumental proportion required David's expertise, adding that he could not emphasize enough the necessity for extreme vigilance in the meantime. He went on to say that all would be explained upon their arrival and *no*, none of their loved ones were in danger, but not to *dally* as he put it.

David had some last-minute legalities to take care of in Broyles. The two planned to meet back at *The Rose* as they called their home—La Petite Chateau Rose, the proper historical name of the structure. The building was undergoing renovations to update the interior with all the comforts of modern life without destroying its integrity. The contractor in charge of the renovations had promised to have it ready before the Christmas holidays. Chloe wanted to arrive back just before to decorate for Christmas. This would be their first and forever home together; she wanted it to hold all the magic for them that she could create.

They had shared a great romantic adventure in the Château Rose at the end of summer, one neither could ever have conceived of being involved in. The place had captured their hearts as they had each other. Chloe had been awakened from her life as she once put it, a life of slumber, with everything in its place—a life with no hardship, one of extreme ease, as a matter of fact—one so perfect, it had given her a feeling of unease as no one's life was meant to be so; for she knew that without obstacles there is to be no progress of the soul. As she had matured, this was a fear she recognized and kept to herself.

Now, on this glorious autumn day she would not allow fear to intrude. Peter had said *all* were fine. That was always her greatest fear, of losing those she so loved, that, she put this aside and concentrated on this glorious moment in time being one with a place she was part of.

She had already packed and need only shower and change as she and David planned to leave his black Citroen at the station in Broyles and take the late train to Paris, then an overnight flight on to Boston with a small town on the New England coast their final destination—Smugglers Cove, as Peter had indicated. He added that Ledger, a member of his scientific team and Chloe's beloved cousin Ombline Patrone would be waiting at the airport to transport them back to Smugglers Cove.

Chloe suspected something big was about to take place as it seemed this was almost some sort of *clan* gathering. David had been low key and within himself since Peter's urgent message, seemingly preoccupied and saying little at lunch. She was sure he knew more from Peter's inferences about being vigilant than he had voiced to her. It seemed that most of her life she was always the last to know. It had been, she knew, a tact of her family to protect her; but she did not need such protections anymore. She wanted to participate in whatever was needed—she had extremely valuable skills as an information gatherer, after all, she *was* a detective of sorts. Her position of unearthing the whereabouts of lost art from the early twentieth century gave her access to much out of the way knowledge not available to others—some of it astonishing in relevancy to historical events. There was also an element of intuition attached to the work she did, sending her on paths of disclosure that technology sometimes could not. Her research (and the grand adventure she and David had been involved in at the end of summer) had contributed to saving all their lives by exposing the plans of a group of dark scientists bent on the destruction of them all. She just resented the fact she supposed, that those she so loved were always protecting her from things she would rather take part in, as if they sought to forever protect her from their truths by refusing knowledge of, or protection from participating in such clandestine affairs as had surely been the centerpiece of their lives for a long time!

There had only been two small cars pass her since she had left the café and started her run. The grey sweats she wore were beginning to feel too warm. She ran two kilometers west past Château Rose and now rebounded back with only a few hundred meters to its small drawbridge. She heard the low hum of a larger engine down the road behind her. Turning, she saw it was a black SUV of a sort she did not recognize. Its windows were blacked out preventing her from seeing its passengers. She stepped off the blacktop to let it pass—it didn't—only slowed alongside her then stopped. She had no time to understand what was happening as two men in black tight fitting hoods jumped out from either side of the vehicle and grabbed her as she fought viciously to free herself. She was crammed in the back and quickly subdued as a syringe was plunged into her neck. Everything went black.

Far down the road David's black Citroen barreled down the road toward the van where he could see the great love of his life was struggling to free herself from abductors. He was too late. The van screeched past him tearing into his driver-side door and running him off the road down an embankment as it sped away.

He had no time to get a license number. The dark vehicle had already disappeared toward Broyles. He called for emergency help. Gendarmes arrived on the scene as David related Chloe's abduction and the best description he could give while he tried to extricate his vehicle from the ditch intending to take up the pursuit himself. He knew though, it would take a tow truck to do this and screamed at the officials who did not yet understand the circumstances he demanded they attend to as if they *purposely* did not understand.

He did not believe that they didn't see the black SUV that would have had to have sped past their car. He wanted to go with them to search for Chloe. This was against the law to take a private citizen in a police car on patrol so they said, but they did alert all law enforcement officials—of course Interpol so they said too. David was beside himself and beginning to question anything he was told by these people, especially the part about Interpol being notified—that, he felt sure would not have happened so soon. It was as if they purposely delayed. He waited helplessly as they sat in their car talking, not able to hear what they talked about, seeming to certainly take their time glancing suspiciously over their shoulders at him. He wondered if they had been paid not to notice the vehicle as it sped away, and, take their time giving Chloe's abductors time to get too far away to catch up to them. He felt they had been put in place to stall the process. In anger and frustration he kicked the door of their vehicle calling them a name better left unsaid as he was reminded of this with a threat of arrest.

He knew that was all that could be done for now. He called Peter. He couldn't leave for Boston now in case there was news of Chloe. He intended to search for her himself, for in his sorrow, fear and distress he had to do something!

Peter disagreed. "It's imperative you come on to Boston as fast as you can get here. There is nothing you can do there now—but here you can—you see, we know who has her—she is no longer accessible to you without the assistance of our group here! We have someone who is on it. Trust me David, she's my granddaughter and I want to find her as surely as you do. This can be done but we need your help!"

David relented and started the trip to Smugglers Cove.

Chapter Thirty Eight

Chloe was regaining consciousness. She felt she had been riding for hours but couldn't tell for sure, her full awareness was returning, but decided to pretend to still be out in case they would take another jab at her. In her predicament she would be her only and best defense—better to lay low for now, for they had not bothered to bind her with the use of the drug.

She could tell they drove a mountainous road by the swaying from side to side and the constant feel of the upward incline of the vehicle; she didn't know how long she had been out. She believed their destination to be somewhere in the western mountains of Austria or Switzerland—possibly foothills. She tried to allay her fears and concentrate on what she *could* do. For now there was nothing until they arrived at whatever destination they had in mind. The people who had abducted her had made no conversation between themselves which seemed odd.

Wondering at the strangeness of this, she felt the vehicle begin to slow and seemed to come almost to a stop as the grating sound of something metallic could be heard moving aside, then, they moved forward. A clanging sounded behind the SUV as they went on through whatever it was, most likely a gate of some sort.

The vehicle rolled to a stop. Fear she could no longer keep a grip on threatened to expose her but still she lay inert. Her captors yanked open the tailgate lifting her under the arms and dragging her to a giant metallic looking oval covered in rough cut crystals. It seemed they had driven into a cavern carved from rock, natural or manmade, there was no way to know—a place of secrecy; it had to be in the Alps somewhere she felt. It was huge inside and low-lit with the intermittent sound of something like giant fan blades coursing somewhere giving rise to the impression that it was necessary to draw in air from outside.

Chloe could no longer pretend the drug affected her, for a presence so diabolical that it defied description stepped in front of the crystal ring—it was the one person in Chloe's life that had provoked her to violence in the life-threatening adventure she and David had been drawn into at the end of summer—Madame Seurat—her old foe!

The woman smiled malevolently at Chloe. "My dear, you and I have so much to catch up on if I so chose, but alas, your disappearance will serve me better—so—!" She snapped her fingers at the two men restraining Chloe as Seurat's face changed in an instant from one of triumphant gloat to one of pure evil venom.

Chloe said nothing, there was no reason to give Madame Seurat even the satisfaction of a response. The crystal ring as yet gave no indication of what it did—was she to be vaporized or what? The double ring of crystals of her grandfather Peter's lab that had resulted in she and David's being transported back to 1937 France in their personal rendezvous with danger had been an overhead array over a sizable plate of Lapis Lazuli—this arrangement reflected a similarity, yet vertical. This was, she knew, another version of space-time technology displacement; but to where did they intend she go and for what reason, just to camouflage her existence? Blackmail she was sure—but as barter for what? Or, some other purpose? She had wished Peter would once and for all just lay it all out but knew instinctively that he had not been completely forthcoming with her. She was tired of always being the one not in the loop of things she became caught up in.

Nothing more was said. A fleeting glimpse of what Madame Seurat held assured Chloe a technology was being engaged. The evil woman snapped her fingers at Chloe's captors. She was dragged to stand in front of what she now knew was a portal transport to somewhere else—just where that would be she rightly feared. Would she ever be able to return home—even survive? These fruitless thoughts stopped as light crawled, snaking its way around the inner crystals finally fully engaged creating a field of pearlescent writhing.

She had not been prepared to be so roughly shoved into it and was shocked when it happened. A cold timeless void with a sort of pulling seemed to encapsulate her in an existence in limbo. No spark of understanding could be felt. It happened so fast, there was no time to reference the transition from one place to another when abruptly she found herself in a dark forest of trees towering overhead to great heights. She turned, looking back to the spot she had been expelled from seeing nothing to indicate anything unusual. It was fully night, for faint stars could be seen through the mighty branches above. She stood frozen to the spot she had been deposited on wondering just what sort of place this was.

The very first step she took propelled her down an incline unseen in the dark. She slid on pungent slimy lumps that she took for fruit considering the alluring aroma and the seeming mushy ripeness of some. The stuff was all over her butt, feet and elbows. Her sweats felt soggy, sticky and gross which for Chloe an admitted clean freak was torture—and, her butt hurt—again reminiscent of a previous engagement with Seurat's people.

She shakily climbed to her feet in shock at her sudden fall down this hill upon arrival. She tried to scrape off as much of the lumpy pulpy fruit stuck to her as she could. The night air was more than chilly especially now that she was wet with fruit pulp all over her sweats. She seemed to shake uncontrollably—whether from fear, trauma or the residual effects of the drug wearing off or all three. Why could she never get into *clean* scrapes like Poirot—a true, armchair detective? Her lot in *field* detective work had always turned out to be more like that of Clouseau or Colombo. These had been her stand-by comparatives forever—they all just seemed to always fit her circumstances. All her life she'd had a penchant for physical mishaps. Ballet had not helped, nor as Ombline and Georgianna chided her would she ever be a finishing school grad! She began to pick her way down the hillside as best she could in the dark. The moon appeared to be close to the finish of its night's trajectory and helped little, so wherever she was, morning was surely not too far off. Barely visible at the bottom of the long hillside was a road following the banks of a winding stream noisy with swollen water. She intended to follow the road when she reached the bottom to ascertain just where and/or *when* she was.

Terror raced through her as a hand came from behind covering her mouth, and another around her midsection pulling her back onto the ground and into the underbrush. She was kept quiet as down below a strange vehicle passed slowly on the road sweeping the hillside above with a light beam in the direction where she lay confined by her captor. It made no sound. A man rode astride a seat at the top front as would a stagecoach driver but this was no stage coach!

Was she on the wrong side—should she try to break free to be found by the searcher with the light or remain calm with the person behind her? *Who were the good guys?*

A male voice whispered in her ear. "Quiet! The Vraang murderers are searching the fruit forest for more victims to burn at the great execution only hours from now—do you want to be one?"

Chloe's eyes were wide at his words and adamantly shook her head sideways with his hand still over her mouth and the other tightly around her midsection.

The sweeping light withdrew and moved on down the road splaying its light on into the darkened forest as it went. She damn sure knew she was not on earth! As little as she knew of the fantastic science Peter was engaged in she believed she was in some other sort of existence, a parallel world maybe, certainly not her own and in that moment her hopes of ever returning home certainly seemed dashed! Her heart lurched, filled with such forlorn loneliness and loss as she couldn't have ever imagined enduring—to never again see any of one's loved ones—to be so alone in a new existence of such strangeness as she had so far witnessed—if ever there was a way home she would find it!

The coach vehicle slowly disappeared down the road into the dark of the night. Her captor slowly stood, pulling her up with him. "Hurry now, we go to join the lady's forces, you will have to go with us." He pushed her ahead of him on back up the hillside she had slid down. He kept his hand on her back to keep that from happening again.

Her heart was racing from fear and the excitement of what he seemed unconcerned with, divulging to her—of the plans of this, *Lady* person. What was she caught up in—some sort of revolution? Whose side had she been scooped up to be on? *If you don't know the players*—she huffed to herself, for now they both clambered up rocks almost as steep as a cliff. She had no time to complain.

Thankfully, she had on her best running shoes not the usual heels such a girly girl as herself (well only a little bit) could be found wearing. Swimming, running and bicycling she varied to keep fit and their rock climb proved no effort, but where were they headed—civil combat of some sort? They finally reached the ridges summit covered by more of the gargantuan trees avoiding patches of the blue fruit that had, in over ripeness, fallen from the fruit-laden branches—the aroma very pervasive considering the fruit paste she now wore.

Her captor took her hand in an unyielding grip, pulling her along a vague pathway for a distance, finally following it down the other side of the ridge into an unlit valley below. She saw people in a frenzy of activity loading the same sort of metallic coaches she had seen back on the road with what looked to be weapons along with large baskets of the fruit. What was going on here—fruit as a weapon—was it poison? If it was she should be dead by now considering how much she wore! Yes, this was a very strange place!

They seemed to find her a curiosity glancing her way in their haste. Shortly all seemed finished and in readiness. Everyone gathered around her, her captor and the man who seemed to be their leader fronted her shining a light upon her face. They were all dressed in high-tech black fitted uniforms with metallic skull caps—a fearsome group they appeared. A look of disbelief crossed the leader's face as he stepped back, questioning what he saw. Her captor took a kind of flashlight of his own shining it over Chloe's face again, she was afraid to move, immobile in its light. The black clad leader came closer, "Lady—Lady Arianne, what are you doing here? Our understanding was to meet you in Handeleine at the appointed time have you changed plans? Why are you dressed like that and without chainmail?" He stepped back looking her up and down suspicious in his assessment of her condition.

"I—I beg your pardon? I'm not this lady Arianne you speak of—my name is Chloe, and," she paused, not knowing whether to mention the fact that she was new here or not but thought it a more positive approach to *fess-up*! "I'm not—from around here!" She watched his reaction, had this been a mistake?

Someone among the group of similarly garbed men shouted. "The only way to know is keep our appointment with the lady and the others. She'll have to accompany us. Let Lady Arianne sort it out. Look at the sky." He pointed back up to the ridge. "Dawn breaks, we must leave now! The burnings start soon."

Shouts of agreement rang out as their leader turned to the man who had found Chloe. "Put her in the last coach." He turned to the crowd. "We go!" He shouted. "To the liberation of Handeleine and its people—death to the Vraang!"

The group of revolutionaries piled into the armed coaches. Chloe was installed in the last one to leave. She was in awe when the vehicle silently rose off the ground. The tops of trees were visible below as they flew over them in a north easterly direction toward the first rays of the rising sun.

What kind of place was this—flying coaches, revolutionaries who took big containers of fruit with them into battle along with their weapons (she still didn't know which was the right side to be on—although, if they burn people in mass (the other side that is) this was definitely the side she wanted to be on)!

Chloe tried making a connection with the men in the coach. She felt there was no harm in telling the truth at this point. She ventured, "I was drugged and found myself here in the forest." She didn't mention the portal not knowing how something like that would go down with these people. "How did you know I was here and so soon?" No one replied to her question, silently they continued to stare out the coach windows ignoring her, awaiting destiny. Chloe could feel the desolate tension from each man in the coach; she well understood they knew they could die, but were determined in their cause.

One of the group broke the silence. "Ma'am if we had not found you first—you saw the searchers coach on the road—if it had been them instead of ourselves, this morning you would be part of those poor souls to be burned as soon as the sun is all up. Now whether you like it or no, you are part of this force— we succeed or we will all be destroyed together and that does include you. Now." He tossed a black bundle to her. "If you are to live, put these on."

Chloe caught it. She looked to the man who tossed to her what she now understood was a black uniform such as they wore, complete with silver skull cap.

"Yes lady, dress here now—it will save your life. You can wear the uniform over your own clothes but later remove it so you will not be mistaken for a real guard once the fighting starts after we land for not all guards are Vraang." He turned to look out the coach window as the others did saying nothing more.

She dressed as quickly as she could, putting it all on over the sweats as nasty as they had become. It was a tight fit. The skull-cap was another matter, it seemed impossible at first to get her dark plum shoulder length hair stuffed into it, it was a help that the ponytail she had been abducted with still held. The skull cap finally fit with her hair hidden inside; it was so tight she was sure she would get a headache—*better a headache than dead.*

All was eerily silent as the line of coaches slowly descended to a vast city below occupying a hilltop similar to middle ages architecture—fortified crenelated buildings, turrets and conical topped towers waving bright coloured standards in the rising sun, but the flavour of time had not settled over these as in Europe—which, certainly wasn't the Europe she was familiar with. This gave rise to a feeling of strangeness—of knowing but not knowing. She had come to believe that this had to be a parallel world, not another planet for that too had crossed her mind, there was considerable familiarity, but nothing so far fit any of

Earth's history, it was all mixed up—strangely off kilter but similar! *Just what one would expect a parallel world to be!*

The man who had tossed her the clothes turned to her once more. "For your own protection, you must stay in the coach when we disembark. We will not return till all the Vraang are dead—dissipated—this may take some time."

Dissipated? What did that mean?!! Evaporated? Did he really mean that? Was that what their weapons did—evaporate people?

There was no time to find out. They and another line of similar coaches settled in an extensive and grandiose city center. Chloe counted 12 coaches on the opposite side of the common; she assumed she was part of that many on this side. Central to the area was a sea of stakes all piled with wood around each. Her heart thumped wildly knowing what this meant. She would help these people she was now a part of in any way she could—whatever these people's crimes this was no way to carry out justice!

Her heart raced—what had been planned? She offered her assistance to the leader. "How can I help?" She pleaded. "I want to do something—please!" Not knowing the circumstances she still felt a part of these people and their cause.

"Stay where you are. When the explosions start, throw fruit at those souls in black, and if they are ours all is well, if not, less Vraang. Use the fruit to protect yourself as it is instant death to Vraang. I feel you do not know this—it is our best weapon—the explosions are only a distraction." He continued. "The high Vraang executioners will all come forth to benefit from the burnings. They are the most important target. The disruption will take place as they are seated. Fruit will be launched and juice sprayed so none escape before any fires are torched. It is necessary to wait until they are seated for only then will the prisoners be brought forth and tied to the stakes. Do not fear when you see men, women and children, for today they will be saved."

Chloe asked. "So, (she hated to think how many times this could have happened before) are all these coaches usually here at the executions? Will the Vraang (she felt strange with this word) executioners expect so many?"

"That is correct, many are brought in late. When they search the forest for revolutionaries we have been able to take their own guards place without being suspected as some of their guards are our people under a form of mind control *or* blackmail with the lives of their loved ones in the balance, they don't seem to be aware of an uncontrolled one in their midst. In that respect we have taken over; still, the city is in the hands of the high elect of the Vraang, but for only minutes more."

He turned quickly away from her and exited the coach. At that moment a heralding of horns accompanied a troop of similarly dressed black guards escorting a group of twenty or so purple-robed men to a grandstand in front of the field of stakes some distance away. They were the high Vraang executioner judges being seated to observe the burnings of what Chloe believed to be as many as fifty prisoners paraded out in a group.

She could feel her very being revile all she was witnessing in disgust at what humanity could be capable of. Could this really be as it appeared? She trembled at the scene and seemed to have no control over her reaction plucked out of her own reality into one of archaic barbarism.

The Vraang guards began tying the prisoners to the wooden stakes when without warning explosions erupted from everywhere. Fruit and its sprayed juice filled the air with its potent aroma, one most enticing and at the same time strangely clean and fresh. It made Chloe crave it then and there, even in this dire circumstance she fleetingly thought how compelling it was. Guards from the coaches ripped off their uniforms everywhere she looked. She did the same not wanting to be mistaken for one of the forces of the Vraang. The Vraang elite had stood and huddled together in terror as the blue fruit rained down on them. Some of the black clad guards around them dissipated into nothingness along with their elite masters in purple as they were bombarded with the fruit; these she knew must be true Vraang—so this was how the fruit affected them. She had never envisioned any thing like what was taking place—human appearing humans just evaporating into extinction!—into nothingness! Her captors words in the coach had been the truth!

It was getting harder to see in the resulting smoke from the explosions and blue flashes from what she believed to be some sort of hand-held laser weapon of the revolutionaries. She thought it best to try to keep track of the revolutionaries progress just in case it didn't work out and she had to make a run for it, to where, she didn't know. She felt it was time to climb down out of the coach and do what she could for she felt she could be of some help in this liberation from what she perceived as evil. She gathered up a load of the over-ripe blue fruit in the bottom of her sweatshirt from the baskets in the coach and began throwing the stuff at the black uniformed ones as two attempted to escape running past her. Seeing them dissipate before her very eyes was the dispersal of ones own view of reality. It was a formidable thing to know this dissolving of another's life came about from her efforts. But in her very soul Chloe knew she had to put this aside and do what had to be done so she continued throwing fruit at any in uniform running past her. If they weren't Vraang it didn't matter, nothing happened. She did this her arms aching with the continuous effort until midday, for now the sun was overhead. The fruit had been Chloe's protection as well as a weapon for she was positive this was her only resource to survival; the revolutionaries were busy with their own work for the Vraang had incorporated some of Handeleine's population into their cruel slavery—this had to be sorted out, the fruit stood in the way of any deceit, in a way she was just a bystander—an observer on the sidelines of a people reclaiming their very lives and souls.

She stood a little ways from the coach cradling fruit in the bottom of her rolled up sweat shirt on alert for escaping Vraang when a little boy with dark hair ran by her in terror. She pitched the fruit back in the coach and scooped him up in her arms. His clothes, face and hands were soaked in the pulp of the fruit, his little body quaked with sobbing in the crook of her neck as she cradled him. Holding him tight she could see that fruit continued to be cast everywhere, it's juice sprayed in the air, while the grandstand stood empty of its evil occupants. She, herself was soaked with it, her hair plastered to her head. From her vantage point the city square ran with rivulets of blue and orange! It had been thrown in windows, doors and down alleys—near inescapable for those having reason to fear it.

In the midst of the fighting the mind-controlled still fought for their Vraang masters. Scores of prisoners ran as far and fast as they could after the dungeons were opened freeing them from possible execution after the first group who had been tied to stakes. A few stayed to fight taking up the arms of fallen Vraang supporters. The only way to tell who was who was by the fact that the revolutionaries she had accompanied had not evaporated but had ripped off their black uniforms (keeping on the skullcaps for they must have allowed for some protection) the true Vraang were finally becoming only a mist of a memory. The fighting was done not only with the short-burst laser with the blue flash but with blades of steel too.

Chloe hoped all the revolutionaries survived as she crawled back into the coach with the little boy. She was terrified when a black clad guard jumped in the coach's opposite door. Vraang or one of the mind-controlled guards? He glared at the child attempting to throw some kind of vile smelling canvas over them both. Either way—*this was not one of the good guys*. She pulled the little boy back and away as she lifted her knee and kicked with all the blunt force she could muster under the man's chin and throat before he could protect himself. She heard the snap of his neck knowing she had broken it. He lay staring up at the coaches ceiling in death. She gave him one more kick to the side of the head—again hearing a snap knowing he could not be more dead—or, dead enough for her. She leaned forward snatching up one of the fruit in revulsion rubbing it into his morbid face watching him vaporize into nothingness—not even the scent of a chemical reaction in the close quarters of the coach. Why would this even cross her mind—a lingering odor from such complete annihilation?

In circumstances as strange as she now found herself in, ones mind most likely landed upon the most mundane of thoughts just to hold onto reality. Now, he was dead enough! And yes—he had been Vraang!—Somehow surviving the onslaught of the fruit—where had he concealed himself until now so successfully—had he been in charge of the child losing him in the confusion of the assault on his masters and only now discovering him?—why was this child so important that a Vraang would risk death from the fruit to gain custody? Had that acrid smelling canvas something to do with the Vraang's survival? Was that why he had wanted to throw it over them? What about the air full of its essence? She did not know these answers—anyway she had kicked the foul smelling thing outside the coach!

The little boy clung to her soundlessly; she could feel his little body quiver as had her own in fear of her plight. She believed him to be no more than three—at the most four, and hugged him even tighter as they hid low on the floor of the coach. Their concealment was short-lived for in a flash a brunette woman in a navy jacket, jeans and high black boots jumped into the coach. Her hair had been pinned up in a French twist but now mostly fell in long strands around her face. She was striking even in the chaos, just past middle-age and obviously athletic. She sat back on the floor beside Chloe and the charge she held so protectively. Chloe believed her to be one of the liberated prisoners. The woman threw her head back and breathed deeply in a sort of relief in escape from a horrible death, Chloe guessed, just from the sheer terror of a narrow escape.

Looking to Chloe's sweats, the woman turned just her head and asked, "You're not from here are you?"

Right away, Chloe realized a kind of unexpected relief. "Hell no!—and I don't believe you are either. I'm from good old Michigan, U.S.A., Earth—and you?"

"Earth too!" The woman again threw her head back taking several deep breaths. "I thought this was it until all hell broke loose. I would join the fight but I can't be sure who's who just yet! Although, I believe the right side is winning. I spent the night in the dungeons after I was picked up in the fruit forest that the Vraang so greatly fear that they burn people alive here for even being in it—including me, had it not been for these brave souls." She nodded her head at the fighting forces clashing with what was left of the Vraang slave guard in the cobblestone center of the commons. The woman's breathing had become more even now. "By the way, I'm Serpentine Pendergast of Smugglers Cove—New England coast—USA!"

Chloe smiled in acknowledgment of a fellow citizen. In the thick of it they shook hands finding comfort in an act of civility and acquaintanceship in the midst of such inexplicable circumstances as they found themselves in.

"Smugglers Cove," Chloe whispered as the child she held had begun to calm and fall asleep. "My fiancé David Stewart and I were to meet my grandfather there on what would be today until I was shanghaied by some very nasty people and transported here, as crazy as that sounds."

"Not in my world it doesn't sound crazy, you must be Chloe Steffington, Peter's granddaughter."

"I am." She said, astonished that in a parallel world she would be fated to make the acquaintance of a familiar of her Grandfather. Momentarily subdued with the oddity of this happening she attempted to get a better view out the nearest window—wrong move. For she quickly withdrew back to her position on the floor as a sword blade sliced by the window.

Serpentine said. "Better we stay put until we know who ends up on top, for if we did run, there's no telling if we would be better or worse off till we know what the story of this place is. Right now we seem to be on the right side."

Chloe could tell that Serpentine, like herself, was not a person who would lie down and wait to be rescued, even now she could see the woman plotted her best outcome as Chloe herself did. She felt they could do better together than each on their own. They needed to know more. Perhaps the revolutionaries could be the key to getting home.

Serpentine asked. "Have you seen how these coaches operate—been close enough up top to the driver's seat to tell how to drive one?"

"No." Chloe said. "This might be the best opportunity we have of finding out."

As time passed by they could tell the fighting was winding down and their side seemed to be the victors. They cautiously climbed out of the vehicle and moved around to the front where a ladder of sorts led up to the driver's seat.

Serpentine climbed above and sat in the seat as Chloe kept watch. She found one of the laser pistols lying on the floor and put it to use right away when an enraged Vraang guard appeared from nowhere and attempted to pull Serpentine off the seat. She shot him in the head feeling no hesitation or remorse. She shoved his dead body to the ground while Chloe grabbed up a piece of fruit flinging it onto what was left of his head dissipating the body into the ethers. Here another Vraang guard had survived the fruit up until now, all she could conclude was that they had been in hiding and intended to escape in the coach for as she thought about it neither one had any of the fruit on them—clean as a whistle—anyway, they were part of the atmosphere now! She felt sure the little boy she guarded had been of value to the Vraang since two of the real Vraang guards had risked death to retake him and escape in the coach. *How had such a little boy been able to get away from them?*

Serpentine determined the layout of the controls, quickly gauging their relevance, judging rightfully, that anyone could maneuver on the ground or in the air in one of these machines—the panel had pictures below each control indicating it's purpose—training did not seem to be needed she found by trying such—then turning off the vehicle after feeling it engage and rise slightly off the ground. She disengaged the panel and jumped down as quickly as she had climbed up. They must learn all they could taking their chances in an unknown world even with its political state in upheaval doing whatever was necessary to find a way home.

Chloe knew that something she had felt uneasy about needed to be brought up. "The technology and the past are so intertwined here I fear we easily could be thought a danger—even"—she hated saying this, "witches—or the like—any sort of differentness could be feared; it's hard to fathom what has happened—the completely archaic combined with a technology superior to our own, if these flying vehicles and medieval architecture are any indication of the rest, it could present a problem. And, besides, I don't feel right handing over this child to the first person freed from prison that comes by." She pushed the hair off the boy's damp forehead, his deep even breathing attested to his trust in Chloe. She would not betray this.

The revolutionaries had not returned, even though, all seemed under their hand for the moment. Several she recognized in the square marching off prisoners of their own people who had abetted the Vraang in their crimes of cruelty; some destroyed in anger and satisfaction the stakes and piles of wood removing it in loads in great carts that ran as silently as the vehicles Chloe and Serpentine now stood beside.

They were in agreement that it was imperative they make a decision soon, afraid of their fate's interpretation by the locals, not knowing how they would be perceived—which way justice fell even with the victors—what if they were just as cruel in their ways as the Vraang they had only minutes before defeated? They did not have to sort this out further as a woman in chain mail, sword and laser belt yelled to them as she ran across the square leaping over the random logs that had rolled from the stakes. She ran with the speed of one let out of hell itself.

It was too late to try to escape in the metallic coach and since Chloe held a little one it could be construed as kidnapping if they ran. They stood their ground; it was the only action that made sense for now. The closer the woman came the more fascinated

Chloe became, for she looked at herself. The woman could have been her twin. She stopped abruptly in front of Chloe only for a moment realizing that she too was looking at her own mirror image—dark eggplant tinged hair, violet eyes, full lips and lanky stature—even the same smattering of freckles. Her determination took precedence over the shock of this as she grabbed the sleeping child out of Chloe's arms. Tears of joy and relief spilled down the woman's face. The little boy roused and looked up into her face, his little hand patting her nose. "Ma'man, Ma'man." He smiled in joy.

The young woman held him tight to her, tears falling on him. She said nothing to anyone until she regained control, murmuring only to him, "Bronwyn, Bronwyn, I have so missed you, my son, are you fine still?" Again, she held him close to her cheek cradling his head, his hair the same shade as her own.

Finally she spoke. "I do not know you, or you," she nodded to both Chloe and Serpentine acknowledging each. "Albert, my commander of guards told me of you," she nodded only to Chloe this time, "and your arrival in the forbidden forest, his confiscation of your person to protect you from the Vraang, and Madam," she nodded this time to Serpentine, "I understand you were part of the freed prisoners. I can never thank you both enough for saving my son." Again, she held him to her. "This great cruelty," she halted for a moment needing to again control her heartfelt emotion at reclaiming her son then continued, "was to force me to surrender myself and the rest of the revolutionaries to the Vraang. They kidnapped my son, the cruelest act of all against me. Other prisoners related how one of the Vraang guards kept a separate hostage, a very small boy who was later seen running in the square while all the fighting was taking place—we looked everywhere until I saw you holding him. I believe his life has been saved because of such kindness." She stepped back and touched her bowed head in a kind of salute; "I am Lady Arianne de Bretagne of Mont Claire."

It all clicked for Chloe, now she understood why they mistook her for this woman. "I'm so glad we could help, he just ran past all alone—you could see he had been terrorized so I just scooped him up as he flew by and attempted to console him; he's exhausted with all I'm sure he has experienced."

Bronwyn's mother straightened, brightening at once, joy splaying across her own freckled face. "I would like you to be my guests, we will exchange stories—possibly we can be of assistance in returning the two of you home—how do I know this?— because most people found in the forbidden forest are deposited there from other worlds since the Vraang first came to ours—it is more of their wickedness; and now I will have Albert deliver you to my Château, Mont Claire, in the countryside. We can discuss this further." Once again she stepped back, bowed her head, gave a short salute, turned and briskly walked away carrying Bronwyn close to cross the square now almost clear of firewood. The grandstand had been set ablaze roaring high into the air.

"Well," Serpentine said, "I do believe we've been invited to dinner whether we accepted the invitation or not! Arianne didn't wait to find out! One's fate changes so quickly here from being burned at the stake one moment to having dinner with the local aristocracy at their Château the next." She laughed as did Chloe. It felt good to laugh, a kind of relief from both their trauma. Nothing was said between them concerning the fact that they had just met Chloe's physical twin who seemed to be a medieval knight in chain mail!

Chapter Thirty Nine

By late afternoon Chloe and Serpentine were well away from the city of Handeleine. The revolutionaries had finished routing out any loyal to the Vraang in hiding. The juice had been liberally used on the Vraang-controlled city, drenching it in fruit purification. There were to be no trials or formal executions, all such evil had been deposed of forth-with. Captain Albert and two of his men accompanied the coach containing the two heroines to Lady Arianne's Mont Claire. The coach followed a winding road through the rolling hills of a late autumn setting. This time there was no flying over the forests as they had on their way to Handeleine, but stayed just above the road surface passing several small villages where people waved and cheered as they passed by. This was done, Chloe supposed, to allow the people to take part in celebration of the victory over the Vraang and the freeing of the prisoners. Captain Albert and his men no longer wore the uniforms smelling of the hated Vraang, but the deep blue and silver of the revolutionaries. They arrived at Lady Arianne's Chateau just before sunset.

It sat on a promontory surrounded by forested land. The blue fruit trees along with others bearing late autumn fruit of many varieties grew in abundance on the estate grounds. Mont Claire was surrounded by a mote of freshwater. Sandstone in colour, the building's four conical topped towers were grey slate. A small drawbridge and guardhouse arched over the mote to the heavy wooden doors of entry, not large enough to admit a conveyance, only those on foot.

Chloe experienced a lump in her throat for it so reminded her of her home in France, her own Château Rose, the convergence of her and David's adventures the previous summer—a time that had been magical in danger uniting them with a finality they could not have imagined. These vague similarities as she was experiencing did not concern her so much as Arianne being her physical twin—herself, as a chain-mail wearing Medieval Warrior. In Sci-Fi stories parallel worlds were expected to almost mirror many other worlds—this one (if truly this was what this was about) did not—it seemed a disjointed version of Earth's history and unknown technology. Regardless of what all this meant, she would find her way home. Peter and David would be on it—the scientific part. For now, she needed to learn all she could to help in her own recovery—to go *home!*

They stopped at the guardhouse where Albert spoke to the only guard on duty, then turned back to the coach attending to his passengers assisting each from the vehicle. Their arrival was met by a servant dressed simply in a navy tunic and straight pants. Being met by this immaculate and aloof man made Chloe feel like she had been rolled in jelly and left to dry in the sun— afraid even that she might leave tracks on the floor when they entered so encrusted with the fruit she was. This was not a first in the life of Chloe Steffington—ending up like something the cat had just up-chucked!

The grand hall was beautifully lit with what at first appeared to be candlelit wall sconces, but a closer look revealed not that of flame but another light source. What energy sources were put to use here Chloe could only imagine. They were unfamiliar science. The soft glow of wood-paneled walls shoulder high to the sandstone composite of the structure throughout the space gave off a welcoming ambience. A sizable bowl of the blue fruit sat on an entry table exuding its compelling fragrance. It seemed the fruit was a big part of life here—it served many purposes apparently. If she had been home and as hungry as she was right this moment she would have taken one of the fruit from the bowl devouring it for a before dinner snack. She always had a good appetite and now was no exception, especially not eating since lunch yesterday.

She wondered briefly how Bronwyn had been abducted with so much fruit around in some form. She and Serpentine could see into a room off to one side of the hall lit by the firelight of an arched fireplace. The unknown light source illuminated sconces on the walls there too. Sturdy but pleasingly upholstered furniture was placed to invoke the comfort of a library since most of the room's walls were filled with bookshelves. An antique gold-framed painting of a man of noble countenance with a small girl at his feet hung over the fireplace. Unmistakably this was Arianne as a child.

Chloe tried not to dwell on all she loved and missed at home, but what she would need to do to have all that back again. She was glad to have run into Serpentine—a most fortuitous meeting in dire circumstances for them both. On the journey to Mont Claire they had discussed the events leading to their individual disbursement to this parallel world, and apparently, all they had in common.

The man employing the position of butler led them into the library to await Arianne. Neither sat down considering the state of their hygiene. Serpentine asked for water as thirst still stirred in her, Chloe also, for on their journey only once did they have water from a flask which all shared.

Arianne appeared just before the water did in clothing Chloe would not have expected. It was very similar in style to the Butler's, but in a subdued green. Simple silver cuffs adorned both wrists with no other jewelry.

She rushed over to kiss both women on the cheek while attempting not to get too close. "Welcome, welcome to my son's heroes! There are adjoining rooms and baths for both of you, please, baths are waiting, then dinner and talk we will have."

Arianne beamed in joy, Chloe was sure this was from finding her son—certainly, not her and Serpentines arrival in their disgusting smelly states. Naturally, she would tell them where the baths were first! They were both glad of that!

Algernon, the name of the Butler, escorted the two women to their rooms via the roughly-hewn stone staircase following up the outer wall of the Chateau. A servant followed with a tray of water flasks and wine. Clothes similar in style to Arianne's had been hung in the spacious baths.

Chloe was surprised to see water faucets already rushing water into a marble tub filled with an aroma of freshness, not perfumery, just a wonderful, clean scent of nature. She undressed and slipped under the water for a moment to submerge herself in such luxury. So wonderful to be clean again!—to be rid of those filthy sweats and into the soft lilac pajama style of clothing was heaven. An ankle high pair of soft woolen boots was provided along with a kind of woven one-size-fits all sort of undergarment. Her outlook was improving.

A soft knock on the door proved to be Serpentine in a dusty blue garment of the favoured style. Algernon came to announce dinner. It would be just the two of them with Arianne in her suite in front of the fire, nothing formal he had said.

They were escorted down the hall and into a room where one felt an immediate welcoming and yes, it had feminine aspects but a strong masculine influence as well. The lit fireplace was the backdrop for an informal table setting for three. A simple deep yellow China, natural flax linens and heavy silver composed each place setting. The lighting that imitated candles, illuminated the table and walls too, no cord or outlet visible. Soft blue roughly woven fabric upholstered the wing chairs that were pulled up to each designated place indicating that this was not going to be a short evening. It seemed Arianne had much she wanted to discuss.

One corner of the spacious room curved out from the rest, most likely part of one of the four towers. Wide wooden planks of flooring anchored the room with strength and warmth for such a large space. No wood-paneling on the walls here, only the bare block walls of the Château's sandstone.

A magnificent roomy bed of white linens and pale blue hangings at each of its four corners almost concealed their hostess admiring Bronwyn asleep in his mother's bed. Arianne bent over the child gently smoothing the hair from his little forehead not realizing her guests had arrived. Neither spoke, afraid of waking him. Slowly, Arianne turned seeing the two and smiled in welcome.

Chloe asked. "Will we disturb your son's rest dining in here?"

"No, he's used to sleeping with conversation taking place. He's a deep sleeper, besides, I just want him nearby." She extended her hand. "Please, be seated. We have much to discuss this night!"

Serpentine and Chloe looked to one another knowing Arianne's words to be veiled, mysterious even.

The sun had set and the clear blue night sky of autumn could be seen through the glass of the thick-walled windows.

Arianne moved to the table seating herself indicating her guests do the same.

Shortly, two servants arrived with wine and a heavy tray laden with an assortment of food. The servants did not bow, only turned and left shutting the door firmly. Arianne quickly got up and locked the two halves of the heavy wooden door together forming one peaked arch above. "So we won't be disturbed." She said, reclaiming her seat.

Chloe, not a meat eater, delighted in the array of fresh food before them but drank sparingly of the wine not having eaten in more than twenty four hours. She had not had the blue fruit before either. This was a new food to her. A much firmer less over-ripe version was included in the offerings on the tray than the over-ripe version used as a weapon against the Vraang earlier.

Serpentine watched as Chloe tried it. Her eyes lit up. "This is delicious! I've never had such a fruit before." She looked closely at the piece she had taken a bite from consisting of bright orange flesh and blue skin.

Arianne asked. "You don't have this on your world? How do you protect yourself from the Vraang?"

Chloe did not understand what Arianne meant. "How do we do what—the Vraang? I—I—don't believe we have those." She looked to Serpentine wondering why Arianne would ask this just assuming everyone had the problem of the Vraang.

Serpentine did not make eye contact with Chloe, for there was so much Peter's granddaughter did not know, but now, of course, she would have to be told all and considered what she would need to say to bring understanding to someone so unfamiliar with such a concept as that of the Vraang.

Serpentine hesitated not sure how to begin. "Arianne, from Chloe's and my discussion on the way here we understand we were both dispatched from our world against our will by the same method, by the same evil woman, a Madame Seurat, but almost a day apart, and, in different locations on Earth, the name of our world." Serpentine was quiet for a moment, gathering her thoughts and then spoke directly to Chloe understanding that she would need to know the reality which her grandparents had throughout her life protected her from. It could no longer be avoided considering their circumstances. She began. "Madame Seurat's true affiliation—she is Vraang, and yes Chloe, Earth is Vraang controlled by their intentioned chaos, always one step forward for humankind, two back to supply the Vraang with their Sesca—a drug component obtained only from human adrenalin that unbelievably enhances only Vraang health and life spans, ultimately changing their very DNA irreversibly." All this she related and the decades old attempt to finally free Earth for ever from this evil branch of human. She went on to explain the sorrows of Earth's condition due to centuries of secret Vraang enslavement of its people and how Chloe's grandparents were part of a small elite group of scientists finally on the verge of freeing planet Earth from this scourge forever.

Chloe took this better than Serpentine had expected. "Why did no one ever tell me about the Vraang—all that you've just revealed to me Serpentine? Our world has such troubles, so hopeless for most, it would have lifted me from many sorrows we all deal with no matter how good our own lives are, just to know there is hope—that there is a reason things are the way they are and that something can be done about it!"

Serpentine put her hand on Chloe's shoulder. "It would have made no difference. There was nothing you could have done with such knowledge—possibly placing you in even more danger than what your family had always feared for you considering the stakes of their involvement." She paused, peering closely at the young woman. "At this very moment everything that has taken decades of scientific advancement and planning is in place to end our enslavement by the Vraang. The blue fruit as it is called in some places has now been seeded over the planet in secret, the first and most important step in any world freeing themselves from this abominable species of human as was done here today—and—other—places." Serpentine went on to explain fully the part the fruit would play in humanity's deliverance and what it did to Vraang as she had witnessed earlier. "Next, after the seeding is accomplished, their collectors in high Earth orbit will be destroyed to fall into the sun or dissipated completely in space, because, if their destruction caused the collected Sesca to fall back upon the Earth it would result in such a depression upon humanity that most might never recover from it—resulting in mass suicide. It could destroy most human life with no hope left for a future full of possibility, releasing us of their undermining our every attempt to claim ourselves."

Chloe slowly shook her head at such unanticipated enlightenment. "This is so hard to believe—like a Sci-Fi movie, how can such a thing be? And, that there is hope for our world, yet if all this is real what is the possibility that something could go wrong? Earth has forever just accepted its state—we all have, not having a clue how things really are or why—or that things could even be different! This is unimaginable!"

Serpentine said. "It's not complete yet. There will be a great effort to portray the fruit as poison—most surely deadly, as so many of the Vraang will evaporate before the eyes of the world through every venue for all to see, accompanied by every conspiracy that can be attached to a visual. Oppositely, the other factions—us—true earthlings will attain almost perfect health—our life span will begin increasing, the fruit will reign as the hungry of the world continue eating it regardless of the Vraang's attempt to disparage it fails miserably. The hungry of the planet will be the tellers of the fruit's true story, their experiences always in every instance far out weigh a few of the evaporated Vraang. People will begin to realize just what has happened as they feel free when these Vraang are no more. A new understanding of our reality will take place."

Arianne looked to her two guests with a so far unvoiced concern. "That is not exactly the way it happened here." She began to relate a tale that was not quite finished and it all centered on what the people of her world considered Europe.

Chloe interjected something she had suspected. "I detect a bit of a French accent. Is this country France on this world?"

Arianne said. "It is pronounced Franze here." She continued. "Almost seventy five years ago we had a much more advanced civilization technologically than today. Our largest cities unbeknownst to us little by little were being taken over and quarantined off from the rest of society. At first we didn't understand what was happening. You saw the painting in the library of the gentleman and the little girl?"

They nodded.

Arianne went on. "That was my father, and me as a child, a father I visit only occasionally now and in secrecy, his life is always in danger for later he exposed the Vraang and where they came from. Their agents would love to take him—the Vraang's greatest prize and parade him through Mezelin torturing him publicly before executing him." She paused. "Or me—or my son as they have no qualms torturing children. Their evil knows no bounds. Always, we must look over our shoulders—suspect every shadow. My father is a scientist of great accomplishment, and I believe he can help the two of you. You see, some years after the Vraang arrived on our unsuspecting world, he had contact through his advanced scientific developments with a fellow scientist from another parallel world, the world the Vraang were refugees from, a world the fruit had taken hold on. My father initially learned of the immense nutritional value of the fruit to health and its protection from Vraang (which we were as yet still unaware that we had been infiltrated by these beings) bringing it back as a fantastic boon to life. Through its purposeful seeding it spread so quickly over all the planet this vile race was exposed for what they were, quarantining themselves inside some of our cities. They gained control of the citizens enforcing their ways through unbelievable cruelty, walling the rest of us out from only occasional rescue as the one you witnessed today."

Chloe asked. "Why didn't they just go back to their own home world—surely there is a place of origin?"

"It seems," Arianne said, "that if a Vraang group lose a world fully functioning as Sesca collectors, they are forbidden ever returning to the home world as punishment, they are on their own. Those few left on Irrieth, the parallel world I speak of, had secretly made a final jump to our world, one uncorrupted by their kind, at first secretly immersing themselves amongst our population. We understood Irrieth had been one of their corrupted worlds but did not realize that that had happened to us of late. Our lives were good and getting better until their gradual takeover. They had been safe and unrecognized until my father brought the fruit back with instructions from Irrieth on how to start the seeding. The foothold of the fruit was their final revelation. Eventually, we were able to liberate our people from most of the cities controlled by these

Vraang. After today, only one city remains Vraang controlled—Mezelin—our largest. Many citizens are in cooperation with the Vraang to ensure the safety of loved ones. They live in constant fear of reprisal. There are detectors at every entry to the city to reveal the fruit. If even a hint should come from the air above many are kept in dungeons below to be executed as you were about to be Serpentine, and you Chloe, if you had not been found in time. We have made many attempts to infiltrate with the fruit or its essence in some form, at times ending in murderous revenge of the innocent. The only way we were able to free Handeleine was using the stolen coaches and innovative surprise. It had to be done very quickly. We can't use this technique a second time for now they will anticipate that form of intervention—we are researching other ways to infiltrate subversively, the fruit into Mezelin. We must act quickly there for revenge will be taken against the innocents as a matter of course because of our action in Handeleine. Still this cannot stop what we must do—a final liberation."

Serpentine lit up at what Arianne had just said about their not being able to infiltrate the fruit into the city because of the detectors. "Arianne, I must interrupt you, I killed a so-called "Honourable Executioner" with the fruit I had inside my jacket. How could they not have detected it on me if they have detectors everywhere—I was scanned when I was picked up in the forest of Kirth with a wand they seemed to trust implicitly?"

Arianne froze, considering what Serpentine had just said. "Where is this jacket?"

"I left it in the bath to be cleaned." Serpentine said. "It's an old lightweight skiing jacket I had on when I was shunted through to here." Serpentine paused as illumination revealed itself. "Gore-Tex—it's got to be the Gore-Tex—it's a special material to protect from the cold, it holds in body heat! That's it—it's the Gore-Tex! You could infiltrate and regain control of your cities and permanently do away with the Vraang!"

The three were caught up in the possibility of such a discovery.

"But wait now." Chloe said. "Before we just assume it's the Gore-Tex we need to see what other components could be part of the fabric, check its content tag. It might be that it's the *combination* of different fibers that works."

Arianne stood. "I'll get it. Most likely it has already been cleaned though—which doesn't matter." She left the room, only to return with it shortly. "They hadn't started yet, we're in luck." She handed the garment to Serpentine.

She searched for the content tag finding it in the left side seam. "It says, also polyester, you see, Gore-Tex is usually laminated, a heat process adhering it to other fabrics for weather protection. No need to give this a test, at least we know this particular combination works."

Chloe thought for a moment. "If we could only get home, we could send back dozens or hundreds of these garments, or as many as you think you need Arianne, this product is used in many kinds of outdoor clothing at home, you can't just buy yardage, only certain manufacturers are authorized to use it, usually in jackets, pants, gloves, etc., cold-weather clothing. You could get the fruit into the city without any detection wearing the clothing. Spray the whole damn place with fruit pulp, throw seeds everywhere!"

The excitement in their voices woke Bronwyn. He sat up rubbing his eyes with his little fists. His nightshirt was up around his waist. Arianne picked him up, caressing his small form, consoling his fears until he fell asleep. She laid him back on the bed and pulled the cover up to his chin. She returned to their table before the fire and looked grimly over to the bed where her son lay. "I'm afraid he will suffer nightmares for some time."

Chloe offered the only consolation she felt was logical. "It's understandable, only time and talking about his fears will help him to get over his experiences—and, being such a young age."

They all agreed.

Arianne took a sip of wine, setting her glass down abruptly. "Back to business! I think we've come upon the solution to both our problems."

Arianne spread her hands on the table. "I have a plan— one that will require the two of you to become part of a travelling caravan, a theatrical troupe on the road. There is a traditional celebration this time of year up in the mountains where we have resorts for winter recreation. It's an autumn event welcoming the seasonal change to winter—saying goodbye to the nature spirit of autumn and welcoming the Ice King of winter. Much frolicking." She laughed with a twinkle in her eye, knowing they understood. "This was one way I secretly met with my father, actually one of the easier. I will not now divulge his location; it is safer for all if you do not yet know, but when it is closer time you will be put in touch if you agree to this. You see—I am sure he can get you home! He is much more scientifically advanced than those long years ago when it was necessary for him to go into hiding to avoid the incessant prodding and danger from the Vraang to shut down his scientific advancements to help our civilization forge ahead into the future. You see, there are Vraang agents, not their own people of course, they can't leave the city, but our people blackmailed into compliance by the captivity of their loved ones, some we fear are even mind controlled. Most of these poor souls, are on the prowl in the shadows, spying against their own will for the Vraang they so despise—then, of course, there are those who do so willingly, looking to benefit from the Vraang— these most dangerous and despicable ones you have to fear most. The Vraang will not be able to hold out forever, their only hope for now is all the innocents whose lives they hold hostage—it is only a matter of time, they know this—so, their desperate cruelties." She paused for effect. "You *are* going home and we *will* have some of this Gore-Tex!" She smiled. "We do good business together—the three of us!" They raised their wineglasses in agreement to a covenant that served all their purposes. Chloe knew in her heart she would find her way home—no longer did she fear—a new sensation coursed through her veins—the anticipation of grand adventure. Her dear grandmother Mona had always said this moment only is your life—*live it*—yesterday is only a dream—the future is completely unknown—*right now* is what you have—live fully in it little one! This night, the three women laid well their plans. High above in the clear blue night sky of autumn the stars glimmered in approval.

Chapter Forty

Morning came very early for Chloe—well before dawn, she awoke on her own in the dark regaining awareness of the reality she existed in for now. She was unable to sleep any longer but at the same time luxuriated in the big turn-screw four poster bed of the chamber where she slept in the Chateau Mont Claire, home of her physical look-alike the Lady Arianne of this alternate Earth—Errith as this world was called. It was only vaguely similar to her world's France, little else here mirrored her own Earth. Just hours before in the dark of night, their hostess, the Lady Arianne, Serpentine and Chloe had formed a plan that hopefully would solve the troubles of all three of them simply because of the almost undetectable physical likeness between Chloe and Arianne—return Chloe and Serpentine home and assist in the liberation of Arianne's people once and for all from the Vraang with Gore-Tex obtained from Earth. Chloe only hoped somehow executions of Mezelin's citizens could be prevented long enough for them to be restored to Earth and find a way to get the Gore-Tex back to Arianne's forces. Lady Arianne had been, they knew, a prominent chess piece in the liberation of Handcleine, thanks to her and the others it was no longer under Vraang control. Now they turned their efforts to the fortified city of Mezelin—Franze's largest and most populated metropolis. It was feared this last hold-out of the Vraang would produce mass executions of the innocent because of their now desperate state. The Vraang had no where to go unless they could jump to another parallel world which would not be an acceptable answer—foisting Vraang upon any unsuspecting civilization. Mezelin's citizens lived in terror of being part of the next group to be included in an exhibition of barbarism. The Vraang controlled all within Mezelin's walls and above its skies—a fortress of fear and cruelty.

Chloe rose, bathed and dressed quickly in the costume provided for her the night before. It was still dark when she stood before the tall deep set windows of her chamber wondering if she would be able to pull off her part impersonating Lady Arianne—she had impersonated the great actress Lillith in Broyles, France last summer, but this was different, this part was actually inconsequential, be the traditional on-site aristocrat accompanying a troupe of actors in an annual autumn festival into the mountains. She wore the full livery that would verify her role and place in local history as warrior noblesse of olden times—including gauntlets, chain mail scarf and over tunic. Accessorizing personal armaments of war indicated her leadership and title—a silver ornamental sword was belted and swung at her hip. The night before Arianne had given both women one of the hand-held laser pistols, the kind Chloe had seen used in the fighting at Handeleine to hide on their person in case a need arose that would necessitate the use of personal arms. "Just a precaution." Arianne had said. Chloe had never used any sort of weapon before and made sure Arianne instructed them in their use—especially a safety lock. It would be stowed in the tight under shirt of her costume. This role she had agreed to—impersonating Lady Arianne on the annual pilgrimage in appreciation for a way home. Chloe's impersonation of Arianne would free the Lady to take part in the planned reconnaissance of Mezelin, concealing her true whereabouts. This trip would take days for it would be a slowly travelled journey like those of by-gone times of horse-pulled coaches, now, only *accompanied* by the sturdy mountain horses in celebration of the season to come, a salute to the prominent Holds and Chateaus along the way, caught up in the revelry at each stop—a reason for feasting and sampling of local wines—a time of harvest and pageantry. The caravan would be spending the second night at Arianne's father, Morgfried's estate, "Moon Cache" where the horses would be left and stabled, then continue on without them winding it's way into the mountains leaving the gentle autumn behind for the increasing evidence of winter to come as they gained altitude, then, arriving at their final destination, the mountain resort of Yuleyoke, where legend said, the culmination of the festival of light would push back the winter darkness with the flames of frivolity.

Dawn was slowly making itself seen on the distant eastern horizon—a faint pink along the rolling hills beyond Mont Claire's orchards. Chloe heard sound out in the hall, so quickly pulled on the rest of the paraphernalia she was expected to wear as Lady Arianne's double.

Arianne had not disclosed what her part would be in liberating Mezelin—only that she needed to appear to be elsewhere for now. She had requested that Chloe and Serpentine relate to her father what they had discovered about Gore-Tex in exchange for his help in returning them home—this they would gladly do also leaving Serpentine's jacket with him. Serpentine was adamant that she would find a way to get more of the garments to them as soon as possible. In the mean time Morgfried, himself, might be able to discover the particular properties of Gore-Tex that so concealed the presence of the fruit from disclosure.

A soft knock at the door indicated it was time to begin the journey. Chloe opened it only a crack revealing Serpentine clad in clothing similar to her own, only in shades of blue, where Chloe's was a lavender-grey with high laced boots for a medieval effect, the lavender brought out Chloe's plum-hued dark hair and violet eyes and being of some height was an inch or two taller than Serpentine lending Chloe additional pre-eminence for her part. Both women had been given long black woolen cloaks with attached hoods, which they only carried for now. Arianne had said other clothing and needful items had been packed and installed into the coach in which they would be travelling. Their comfort would be provided for along the way stopping and spending the night at each Chateau of the district they would be crossing through that day. The stops for the actors and their play would only require an appearance of Chloe as Lady Arianne lauding the celebrations at the end of each performance along with her companion played by Serpentine. The manager of the troupe, Elfen, would advise them of the accommodations of each day's destination once the caravan was underway. Edouard, was master of wardrobe and all things needful of a theatrical group, this, being his area of expertise. He relished his duties with great enthusiasm and efficiency. Either of the two would be available for any questions Serpentine or Chloe might have—both had been with Arianne's family for some time. It certainly seemed simple enough—*what could possibly go wrong*? Chloe knew better than to even ask such a question for it could only confirm her unease! From experience, she knew full well, simple-nothing to worry about usually meant trouble.

The two Earth women moved along the hall and down the stairs to the library where Arianne had indicated the night before they would meet on the morrow. She was already seated at a small table containing a light breakfast of scones, butter and slices of the fruit. No servants were about. A beverage similar in aroma to coffee topped off sizable mugs and drew Chloe like a magnet to its source—being an avid coffee drinker she could at least begin this adventure full of fuel as she equated coffee. Arianne indicated they be seated, that there was need for haste to leave before full sun-up.

Arianne wore clothing similar to the previous evening. Just what her wardrobe would require Chloe wondered—more of the black Vraang uniform? What would be Arianne's part in Mezelin's liberation, this reconnaissance she spoke of—violent—dangerous—or only information gathering for now—surely there was an underground group inside Mezelin ready to spring when the time was right? Clandestine, she was sure. Arianne could lose her life or even worse, be captured by the Vraang. She knew this to be a surety. The Vraang's methods mirrored those of Earth's Inquisition. This being so, it was imperative they do what they could concerning the Gore-Tex.

Chloe considered how innocent she and Serpentine's parts were compared to Arianne's—a mission fraught with such danger that she might not return from it. She thought of Arianne's small son, Bronwyn and the loving bond between the two, what would happen to him without his mother—surely Arianne had made provisions for such an event.

The previous night Arianne's instructions to Chloe in the impersonation of herself had been to say as little as possible—even feign illness and lay low if need be, otherwise, ooze an air of authority in the event of any suspicion. She had laughed, "act superior!—in other words, just wing it!—it is not supposed to be a serious journey or destination, so don't make it more than it is—all you have to do technically is just show up!"

They were told that they would be contacted the nearer they came to Yuleyoke and met upon arrival by someone not yet revealed to them, so as to maintain the stealth of their mission. They would then be escorted to the secluded mountain facility where her father delved (as he put it) into the secrets of the universe. (Where *indeed*, and how many times before had Chloe heard that in her life from her grandfather Peter)! With his help Arianne believed they would be able to return home.

Mont Claire was still under the spell of dawn as Chloe and Serpentine said their goodbyes to Arianne. Both women thanked her profusely for all she had done and wished her great success and safety in her dangerous crusade to finally free *all* of her people from Vraang control. Being the leader that she was, Arianne stood tall in front of the unlit fireplace and in a gallant gesture saluted them, saying only, "until we should meet again good friends—may it be only in the satisfaction of our desires fulfilled—your coach awaits!" With that she extended her hand indicating the door they had entered upon arrival then briskly turned and ran up the stairs to continue her own destiny.

The two women exited Mont Claire for the six waiting coaches lined up hovering only inches above the roadway across the drawbridge in front of the chateau. They climbed in, the horses waited alongside each coach, their soft woofling and shuffling implied they were eager to get on with it, and they did.

Chapter Forty One

Magnificent beige-coloured horses walked beside the slowly moving coaches of the caravan making heavy clomping sounds as they ambled along. In size and sturdiness they resembled the Clydesdales of Earth. Their heavy pale manes were woven with coloured crystals that also hung draped across their great chests amongst brightly coloured tassels swaying in rhythm to their constant gait. Little silver bells in their livery filled the air with a light musical sound. The silent coaches maintained only a slightly greater differential above the roadway than earlier when they had waited in front of Mont Claire. It appeared to Chloe to be a good two to three feet off the surface they were above for now. Autumn was gloriously triumphant in its majestic beauty as they wound their way through the countryside—it was hard to imagine eventually their final destination would be one of snow covered mountains for here the temperature was a warm autumn day. The afternoon sky was a deep beautiful blue without a single cloud to mar it. It was inspiring in beauty and peace of season, an autumn usually seen only on brochures back home. They passed the occasional keep of local land owners, their orchards flowing on into the distance dotted every where with the blue fruit trees standing magnificently amid the other trees of the orchards— almost their guardians—protecting those less capable of defending themselves.

By nightfall the caravan would make their first overnight stop engaging in the troupe's first performance of the trip. Chloe and Serpentine had rode inside the coach first in line since early morning when it awaited them in front of Mont Claire—theirs being the lead transport with Lady Arianne/Chloe. She and Serpentine agreed the slow pace and beauty of the season needed to be experienced first hand so they called out to the driver if they might ride along side him in the driver's seat up front. He slowed and dropped down to the road surface just enough for them to disembark and climb above.

The fresh air was invigourating. Their small group had stopped for lunch at an inn sheltered by the towering fruit trees. The aroma from the mixture of blossoms and fruit in various stages of maturity was an addictive beacon to Chloe who had just become familiar with it. Serpentine explained that the trees were in a constant cycle of reproduction, producing all year. A light lunch of hearty soup, crusty bread and a yellow sharp cheese was accompanied, as were all meals so far, with slices of the fruit. A drink mixture of dark ale, cold tea and juice of the fruit proved an energizing combination for the rest of the afternoon. Chloe wondered if they even made wine from it. Somehow she didn't think so and would remember to find out about this later—for now, the sustenance from the fruit and the pleasure of the trip in this modernistic caravan was too enjoyable to break the spell with conversation. When Elfen had greeted them earlier in the morning thinking she was addressing Lady Arianne, she mentioned a container of the juice was available in their coach as in all the others. It seemed to be kept on hand for just about everything. Later, after lunch, Serpentine had even suggested that they apply the juice for sunscreen causing Chloe to wonder just how long Serpentine had known about the fruit and all the good it could do, most likely a very long time.

She knew now, after the dinner conversation with Arianne and Serpentine revealing the tragedy of the Vraang, that that was what Peter and her immediate family had been part of for so long—the ultimate destruction of the Vraang—keeping her in the dark for her own protection. In a way she resented this, but if the situation were reversed, she too, would protect a young person in her care from such knowledge, definitely not for the faint of heart of even an adult, yes they had done what had been their only option, for she had been given the best life anyone could hope to have while they had dealt with this in the background. Always her life had been filled with love, kindness and protection from such a frightening concept. She was thankful for this knowing that they must surely have had many painful moments with such knowledge not yet able to do anything about it until now.

Eventually the day ended with the sun setting behind the rolling landscape to the west. The first twinkling stars of evening appeared over the crenellated towers of a square boxy grey chateau on a hilltop unlike the setting of Mont Claire. The difference being, the more fort-like building was not surrounded by orchards, but a steep banked stone wall did surround it with a sizable halved gate large enough to admit any sort of transport vehicle. It appeared old and militaristic in structure. Their caravan moved through the gates into a courtyard and pulled into a circle. They were immediately met by a group of people welcoming them for the night. They were presented to Lord Marcus and Lady Astraca of Gaastead, as this manor was called. Chloe said little not knowing whether she was to be familiar with these people or not. They gave no indication of this either so she went with their lead presenting herself as the representative aristocrat of old with the pageant. She left Elfen to settle the details of tonight's performance with the estate's personage of equal status as her own.

All the actors piled out of the other three coaches while Edouard attended to the troupes trunks with help from Gaastead's servants into an area designated for the evenings festivities. One of their stable masters took over the care of the horses. Chloe and Serpentine were shown their chamber for the night—one to be shared as two beds sat against a far rough wall of block, not as accommodating as those of Mont Claire's but at least not out of doors was the best that could be said of their quarters. Bags were brought in for them from their coach. A maid servant offered to unpack for them, but both declined. She gave a curt nod, turned, and left them to themselves.

"You certainly weren't "Chatty Kathy" with our hosts, *Arianne*." Serpentine said, remembering to use Arianne not Chloe.

"I'm just taking the advice provided—know nothing—say nothing—act superior!" Chloe said rolling her eyes.

"Well, I believe it worked as we weren't questioned—at least not yet."

Chloe bent over to the bags. "Let's see what are in these." She proceeded to unhook the latches on the canvas containers pulling out nothing but under garments and sleepwear—a few toiletries. "Looks like we're supposed to be in costume for the whole trip—just clean under things." She looked around the room. "I wonder if there is a bathroom here—I don't see any sort of adjoining door—do you?—and something else Serpentine," Chloe turned to look directly at her companion, "I haven't noticed any kind of communication devices—you know—cell phone—internet—TV—yet these people have levitating transportation—an unknown power source for lighting—if I had chosen a parallel world myself I couldn't have chosen a stranger one. How can you have all that and not communicate?"

"I'm not sure, I've been curious about this too but I have to believe it has something to do with the Vraang—communications must be shut down. With everything happening so fast I just didn't pursue it—before we leave I would like to know about that as it makes no sense as you say and what about Mezelin and their imprisoned innocents—once that Vraang controlled city hears of Handeleine's liberation won't there be executions right away? Maybe the revolutionaries have somehow blocked all technological communications so they can't know so soon—you know, stalling for time to protect the prisoners until a new plan for liberation can be worked out."

Chloe was in agreement. "That makes sense Serpentine, for if there was communication, executions would start immediately with the knowledge of what happened at Handeleine—that's got to be the answer—some sort of communications block." There were times it still crossed her mind that this was all a dream.

With such conjecture not settling anything they went on to examine the walls thinking a bathroom door might be disguised in a building with such a militaristic appearance, but they found none.

Shortly, a soft knock on the door from the hallway brought their investigation to a halt.

"Enter." Serpentine called, raising her eyebrows to Chloe who quickly sat on the larger of two chairs in the room indicating her supposed *superiority.*

It was the maidservant followed by two men servants carrying a metal tub and water for bathing.

"If you please Ma'm, this is all we have for the bath as this is a very provincial outpost and convenience is frugal here. Lady Arianne, once you finish, we will return to take this away," she indicated the tub, "and bring fresh for your companion. There is a little "room" out in the hall, next door to your right for your necessary convenience."

The two men poured the water into the metal tub. The three once again, gave only short head nods, turned and left.

Chloe said. "I hope she meant the *toilet*."

"I *do* think that is what she meant. At least the servants here don't seem to be the frightened bowing and scraping kind indicating that general life hereabouts is somewhat civilized." Serpentine made this observation then changed the subject. "Well, *exalted one*, since you're supposed to bathe first I'll leave you to your privacy and check out what's on the schedule for tonight without seeming too ignorant of these annual proceedings of merriment."

She turned and swiftly left the room leaving Chloe to a tub she would have to fold herself up like a Praying Mantis to fit into.

Later after the evenings celebrations were done with and everyone was abed, Serpentine awoke to the sound of someone softly scuttling past their door. She quickly jumped out of bed without benefit of a light, cracked the door, curious as to who would be up so late for the caravan would be leaving very early once again at sunrise. She watched as Elfen moved down the hall. Serpentine followed in pajamas and scuffs at a discreet distance behind the slender almost waif-like pale woman as she descended the stairs and on out to the courtyard curious as to just what Elfen was up to so late. Serpentine abruptly ducked around a corner when Elfen stopped under an overhang of the courtyard, looked around thinking she was alone and pulled a small device she had been holding from behind her and spoke into it as if in consultation with someone—verifying orders or taking them—more listening than talking. This did not take long. Elfen clicked what she held shut, disguised it in her hand and proceeded back inside. Serpentine stayed put where she was considering what had just taken place—so there was technological communication here but apparently for whatever reason not everyone used it. It appeared this was something to be hidden. *Damn!—if only she had brought this up with Arianne!* She crept back to bed seeing no one else about and slept until a knock roused them to the continuation of their journey. After Serpentine dressed she relayed what she had seen in the courtyard and it's strangeness to Chloe. Chloe had a bit of her own sleuthing to report.

"You know Serpentine, this may be just a coincidence, why I've picked up on this I don't know, but I have not in this short trip we've companied with that woman, Elfen, seen her eat or drink any form of the fruit—doesn't that seem strange to you—everyone here seems addicted to it—myself included. It's sustaining, delicious and unavoidable once you're exposed to it. And now with what you saw I would believe we have some sort of agent provocateur that Arianne warned about. Eyes open!"

"Agreed, stay vigilant, leave nothing to chance that could interfere with our plans or Arianne's. Elfen is problematic and suspect from now on—and—apparently, there is some communication of a technological sort—and discreetly limited in some way.

It didn't take long to get back on the road and away from the grim first nights stop of the trip.

They saw little of Elfen during the day. She did not appear to want unnecessary interaction with the rest of the troupe and kept much to herself and away from observation.

Chloe and Serpentine were guarded in conversation feeling an undercurrent of unknown intrigue. For now there was no action to take other than be observant so they enjoyed the beautiful autumn weather sitting up atop the coach with their driver Theeves.

Chloe said to Serpentine when they stopped at an inn for lunch. "Has it crossed your mind Elfen is not the Elfen Arianne is familiar with—I guess what I'm saying is—maybe a stand-in, because I can't believe this strange woman is someone Arianne would have kept in her employ, after all Arianne didn't go out to see us off at the coaches when we left since of course I'm supposed to be her."

"But what about Edouard? Wouldn't he know who Elfen is *not*? I had the impression they had worked on this pageant together before."

"Don't know—just don't know, there are so many *unknowns*, for now it's like Arianne said, say little and lay low till we can get to Yuleyoke. Now though, we have to be even more diligent about watching our backs on the way."

Serpentine agreed nodding, saying nothing further.

Chapter Forty Two

In the afternoon the coaches had begun to noticeably ascend more lofty foothills abutting the magnificent snow-capped mountain range dominating the Easterly direction. They wound through a region quite picturesque, (populated with fewer of the orchard farmer's keeps) beautiful in its own way as the altitude escalated and the scenery began to change. The road below the coaches narrowed around steepening hillsides giving more distant views of Franze. Even here, the mammoth fruit trees thrived, fertile with bloom and fruit sporadically dotting the view. Fewer areas of roadway were now fringed by old forestry easing off into more rustic terrain. Just before sundown, the caravan wound around a mountain road revealing in a protected valley far out below, a vast parkland of lakes and plots of orchard all surrounding a hillock occupied by a stately sand-coloured castle of towers and turrets capped off with blue slate roofs visible even so late in the day.

The caravan slowed it's descent into the wide swath of valley. It seemed, just so the beauty of it all could be enjoyed upon their approach. For this was surely their destination for the night—Moon Cache, Arianne's father Morgfried's estate.

The sun finally slipped on down behind the mountains leaving the travelers in a darkened landscape except for a full autumn moon just on the horizon ready to rise into the night sky soon to illuminate the countryside and the pageantry of its citizens celebrations.

The closer they got to the Chateau it was obvious the music and celebration had already begun. Chloe could hear tambourines, violins and other musical instruments she could not identify—the unfamiliar music was both beautiful and bewitching. The locals had not waited for the main event entertainment to arrive before commencing their own celebrations. Laughter and merriment wafted through the night air. They had started early.

The line of coaches pulled up in front of a very grandiose Chateau banded by a wide moat of dark water. Revelers ran out over the sizable drawbridge welcoming them pulling some of their troupe out of the coaches and on into the courtyard. A stable master and assistants came to escort the horses to their quarters where they would remain behind at Moon Cache when the troupe moved on. Shortly a person of some authority came to welcome them. Chloe knew she had to *be* Arianne, and not knowing who was who, once again, avoided using anyone's name while making small talk. Familiar at a distance had become her modus operandi and so far it had worked well. She asked to go to her quarters for the night to prepare for the event as an immediate escape from too much scrutiny.

Their accommodations were resplendent with amenities compared to the previous nights stay at the outpost. A silk hung bed on a dais, actual chests of drawers, a settee and table. An adjoining room provided a bath as luxurious as Mont Claire's. Serpentine was in a suite next door. Chloe had just finished bathing when Serpentine knocked on her door.

"Have you looked in your cupboard yet—it has clothing that you might do well to wear tonight—*fancier pants, Arianne*, along with your sword of course, since this is part of your home ground so-to-speak, lady of the manor and all that sort of thing."

"Good idea." Chloe said. "Although I doubt anyone will even notice, it's getting more rowdy and noisy by the minute—they party early and hard here—unless the fruit keeps them going it will all be over before midnight."

They took their time going down to the buffet in the chateau's ballroom. Chloe noted surprisingly, that bakery products were a favorite with Errith's people—at least at this party considering the colossal display of such on the buffet table. She just smiled. *I know a few folks back home that would just love this aspect of Errith life!* The buffet ran the length of one wall. Chloe, who always had a good appetite, tried many of the foods she assumed must be from the countryside ending always as had become her habit, with some of the fruit.

Serpentine watched the crowd as she and Chloe ate standing. Arianne made her appearance at the end of the troupes play raising her sword in victory as Arianne had explained her part was to be—show up—be the aristocrat on call—go home! None of the crowd seemed to even notice—this was just party—party—party! Perfect, for it did not draw attention to her. She could have stood on her head naked and no one would have paid any attention!

After midnight, the celebration wound down quickly. Servants began to appear clearing away much of what had been left behind. The coaches were lined up outside and ready for an early mornings start. Chloe and Serpentine climbed the long marble stairs to bed. Chloe had managed to acknowledge personages throughout the evening who seemed to know her without saying much or revealing her charade. She was tired in spite of the fruit and eager for bed. Even the fruit couldn't wipe out the need for sleep—maybe made it a more rewarding rest, she didn't know. Serpentine stopped Chloe at her door before she entered her room.

"Just so you're aware, I haven't seen Elfen all evening—I can feel it, something is up Chloe, be very careful for you would be the subject of any subversive goings on as Arianne. Don't hesitate to use your *firearm* if necessary—this is no child's game—we might have to deal with a saboteur." Serpentine looked around once again, then turned and entered her own room.

Chloe lay awake for a while wondering if they would be able to avoid the danger seeming to lurk in their midst before arriving at Yuleyoke—if laying low and out of notice *would* be enough. All this time she had avoided thinking of David knowing how distraught he would be and that there would be no purpose to indulging in the worry of things she for now had no way of relieving for either of them. She finally fell asleep thinking what a bewitching place Moon Cache was, wishing that David could see all she had so far experienced. The estate was entrenched in such a bucolic setting—there had even been Swans swimming around a small island occupied by a gazebo and surrounded by reeds where they nested in the lake fronting the chateau out beyond the road. She wondered if all the merry-making had disturbed them—such a peaceful place, Moon Cache, all that nature and man coming together could create in harmonious beauty, and, as she lost herself to sleep—*this soft clean bed and comforter feel wonderful.*

Chloe awoke with a start! How long had she been asleep—and what had brought her to full wakefulness? All seemed quiet—she was somehow sure it was very late. Only now did she become aware of the soft ticking of a clock and turned over to see where the sound came from. Three o'clock. Something did not seem right—what—she could not rightly say. She rose with as little sound as possible and pulled on her travelling clothes and boots remembering to install the laser pistol in her under Jerkin, fleetingly thinking how vastly her idyllic life had changed to one of carrying a weapon on her person. Not feeling a need to alert Serpentine, she moved out of the room and quietly down the hallway to the stairs, creeping slowly down the wide treads not knowing what she expected to find. The grand staircase wound along the outside wall of the chateau guided by tall slits of windows along the way. Across the sizable space of the entry hall below, a chandelier of pale blue crystal stars and moon crescents gave off only the slightest indication of a disturbance in the air. She wasn't sure if she imagined it or she really heard a tinkle of crystal pieces.

She could smell the blossoms of the fruit—their branches had been used as an arrangement on a table in the hall below where moonlight splayed across the pieced stone floor. The hall was bracketed by white marble benches carved with the graceful forms of Swans on each end. Even with the unease she felt, Chloe knew she would always recall this setting in time—it was for some reason that important—and, beautiful—all her senses seemed so very alive in this moment.

She halted in the middle of the stairs and turned to the nearest window. A stilling of time seemed to settle over all. The window's glass was slightly rippled as old glass can be, but for what she saw that did not matter, for down near the lake of the Swans under a low hanging tree a figure emerged from the shadows that brought instant recognition—Elfen—another figure approached her from the opposite direction—dressed all in black and wearing the metallic skull cap of the Vraang. Chloe sucked in breath afraid to let it out. It had to be one of their controlled ones for their own could not survive outside the city with the fruit everywhere. What was Elfen—one of the blackmailed controlled ones herself, or someone of no moral values looking to profit from her association with the Vraang? Arianne needed to know of this right away. This woman—Elfen, certainly presented herself as a danger to all—what other possible explanation could there be—her secret communications under the cover of darkness and now in league with one of the Vraang's own?

She watched until the two separated, the Vraang uniformed figure disappearing back into the trees and Elfen turning to walk slowly back toward Moon Cache.

Chloe waited, hesitating until she felt sure their meeting was finished before leaving the window. What caught her attention next was apparently not noticed by Elfen. A barely distinguishable bluish glow emanated inside the gazebo for only seconds before blinking out followed by a disturbance—a rippling of sorts in the water surrounding the Swan's island spreading outward in evenly spaced concentric circles away from its sheltering reeded cattails and then back toward its banks in reverse. It stopped just as suddenly as it had started. The water was as calm as it had originally been before the disturbance. This Chloe knew was not a natural happenstance—it was too geometric and precise—an abrupt beginning and ending—and—glowing. What had caused such an event? There was nothing in her field of vision from where she viewed this to suggest an answer to such strangeness.

A little arched stone footbridge extending from the far side of the lake bank to the backside of the Swan's island was just visible from her present vantage point that had not been observable from the road when they had arrived earlier. Nothing else was to be seen.

Chloe did not want to cross paths with Elfen. She turned and stealthily ran back up the stairs to Serpentine's room and rapped on her door as loudly as she dared.

A sleepy eyed Serpentine opened it only a crack, then seeing it was Chloe opened it just wide enough to admit her.

Chloe quickly told Serpentine of the disturbing meeting she had witnessed between Elfen and the Vraang guard under the cover of darkness believing they were unobserved. As for the strange occurrence surrounding the gazebo neither woman could explain it. Chloe was of the opinion that since Arianne's father Morgfried was a scientist on the same sort of path as her Grandfather Peter and David, it had something to do with Morgfried's work—even so, here was another unanswered question of this world—one only witnessed in passing without answers as many others they had no part in during their attempted journey home.

The two women were in a dilemma—afraid for Arianne *and* themselves—how to get a message to her and not expose themselves for they couldn't turn back to Mont Claire now. Arianne most likely would have gone on to wherever anyway, with no way to find her and no one they could trust—no! Arianne had made no contingency arrangement for communication between them. Now their only hope rested with Arianne's father Morgfried. Surely he would know what would have to be done. It had seemed just perfectly settled at the time of their planning—so simple. They had to go on to Yuleyoke regardless of the nefarious events!

Chloe hissed. "All along I knew this sounded too damn good to be true!"

Chapter Forty Three

A swirling thick fog had moved in from the Atlantic settling a distance westward back from the coast late in the day, cloaking the ridge around Dragons Roost in its white swirling masses. The hardy green leafed fruit trees stood out strange and fertile flaunting their blue progeny amidst their autumn counterparts readying for their winters sleep—a sleep never needed by the fruit trees; they stood as if guardians over the others while they renewed themselves.

It had been over forty eight hours since Serpentine had been taken from them and now Peter had told them the sad news of Chloe's abduction as well, and that David Stewart was enroute to Smugglers Cove to add his expertise—particularly Peter understood, to that of Chloe's recovery of course. David Stewart was a physicist of great intellectual accomplishment admired by those who knew him to be a man of honour. Now this evil perpetrated on humankind by the Vraang had become personal for David and he would find his Chloe!

The abductions had been blackmail to get them to stop their work, a futile attempt on Seurat's part. Now that all the seed had been disbursed and the trees were literally part of the planet their next step would be the use of the weapon on the estate.

Zorloff said little lost in his own sorrows; he concentrated as he knew he must with the problems at hand saying only that they would first complete what they had set out to do—for him it would be for his Serpentine, who had been his partner as well as the love of his life. It was for his love of her and her devotion to their cause that he would continue with what must be done, then, he *would* find her. The two of them had always been a destiny to one another. Not even the Vraang could keep them apart.

Everyone felt uneasy even with the success of the sowing— edgy, wondering what would be the repercussions now from the Vraang, understanding such a volatile feral human species would not go down without destructive revenge. As darkness had set in Ombline and Ledger had begun to prepare dinner when a knocking began on the door. Ombline, found Thad and Prudence on the stoop beaming in excitement. They rushed into the room talking over one another telling everyone to turn on the telly quick!

Thad said. "Haven't you guys heard yet? It's all over the news about the trees and the fruit. I never thought in a million years it would go like this—at least not this fast! People all over the world are eating it—it's like a miracle—so soon—and yes, as we suspected, there are those who predict it will kill us all, for even now they're showing films of people diffusing into nothingness—their so called proof of its deadliness. But," he smiled broadly, "no one's listening, they're eating up! It's unbelievable! The trees are coming up all over the planet! We did it!"

They turned on the news channels—every station was consumed with the story of the miraculous fruit that had shown up almost overnight—such a mystery no one had answers for—not even Earth's greatest scientists, but so much speculation—great evil or great good—the negative was being overridden with all the good coming from it. They watched until the story became repetitive and turned it off. They could only wait, for it was done, there was no going back, humanity and all life on this planet had a future!

Peter lit a fire in the fireplace and proceeded to pour one of Serpentine's favourite white wines for what should have been a time of great celebration. They sat around the fireplace sipping the wine each quiet in their own thoughts realizing their victory had been at a very high price—a precious three of their number taken from them. Thad and Prudence stayed for dinner as did Marc. As gratified as the group felt about what they had accomplished, they would be able now to turn their attention to the recovery of their loved ones dispersed to destinations unknown for the moment, by the stealth of Madame Seurat. They all needed rest and a fresh start on the morrow, and with the arrival of David Stewart in the morning there would be a renewed tenacity of spirit and determination of each their tasks. Eventually too, it would be necessary to uncover any secret stashes of Sesca by the Vraang on the planet, for, from previous experience Zorloff knew there would be those and the substance could be deadly to any accidentally coming across it. By then they would know what form the Vraang as a last revenge upon humanity would take—what they would have to deal with for Peter fully expected humanity's deliverance could come at a painful price. Fear was not a luxury any of them involved in this liberation of Earth could indulge in—fearlessly forward was the only option since the *sowing,* whatever the cost there was no turning back now!

After dinner, Peter made expresso and opened champagne for any wanting one or the other. He knew it was important to keep to a semblance of civility. He had found that routine always helped to ground people in difficult times—steady the nerves.

Ombline could sense a kind of disquiet in Peter—like one who had long lived on the edge. He had always been a strength to all their family. She knew in the beginning none of them had really believed they could be in such danger as had befallen them—it had seemed such an exciting adventure fraught with danger but doable—now reality had set in.

Peter swirled the liquid in his glass studying its motion knowing the time had come to reveal all—every bit of it! "We're going to have a visitor tonight." This he said looking to the others in turn as if waiting to be questioned by them. "We're going," he said slowly and precisely, "to have a *portal* guest."

Ombline and Ledger looked one to the other and then to Marc who seemed nonplussed at Peter's statement.

"Who?" Ledger asked, wrapped in hypnotic curiosity.

"Someone of your age Ledger, someone from my home world Irrieth, someone to help us."

No one moved or breathed, it seemed time had stopped at Peter's words filled with more innuendo than any of them had anticipated—a final confession they had up to now only suspected but never dared voice—that Peter was not one of them—not from here.

"What—what do you mean Peter?" Ombline ventured, still not sure what he said, was really what he had just said; for always, she had intuitively felt an aura of differentness encompassing Peter—even as a child she knew there was something discrete and individual about this kindly man she had never been able to put words to.

"Are—are you saying you're an alien Peter?" She was hard-pressed hearing this come from her own mouth instead of Georgianna's. The question about aliens would have been more natural to her sister's mindset than her own.

Peter ignored her *alien* question thinking this was just a way of grounding her own reality with something she was familiar with. "When David arrives from Europe in the morning, he's coming straight here and along with our guest tonight we're going to have a meeting, all of us. Believe me when I say we have truly felt your curiosity and wonder—respect your unquestioning allegiance—you certainly deserve to have answers to how all of you have been accomplices to the beginning of a new age—and what is behind it. Each of you have freely given with few answers from me or Zorloff in the hope for a bright new future for the world—no more could we have asked of you. There's so much more to this story—its tale is way over due. Also, it is imperative you must understand fully the danger we are all now in—not just our small group but all human kind. Always be on guard for your own safety—if something doesn't seem right—assume it isn't—take no foolish risks." Peter looked directly at Ombline as an unvoiced example. "There is only so much any of us can do to help one another—even so, this must always be a consideration—keep in constant touch—do nothing—go nowhere without alerting at least one other member of this group."

Before more could be said, the air in the room suddenly became cold and electrified, charged with a sort of anticipation. Everyone's attention turned to the blue frame seemingly the source of the disturbance.

Ombline faced the blue portal on its stand remembering the initial engaging of the technology, the reverberation in her very being. She realized what was happening—it was coming to life. For some reason she had not expected this so soon.

Zorloff and Peter stood up, quickly setting their wine glasses on the table with a thud. Both ran over to check instrumentation at the far end of the room bringing back a black held apparatus not unlike the one Madame Seurat had used. A soft violet crackling snaked its way around the ornate blue metal frame now waking to its full purpose. The two physicists stood expectantly on either side of it. Blue frosted lightening flew across the inside of the frame finally filling it with a deep pearlized blue swirling. It stabilized. Peter and Zorloff stood aside as a lofty male figure with thick brown hair and piercing grey eyes stepped through the surface of the swirling portal and into the room.

Ledger was in awe never having witnessed this without a gun being held to his head before, as in Serpentine's abduction.

Zorloff put his hand on the young man's shoulder who had just stepped out of the portal and into their world. "Everyone, meet Jack Stewart, Guardian and esteemed physicist from Irrieth, parallel world to Earth."

Jack took a step forward ready to acknowledge his introductions to everyone in the room when something huge and white flew through the still active portal behind him landing on his back like a giant white crab taking him to the floor under it.

Everyone froze where they were. Jack turned his head to the side trying to see what had landed on him. He pushed the attacker off to one side as he rolled over to the other staring in disbelief. "*What the hell?!*"

For there lay Georgianna, up on one elbow wearing a white HAZMAT suit, her Topaz cat eyes framed by her blue-black hair once more splayed across her face as in their first meeting.

She smiled mischievously at him. "Well Mr., the last time I saw you, you needed one hell of a hose down!"

They grabbed each other laughing uncontrollably rolling over the floor together.

Everyone gathered around them with a thousand questions. Marc pulled Georgianna to her feet hugging her unmercifully as did Ombline in voiceless joy as tears streamed down her face.

Georgianna, pulled back from all the hugging. "Oh, Peter," she said smugly. "You better close that portal quick. There's a very angry Vraang that just might be on my tail."

That, he did.

Everyone talked at once. Long ago plans were finally in place. Stories had to be quickly told, for tomorrow all their strengths would be needed for mankind's long overdue emancipation from its dark enslavers. At long last, all their forces were to rally. But for tonight, a homecoming before everything fired up and a new beginning awaited, while on a parallel world, two women are in the beginning of a grand adventure in their quest to come home, and, help save another world's people not unlike those of Earth from the dreaded Vraang!

Not the end...just the beginning!

ABOUT THE AUTHOR

Ethylind Griffieth, author of the previously published novel, "Summer's Portal", the prequel to "Indigo Autumn" has lived a life immersed in creativity.

Growing up in north central Maryland in an old Victorian home was a catalyst to an overly fertile imagination leading to a love of theater arts, fashion design and all the mysterious unanswered questions concerning things that go bump in the night.

These are and will be the pursuits of one whose toes have been accused of never having touched the ground.

40140882R00222

Made in the USA
San Bernardino, CA
12 October 2016